PRIMED TO KILL

Steller's big metallic fist came down in an arc, burning in toward Horn's head like a laser-guided warhead. Horn's own modified arm rose up on an intercept course and deflected the blow in a shower of sparks and a crashing of titanium appendages.

The blond assassin lunged and wrapped both his arms around Horn's chest. Steller tightened his grip, squeezing out Horn's breath, but Horn managed to wedge his right arm between the titanium death clamps and pry them apart enough to keep breathing.

Horn swung his knee up three times in rapid succession and watched as the color drained from Steller's face. He delivered two more blows before knocking Steller's polished arms away.

Gasping for air, Horn struggled to his feet. He grabbed the edge of the beam with his hands and raised his right boot over Steller's head. Just as he slammed it down, Steller's hand shot up and seized the leather sole. Horn tried to jerk his leg away as the pain lanced up his groin.

"Damn!" he yelled out, and suddenly felt himself hoisted into the air.

HORN
HOT ZONE

BEN SLOANE

A GOLD EAGLE BOOK FROM
WORLDWIDE.

TORONTO · NEW YORK · LONDON · PARIS
AMSTERDAM · STOCKHOLM · HAMBURG
ATHENS · MILAN · TOKYO · SYDNEY

For Pamela Susan,
wherever she may be

First edition March 1990

ISBN 0-373-64001-3

Special thanks and acknowledgment to
Stephen R. Cox for his contribution to this work.

HOT ZONE

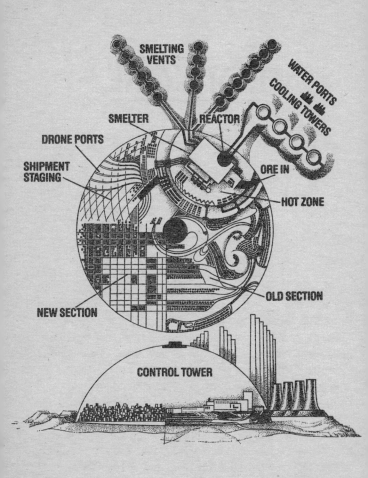

SMELTING VENTS

WATER PORTS

COOLING TOWERS

SMELTER

REACTOR

DRONE PORTS

ORE IN

SHIPMENT STAGING

HOT ZONE

NEW SECTION

OLD SECTION

CONTROL TOWER

NEW PITTSBURGH ASTEROIDAL MINING COLONY
OWNED AND OPERATED BY TITUS STEEL

CHAPTER ONE

HORN STOMPED HARD on the accelerator and rocketed the dirty Buick between a cement truck and a taxi, clipping the rear fender of the metrocab. They had just made the transition from the West Side Highway onto the Henry Hudson, doing ninety, the big rotary engine screaming its lungs out. Horn glanced over at his partner, who was fumbling with the switch on the magnetic base of the emergency light, which should have been flashing on the roof of their unmarked car miles ago. "Come on, Riddle," Horn said loudly enough to be heard over the din as he dodged in and out of the traffic. "Get that light out there—these idiots think I'm just one of them."

Riddle sucked in his breath as Horn jerked the wheel hard over, barely missing the rear end of a stalled bus. "You're gonna get us both killed."

Horn smiled crookedly and ran his fingerless gloved hand through his short black hair. "Trust me" was his only response.

"'Trust me,' he says," Riddle muttered under his breath, then raised his voice. "You know, Horn, every time you say 'trust me,' we wind up ankle-deep in you-know-what."

Horn didn't bother with that remark, which didn't make Riddle feel any more comfortable. "There they are, Max!" he suddenly yelled and pointed to an old Astrial sedan that was weaving in and out of traffic less than a quarter of a mile ahead.

"They're getting off on Ninety-sixth. Hold on." Horn cut across three lanes of traffic, creasing a dilapidated crash barrier as the Buick hit the off ramp sideways. "Looks like they're cutting back on Broadway."

"Damn," Riddle barked in obvious frustration. He jerked the wires of the light from beneath the dash and tossed the whole mess out the window as Horn slid the big machine onto Broadway in a cloud of tire smoke.

Horn got the speed back up to ninety, which was about all the rotary could do, since it had been converted from gasoline to propane and back again about twenty times. Whenever a gasoline shortage occurred, the New York City council would dictate that all city vehicles be converted to propane. Horn was glad that the world was currently experiencing an oil surplus, for gasoline got an extra ten miles per hour out of the old engine, which now sounded like an afterburning cruiser headed into orbit.

Horn felt the muscles in his right leg cramp as he floored the accelerator, trying to coax another couple of miles per hour out of the tired machine. Things were moving fast, but not fast enough to keep up with the fever-pitch speed at which Horn's adrenaline-fueled mind was working.

Less than fifteen minutes earlier, Max Horn and his detective partner, Dan Riddle, had responded to a robbery-in-progress call at the Lincoln Tower offices of Bowen Brothers Construction Company. The two cops had nearly had their heads blown off when they caught a couple of Hispanic machine gun-toting males in the process of ransacking the firm's walk-in safe. A female receptionist, along with a security guard, lay dead on the floor, framed in pools of their own blood.

In spite of the element of surprise, the two perps shot their way out a side door and made it to their vehicle. It was now smoking down Broadway ahead of Horn and Riddle's straining Buick.

"Why do you think they hit a construction company?" Horn yelled the question as he danced the car in and out of traffic.

"How the hell should I know?" Riddle was in the process of stuffing caseless shells into the magazine of an auto 12-gauge. "But don't you think we ought to get some assistance?" he asked, glancing briefly at Horn.

Horn shrugged. "Hell, go ahead. Somebody might show up this time next year."

"Hey!" Riddle broke in. "There they go!" He pointed as the primer-red vehicle they were pursuing cut off Broadway and turned east on Delaney.

Horn cranked the wheel over and followed, the Buick skidding on two wheels. Riddle grabbed the dash and closed his eyes. "Damn!" Horn muttered as the wheels touched down only to land on the ice and snow that lined the gutters on either side of the street. The car jumped the curb, sending trash cans flying into the air.

Horn got the machine under control and drove it back into the street in a shower of sparks, the front bumper bouncing off the concrete like a ricocheting bullet.

"Goddammit, Horn!" Riddle yelped as he flew up and cracked his head on the roof of the car.

Horn had gained on the fleeing vehicle, which was less than a block ahead. "I'm going to try and get a little closer so you can use the shotgun."

Riddle rubbed his forehead and said suggestively, "The tires?"

"What?"

"You want me to shoot the *tires*?" There was a look of concern on Riddle's face.

"You saw what these assholes did back there," Horn snapped. "Try to take out the driver."

Before Horn could coax the Buick into making a move, he watched the Astrial whip onto a side street and slide to a stop in front of a crumbling eight-story tenement. "Damn!" he growled, sliding the machine sideways, smashing into the perp's car. He watched as the two men barreled up the steps and disappeared into the doorless black hole that served as an entrance to the tenement.

"Let's go!" Horn yelled, pulling a 9 mm laser-sighted automatic from his shoulder holster as he climbed from the car while the Buick chugged in afterignition.

Riddle reached for the handset. "I'll get backup!"

"Forget it," Horn said, grabbing his partner by the front of his coat and dragging him out the driver's door. "We gotta go now before those two find a hole to crawl in."

Riddle shook his head as he slammed a number 4 caseless shell into the shotgun's chamber. He followed Horn up the steps and into an eighty-year-old building that looked more like a battle zone than an apartment house.

The two detectives quickly swept the first and second floors, finding nothing. Riddle started up the trash-littered stairs to the next level, but Horn stopped him. "What's wrong?" Riddle whispered.

"They're on the third floor," Horn answered matter-of-factly. "Be on your toes."

"Bullshit." Riddle broke into a skeptical grin and eyed his partner. "Just how the hell do you know that?"

"Brute fucking experience." Horn looked straight into Riddle's eyes to let him know the decision had been made.

"I'll check it out," Riddle said as he started up the stairs. "You cover me."

In spite of the cold, little beads of sweat formed on Horn's forehead as he slowly eased himself to the top of the stairway. It was freezing in the run-down tenement, and his breath rolled out of his nostrils in ghostly white puffs in the half-lit gloom. He controlled his breathing and began to scan the darkness. When he detected movement, he swung the big 9 mm automatic around, the pencil beam of the laser sight searching for a target. The red light reflected off the eyes of a huge rat. Horn eased pressure off the trigger, just enough to cut the beam.

He peered down the dimly lit hallway. His partner was cautiously approaching the last door at the far end. Riddle pulled a small device from the pocket of his trench coat and pressed it against the door. As he leaned toward the device, he raised the police-issued 12-gauge in his right hand and let the end of the barrel rest against the door, just inches from his face.

Suddenly Riddle pulled away from the door and stepped to one side. He looked down the hallway, and the two cops made eye contact. Riddle jerked a thumb toward the door and nodded his head vigorously. After raising his hand in acknowledgment, Horn waved it slowly downward in a motion that was meant to calm Riddle, whose eyes were wide with fear.

Horn started to move toward his partner but quickly backed a couple of steps down the stairs as Riddle broke toward him in a noisy, crouched run. "Goddamn!" he gasped as he slid into the stairwell next to Horn. "We gotta call for backup. They're holed up in there—" he pointed toward the door with the barrel of the 12-gauge "—C-17."

"You sure they're both in there?"

"Yeah, they're both in there. Hostages, too. We gotta call—"

Horn cut him off. "What? They've got hostages?"

"Yeah, we gotta call for backup."

"Gimme the glass." Horn held out his hand.

"Come on, Max," Riddle pleaded as he pulled the electronic listening device out of his pocket and handed it to Horn.

Horn slipped out of his knee-length black leather coat, eased to the top of the stairs, then moved down the corridor in a crouch. Once at the door he placed the little silver box against the worn wood, pressed the button and angled his right ear against the rubber cup.

The voices coming from inside the apartment were a mixture of anxiety-filled whispers, strained orders and stifled sobs. Horn was trying to filter the vocal jumble to determine how many civilians might be involved. He was certain there was a woman and maybe a teenage boy in addition to the two perps. He turned back toward Riddle and was about to signal when another sound came through the earpiece that made him reassess the situation: there was no mistaking the frightened cry of a baby.

"Shut that kid up or I'll do it for you," a Spanish-accented voice suddenly barked, making Horn momentarily jerk his head away from the electronic glass. Instead of giving Riddle the go-ahead for the backup call, Horn motioned him to approach the apartment door.

"Mickey!" A woman's frightened voice became audible, mixed with the heightened screams of the infant. "Try to keep your sister quiet!" A loud smack was followed by the sound of a door slamming. Horn was puzzled, but was sure it was a refrigerator door. There was uncontrolled sobbing from the woman, but Horn could no longer detect the whimpering of the baby. He backed away from the door and turned toward Riddle whose face had become a pasty white.

"Let's get some blue shirts in here, Horn. Don't do this to me, goddammit!" Riddle whispered.

"Shut up, Dan," Horn said, very slowly and quietly.

"You want to wait forty-minutes for backup?" He shot a sideways look at Riddle, who rolled his eyes helplessly. "Of course you don't," Horn continued. "That could be your kid in there...." Horn locked onto his partner's eyes and could see that the panic level had receded.

"Okay," Riddle said as he took a deep breath, "I guess this'll do for backup." He patted the barrel of the shotgun with his left hand. "What're you gonna do?"

Horn looked up and Riddle followed his gaze. The ceiling in the hallway was made up of old square tiles, yellowed and stained. Several were missing, revealing the black hole of a crawl space. Riddle immediately understood Horn's intentions and moved beneath one of the missing tiles to give him a boost.

Horn shoved the 9 mm into his shoulder holster and stuck his penlight between his teeth. Riddle leaned the shotgun against a wall, cupped his hands, and Horn went up and into the ceiling.

The first thing he noticed was the cobwebs. They covered the crawl space, hanging like a gray gauze curtain before the greater darkness beyond. The space was about four feet high and contained a maze of wires and pipes that were covered with dust. Horn duck-walked gingerly along the support braces, picking up a veil of cobwebs that shrouded his body. Through the dust he could see dozens of red eyes reflected in the flashlight's beam. Rats. "Jesus," he breathed softly, and awkwardly made his way toward the apartment.

It wasn't hard for Horn to tell when he was above his objective, because the voices below were coming in loud and clear. Apparently the people down there could hear his scuffling just as clearly. "Shut up! Shhhh ... there's something up there."

"It's just rats, man.... Keep your eye on the door and quit makin' so much noise. Those cops followed us into this goddamn place, and they ain't gonna leave without a half-assed effort or at least lookin' like they're doin' their jobs."

Horn pulled the 9 mm from its holster and cocked it as he moved toward the voices. Suddenly a loud cracking sound echoed through the crawl space, and he immediately felt his right foot slip. He lunged forward and felt himself dropping like a stone straight through the flimsy plasterboard. He started to let out a startled shout but was choked off as a length of electrical wire clotheslined him, swinging his lower body down through the ceiling.

One of the crooks let out a howl of panic as Horn crashed through the ceiling in a shower of plaster and dust. His 180 pounds landed butt first on the end of a worn-out sofa, which collapsed and threw him onto his back.

Even as he was falling, Horn's instincts and training had shifted into gear. His eyes were taking in the situation, allowing his mind to pick the targets. Without trying to rise, he rolled off the broken couch and took aim with the 9 mm. The red beam of the laser sight cut through the dust and rested between the black eyes of a squat dark-haired man, who was swinging an ultralight Stoner Arms submachine gun toward Horn. The 9 mm barked loudly, and a hole appeared where the beam had been, the impact snapping the man's head backward, swinging his long greasy hair in a crazy slow-motion arc.

Horn rose to his knees just as another automatic weapon began its loud stuttering chatter, stitching bullets across the dirty wall above his head. He dived behind the remains of the sofa just as the front door burst open and Riddle plunged inside.

The remaining machine gunner stopped his firing, grabbed the woman huddled next to the window by the hair and held her between himself and Riddle, who was aiming his shotgun from the hip. "I'll kill her! I'll kill her!" the gunman shouted, shoving the barrel of the weapon against her temple. She immediately cried out in pain and jerked her head down as the hot muzzle seared her flesh.

Horn swung the 9 mm up just as the woman pulled away. He squeezed the trigger, and a lead torpedo tracked the beam straight to the Adam's apple of the perp, who was attempting to yank the screaming woman's head upward. The man's face suddenly took on a surprised look, and his tongue limply lolled out from between his lips. His grasp on the woman loosened, and she slipped away. As soon as she was clear, Riddle cut loose with the 12-gauge, sending an X-pattern of number 4 shot through the guy's chest. The gunman's body flew backward, slammed into the wall, and the machine gun fell from inert fingers as he slid to the floor.

Horn got to his feet, walked to the first man he'd taken out and kicked the weapon away from the body, before leaning down and checking for a pulse. There was none.

"No kidding," Riddle remarked, "you really expect to find that cat still pumping? Look at his brains." He waved toward the floor, which was splattered with blood. "You spread his mind out like linoleum, for God's sake."

Horn got up, walked over to the perp against the wall and said out of the corner of his mouth, "You really didn't have to blast this guy, Dan, but I appreciate the backup." He turned toward Riddle and saw him helping the woman to her feet, then cocked his head when he heard a whining sound coming from somewhere.

Horn walked over to the only closet in the shabby one-room apartment and opened the door. The whining got louder. He reached in and pulled out a skinny boy, who really started sobbing when he saw the carnage. "Go over to your mother, son." Gently he pushed the boy toward the woman.

Riddle spotted an outdated CRT telemonitor on a pile of trash and dirty clothes on the floor. He leaned down to pick it up.

"It don't work," the woman said unexpectedly.

"Huh?" Riddle said, surprised she could speak so soon after what had just happened.

"The monitor," she added shakily, "it ain't workin'. We didn't pay the bill."

Riddle made no comment and dropped the dead unit. He turned toward Horn. "Listen, partner, I wish you wouldn't pull this one-man wrecking crew bullshit—"

"Wait a second," Horn interrupted and held up his hand while squeezing his eyes shut in an effort to recall something that had nagged at him. Then, suddenly remembering, he walked over to the refrigerator, opened it and pulled out a gasping baby. Horn thought it couldn't have been older than six months.

"My baby!" the woman exclaimed and grabbed the child from Horn's arms.

Riddle shook his head. "I'm glad you remembered the kid, Horn. I don't think she would have."

"You go to hell!" The woman clutched the child tighter and spit at Riddle, displaying a set of decaying yellow teeth in a face that had been pretty once but was bloated-looking from the effects of poverty and drugs.

Horn looked around the shabby cold room and then at the child who was destined to grow up amid the rats and filth. He thought of his own daughter, Julie, and was momentarily overcome with a feeling of sad helplessness.

While Riddle went down to the car to use the vehicle commo, Horn unloaded the dead men's weapons and rifled through a leather satchel one of them had been carrying. He thumbed through a package of documents that he assumed to be the take from Bowen Brothers.

Riddle stomped back into the apartment and tossed Horn his coat. "Blue-suiters are on their way," he said. "What have you got there?"

"Looks like blueprints of some kind," Horn answered. "No money. Sure doesn't look like something the likes of these two would make a hit for."

"Lemme see." Riddle picked up one of the folded blueprints and examined the legend. "They're plans all right, but for what, who knows. Says here—" Riddle squinted as he turned the paper sideways "—prepared for Titus Steel Corporation."

"We'll check it out with Bowen Brothers tomorrow," Horn said as he stuffed the papers back into the satchel.

The uniformed policemen finally arrived, and after pointing out a number of specific items they wanted photocorded, Horn and Riddle left. It was getting dark and beginning to snow as the two detectives climbed into the beat-up Buick.

"Call up dispatch and tell them we're going to call it a day," Horn said as he pulled the car onto First Avenue and took off in the direction of Manhattan.

"Sure," Riddle answered, "but what about that?" He nodded to the satchel Horn had placed on the front seat between them.

"Shit!" Horn muttered. "I'll take them home with me tonight. Good thing it's not money or dope."

Riddle just shrugged and punched the commo switch. After he made the call, the two rode in silence up First Avenue. They passed Bellevue Hospital, then the burned-out hulk that used to be the United Nations headquarters, done in by a terrorist rocket attack ten years earlier. Horn cut a left on Fifty-second Street and headed toward the West Side, where the two detectives lived.

New York City hadn't undergone many changes since entering the twenty-first century. The evolution of civilization in the United States had become stagnant and was reflected in the city, which continuously crumbled down around itself. While the rich had gotten richer, they had also gotten fewer. The ranks of the poor had increased, and the slums had spread. Corporations formed their own security forces to cover for the state and city police, who waged no more than a token battle against crime.

The city was run-down and virtually devoid of new construction. The once famous skyline had remained for the most part unchanged for more than a decade. The megabuildings of concrete and steel still pushed through the smog to scrape the sky, hanging there like an archaic curtain of cold armor, which in fact they had come to symbolize.

New York was still one of the key financial centers of the world. Corporate America continued to grind on, building the pyramid so that more would continue to support the few, squeezing the last drops of juice from the aging capitalistic apple.

In the streets, on the level of daily living, there was a kind of advanced anarchy. New Yorkers had never been strangers to crime, and as the slowly petrifying city limped into an unchanging future, the criminals took their places on the social ladder—albeit on a low rung. They had become tolerated, and in a way, almost accepted.

For the average citizen, the drive to merely survive had evolved quickly, with each generation preferring to patch together a day-to-day existence and avoid planning for the future. Those who were born in New York tended to die there. Generation after generation continued in neighborhoods that became cities within a city.

An editorial appearing in the *New York Times* stated: "New York City has become an island of despair. Its citizens are prisoners of poverty and crime, kept in place by a social structure that feeds on itself. Once a New Yorker, always a New Yorker—literally." The New York City aura of romance, fame and fortune was as dead as one of the homeless derelicts often found frozen in tenement doorways during the winter.

Horn surveyed the city as he drove. He felt resigned about the overall problems and was only glad that he had a safe haven. Near the old American Museum of Natural History he dropped off Riddle at his brownstone, then drove on up past Columbia University. He pulled up in front of his apartment building just off Amsterdam Avenue and immediately got a warm, comfortable feeling, knowing that in a matter of minutes he'd be getting a hug and kiss from his wife, Sharon. He almost laughed as he wondered what his daughter, Julie, would try to pull on him this time. Every time he came home, it was something different from the little four-year-old. Yesterday she had told Horn that her mother had tried to sell her to the Gypsies. "The Gypsies?" he had asked in mock surprise.

"Yes, Dad," Julie had answered, "but don't worry. I still love her."

Horn got out of the car and cast a quick glance around, noted a dirty Ford that had pulled up on the other side of the street and thought that the times were catching up with the neighborhood. He entered the building and pressed the button that would admit him to the bright, warm refuge called home, idly looking on as a trench-coated man got out of the Ford and began to cross the street.

Turning away from the street, Horn reflected that he loved his home and family in a way he didn't fully understand. But he knew his home was his safe haven amid the everyday danger in the city. It was like a magical island that he escaped to every night. No matter what he'd gone through during the day, it all melted from his mind when he stepped through the door and heard the little footsteps running down the hall, followed by the sweet words, "Daddy's home!" That was exactly what now soothed his ears as he stepped into the hallway and bent over to give the blond curly-haired moppet a big hug.

Horn straightened his lean and muscular five-foot-ten-inch frame and stretched as Sharon came out of the kitchen and gave him a quick kiss. Her sandy hair swirled around her face pertly as she started to walk into the living room, but Horn grabbed her and kissed her roughly on the mouth. She laughed, and beat Horn's rock-hard chest in mock anger, while Julie grabbed his pant leg and screeched, "Let my mama go, you beast!"

"This kid's been getting too much screen time," Horn said, looking down as he released his grip on Sharon.

"Have an exciting day, sweetheart, or did you just miss me?" Sharon asked, still flushed-looking from his kiss.

"Just missed you, babe," Horn answered as he walked into the living room and tossed the satchel onto the sofa. Sharon took his coat, and Horn flopped down in an overstuffed armchair. Julie was immediately on his lap, talking a blue streak and fiddling with the panelvision's remote control.

"The paper's on the end table. Supper in thirty minutes," Sharon called out as she went back into the kitchen.

"I'll go help Mommy," Julie piped up as she climbed from Horn's lap.

"Gimme a kiss first," Horn demanded. The little girl beamed at him and gave him a quick peck before running after her mother.

Instead of taking a look at the evening news, Horn stretched out his legs and propped them on a worn ottoman. He willed his muscles to relax and let the tension seep out of his body. One of his instructors at the police academy had called being a cop a job of extremes. As Horn unwound in his modest but comfortable living room, he knew exactly what the instructor had meant. It was quite a switch going from a bloody shoot-out to a quiet family meal in less than an hour.

Horn often wondered if he should have chosen a different career. But every time he thought of himself wearing a coat and tie, punching numbers into a computer terminal or doing *anything* other than beating the streets, he laughed. All the time while he was growing up on the East Side he'd never considered another vocation in his future. Not just any cop, either—he had to be a New York City cop, as his father had been.

Horn's father, a decorated veteran of the 1960s war in Vietnam, had spent almost thirty years in a blue suit, walking the same beat and working out of the same precinct station. He had trained his only son well—not in conventional police matters, but in street survival techniques.

When Horn was eighteen, his father was killed answering a robbery in progress at an East Side bowling alley. Two years later his mother waned away to her death. But that hadn't deterred Horn from entering the police academy in the spring of 2007. He had progressed through the ranks, and at age thirty-eight had achieved full detective status, assigned to a West Manhattan CSU—Crime Suppression Unit—a two-man plainclothes team.

Horn had been with the CSU for the past three years, and for the entire period his partner had been Dan Riddle. A couple of years younger than Horn, Dan had grown up in the same West Side neighborhood and still lived with his aging parents in a run-down brownstone. Horn and Dan were not only partners, but also good friends. Sharon thought of Dan as Horn's younger brother, and Julie called him Uncle Dan.

Horn startled when his head began to droop, and he realized he'd nearly dozed off. He could hear Sharon in the kitchen, explaining to Julie why pasta had to be boiled for such a long time. He felt a comforting warmth spread through his body. His idle glance came to rest on the satchel, and out of curiosity he reached over and picked it up from the couch. He pulled out the sheaf of papers and thumbed through them. "Hmm, wonder why they would want these," he mumbled to himself, then stuffed the papers back, deposited the satchel on the end table and picked up the newspaper.

Sharon stuck her head into the room to say that supper was on the table. "You forgot your gun," she added. "You know I don't like you wearing it around Julie."

"Oh . . . right, babe." Horn got up, walked into the hall and hung his weapon on a peg inside the closet door. He was just turning to walk back toward the kitchen when he had the sensation that he was in the midst of an underwater shock wave that flung him facedown in the hallway, with pieces of the front door covering the floor around him.

It seemed to his stunned mind that something had exploded. A wave of panic spread over him as he instantly thought of Sharon and Julie's safety. He tried to get up, but his legs didn't seem to function. He managed to raise his head about six inches, when a shadow blocked out the hall light and a highly polished black boot stepped down in front of his face. There was a loud pop, and Horn felt his right shoulder explode, setting off a crazy flashing pattern of lights before his eyes. He heard a bloodcurdling scream, and half a second later realized it had come from his lips.

Horn cranked his head sideways and watched the boot move away, followed by another, his blurred vision finally moving upward and taking in the trench coat covering a massive frame well over six feet tall. The figure moved deliberately, almost casually, like a lion that had just crippled its prey and was now preparing to kill at its leisure.

Horn's mind was a tangled mass of disjointed thoughts. There was no logic, no reasoning that could explain what was going on. His eyes and nerves were relaying to his brain what was taking place, but it didn't *fit*. This was home... this was his safe harbor....

"No!" Horn screamed as he watched Sharon run into the hallway. The towering figure swung toward her and pulled the trigger of the massive .44 held in a gloved hand. The slug caught Sharon in the left breast and drove her body back into the kitchen in a strange jerky puppetlike motion. The figure followed her, and Horn heard his wife's moaning silenced by the booming of another shot.

"Daddy!" Julie's shrieking drove into Horn's heart with anguished pain. Despite his trancelike state he went into overdrive and somehow managed to haul himself to his knees, then to stumble toward the hall closet. Julie's screams heightened in intensity, trapping him in a nightmarish slow motion. He finally reached the door, jerked it open and pulled the 9 mm down from the peg. He swung toward the kitchen, his right arm dangling dead like a shredded rag. There was an odd momentary sound that reminded Horn of a twig snapping, and suddenly Julie's screams for help stopped cold.

Horn struggled to his feet, grasping the 9 mm awkwardly in his left hand, and aimed it at the doorway as the trench-coated man walked from the kitchen carrying the limp little body under his left arm as though she were a rag doll. Her head hung at a strange angle, and Horn knew her neck had been broken.

"You son of a bitch!" Horn cried out in animal agony and grief. His rage ripped through the air as he squeezed off three quick rounds toward the beam that had centered on the assassin's massive chest. The bullets shoved the man backward a half a step, and he dropped Julie's body. Horn fired off another three rounds as the killer raised his .44 and took out Horn's right knee in a shower of blood, muscle and bone. As Horn started to topple, the attacker reached down and jerked the 9 mm out of his hand with such force that it nearly ripped the trigger finger off his hand.

Horn saw the toe of the boot swinging toward his face, and some deep-seated instinct of self-preservation made him roll his head enough that he caught only a glancing blow on the right cheek. He thought his head had been taken off and felt blood flowing down across his face in a warm flood.

Surprised that he could still see, Horn watched in shock while the man strolled casually into the living room as though he were looking for something. He turned toward Julie and his eyes immediately filled with tears. She lay in a heap upon the floor, her body twisted unnaturally, with a look of fear still in her eyes.

Horn shifted his gaze at the sound of approaching footsteps. The man walked in front of him and stopped. He held the satchel in one hand and proceeded to return the .44 to a holster beneath the bullet-riddled trench coat. Horn stared at a side view of the man's face. He had short blond hair so thick it stood up like a wave, a square chin and a nose that had been broken a few times.

The assassin slowly turned his head and locked eyes with Horn. Horn's numbness suddenly vanished, instantly replaced by the supertormented acuteness of all his senses. Steel-blue spikes drove into his very soul, and an insanity that was like a contagion enveloped his mind. He etched the face forever into his brain, and watched in disbelief as it broke into a grin that could only be described as one of madness.

CHAPTER TWO

TITUS STEEL'S corporate tower was ninety-nine floors of concrete and glass, driven into the heart of Manhattan like a tombstone spike. The entire top floor of the monolithic structure was home and office for Oasis Fine, president and chief executive officer of the heavy metals conglomerate. It was six in the morning, and Fine was sitting behind his massive walnut desk, watching the rising sun turn the polluted sky into shades of red layered with rust. The drab ribbon of the Hudson appeared before his bloodshot eyes, stretched still and cold in the frozen haze of New York City winter.

Fine opened a drawer of the desk, took out a bottle of prescription amphetamines and downed one of the black capsules with a choking swallow of cold coffee. He buzzed the executive-level lobby for the third time within an hour and asked the guard if Steller had arrived.

The guard on the telemonitor rolled his eyes toward his partner before punching on and answering, "Ah, no sir... I'll be sure and notify you as soon as he arrives, sir."

"Very well," Fine answered. He punched off the intercom and stared across the river at the broken sack of garbage known as Union City, New Jersey. Almost as an afterthought he pressed the button again. Downstairs, both guards cringed and glanced apprehensively at each other. They knew no one else would be calling them at such an early hour.

"What the hell does he want now?" The guard nearest the com pressed the Talk button. "Executive entrance, security."

"Yes," Fine said. "My order for you to notify me when Mr. Steller arrives stands. However, I also want to see Alex Glass as soon as he gets in."

"I understand, sir," the guard answered quickly. Almost as soon as he had punched off, the doors to the elevator slid open, and Alex Glass, vice president of strategic planning, stepped into the lobby. He began pulling off the overcoat covering his bulky 240-pound body.

"Ah, excuse me, Mr. Glass," the guard called out, raising a finger to get the man's attention.

"Yes, what is it?" the rotund vice president snapped, his dark eyes reflecting extreme annoyance. He folded his coat over one arm and brushed the frost from his bristling little mustache. "Well, what do you want?" He glared at the guard resentfully.

"Ah, Mr. Fine wants to see you...ah, first thing. Now...sir," the guard stammered.

"Wonder what the son of a bitch wants now?" Glass said, more to himself than the guard.

"Excuse me, sir?" the guard asked timidly.

"Nothing," Glass spat out as he brushed the man aside and stepped into the limited-access express elevator. He slipped the coded edge of his badge into a slot next to the digitized control panel and pressed the double nine. The elevator immediately rocketed upward, making Glass grunt loudly as his body weight more than doubled. A few seconds later he experienced a brief moment of weightlessness as the elevator decelerated. The door slid open, and he stepped into the long hall that led to Fine's office. Straightening his tie, he walked briskly, knowing that the CEO would be watching him on a closed circuit monitor.

He shoved his badge into a reader next to double glass doors. The doors swung open, admitting him to what those in the lower tiers of management referred to as the Crystal Shithouse.

"Hello, Alex." Fine swung around in his chair to face his chief strategist. "Coffee?"

"No thanks, Oasis." Gingerly Glass settled himself into one of the chairs across from the huge desk and fidgeted uncomfortably.

Fine locked his copper-colored eyes onto Glass's face. "We have a problem, Alex."

"Problem?" Glass said nervously. He felt a bead of sweat roll down the small of his back and shifted his eyes in an unsuccessful effort to avoid the snakelike stare.

"Our plan to gain the intelligence we needed to be able to, how shall I say it—" Fine ran a hand across the top of his desk as if brushing away a speck of dust "—to disinstall our New Pittsburgh operation experienced an unfortunate glitch."

"What glitch?" Glass asked cautiously and almost timidly.

Fine sensed his vice president's anxiety. "The two clowns sent to appropriate the goddamn plans got picked off by a couple of cops." Fine dropped his voice down to about the level of Glass's knees. "I thought you had a reliable connection for that kind of errand boy."

Glass swallowed hard and made himself breathe deeply through his nose. "What's the status?" he asked, trying to force calmness into his voice.

Fine leaned back in his chair and squinted. "The two Puerto Ricans got nailed, and one of the cops apparently took the plans home with him." Fine rubbed his high sloping forehead, which faded into thinning dark hair. He watched Glass squirm in his chair before coming out with his trump card. "I sent Steller."

"Oh, shit!" Glass blurted as a mild shock tripped up his spine. Anybody who was a member of Fine's inner circle knew that Steller was brought in on an operation only when Fine needed the real dirt work done, when something got screwed up and needed fixing—with force. Glass felt the bottom drop out of his stomach and would have bet his firstborn that somewhere in the city a cop was getting stiff. "Did, ah, Steller g-get . . ." Glass stammered.

"Did he make the recovery?" Fine asked, then answered the question for Glass. "Yes, he made the recovery and saved your fat ass once again."

Glass could feel his shirt getting soaked and wondered how long Fine was going to rake him over the coals.

Fine sat up straighter as he suddenly reverted to the purely businesslike manner he had displayed when Glass entered this office. "Run through New Pittsburgh's financial status for me, please," he requested calmly, and in an attitude of expectancy, cupped his hands behind his head in a relaxed manner.

The request, and the manner in which it was delivered, shook Glass up even more. "May I?" he asked, and leaned toward the desk. Fine nodded, and Glass picked up a small device resembling a hand-held calculator. He punched in a sequenced code, and a colored, backlighted view cell appeared on a side wall of the office.

Glass swung his chair around and summarized the projected numbers: "With the price of titanium the lowest it's been since the strikes in 2000, we're losing 500 to 650K a week depending on the market fluctuation. You've heard this before, Oasis," Glass summed up without turning his head.

"Go on. I want to hear it again."

Glass switched to another set of numbers. "We've tried to improve the efficiency of the asteroid's operation by busting the union and tapping the migrant labor market, but the reactor is running at less than fifty-percent efficiency. It's worn out and burning dirty."

When he spoke, Fine's voice was laced with sarcasm. "I don't know why everyone doesn't jump at the chance to spend sixty grand a week for the privilege of mining and smelting titanium on a rock in space!" He looked wide-eyed at Glass, who couldn't tell whether or not Fine was making a bad joke. Glass grunted nervously.

"You're my goddamn planner!" Fine snapped, working himself into a heightened state of agitation. "What the hell were you doing screwing around with a couple of punks? You don't send a goddamn hubcap thief to steal a car.

"Now listen to me." Fine lowered his voice and leaned forward across the desk. He seemed to be hovering between the extremes of violent anger and calm logic. "Listen to me, Mr. Planner," he almost hissed. "I'm losing ten times as much on the South American operations due to volume alone. If we zero out New Pittsburgh's production and buy out the Melbourne Company holdings, we can raise the world price of hard metal by maybe a point and a half."

"Ah, I see." A light came on in Glass's mind, and for a moment he forgot his anxiety. "That would put the South American ops way in the black." Glass realized in a flash why he had been given the task of appropriating the reactor plans for the smelter. "If New Pittsburgh goes out as a result of the reactor meltdown, then the insurance payoff could be used to leverage Melbourne."

Fine leaned back in his chair. "Doesn't take a rocket scientist to figure it out. What took you so long?" The CEO's voice was calm again.

Glass thought about it, but couldn't really answer his boss's question. Up until then he had carried out orders, crunched numbers and chimped out reports, mostly in fear of Fine's demented wrath if he screwed up something. Now he had really screwed up, and Fine was letting him glimpse the big picture. It made Glass even more nervous.

"Now I hope this has taught you something, Alex." Fine drummed softly on the desktop and spoke with a funeral director's voice. "Since I had to send Steller to finish your assignment, I am certain that by now you are once again an accessory to murder."

A cold shock slammed into Glass's spine. He tried to say something, but his vocal cords were frozen with the same fear that dropped his stomach through a trapdoor into a bottomless pit. "Jesus," he managed to gasp weakly.

A thin ghost of a smile crept across Fine's lips and little crow's-feet flagged the corners of his eyes. He seemed to enjoy the anguish Glass was experiencing. "Oh, come now. I know this is not your first page of sin, Alex." Fine stood and gestured nonchalantly. "You've worked for me long enough to know that...fools die in this business!" He slammed his fist on the desk, enunciating the last part of the sentence with chilling emphasis.

Glass jumped in his chair and felt himself getting sick to his stomach as Fine elaborated for his benefit. "Those two punks you sent to Bowen Brothers killed a guard and secretary during their little foray. Steller, no doubt, has added at least one cop to the list."

"But I didn't figure anyone would get killed," Glass protested weakly.

"Don't be so naive, Alex. The police aren't going to get near us. I'm sure there is no link to Titus Steel, is there?"

Glass racked his panicked brain a few moments before answering. "Ah, no. I don't think so."

"And anyone who could even speculate about such a connection is occupying a slot in the wall of the city morgue now, so relax."

"Wh-what about Steller and the cops?"

"The cops? Don't worry about—" The buzz of the intercom interrupted, and Fine pressed the button.

"Mr. Steller is on his way up." The guard's voice rang strange and hollow in the huge office, adding to the fear that coursed through Glass's mind.

"Thank you." Fine punched off and watched Glass's eyes turn fearfully toward the office doors. "You've met Steller but once, is that correct?"

"What?" Glass jerked his head toward Fine.

"I said," Fine said with mock annoyance, "you've met Mr. Steller but once."

"That's right." When Fine's words finally registered in Glass's brain he remembered with dismay the only time he'd met Fine's secret weapon.

Glass had been a passenger moving across town in Fine's limo when the CEO received a call on the Digicom. Glass didn't quite get the gist of the conversation but he could tell that Fine was excited over what was being said. At Fine's direction the driver changed course and drove to an abandoned waterfront dock near West Twenty-third Street. They pulled up next to a nondescript sedan at the end of a shabby pier. One of the biggest men Glass had ever seen got out of the driver's door and walked over to the limo. Fine pushed the button, the smoked glass window slid down, and Steller stooped to look in. Glass had retained a vivid image of the big, square-jawed blond man glancing past his boss and staring at him for what seemed like an eternity. Steller finally pulled his blue knives out of Glass's chest and asked Fine, "Who's he?"

"Oh," Fine said as though he'd made some social error, "pardon me. Mr. Steller, this is Alex Glass, my vice president of strategic planning." Glass extended his hand toward the open window, but Steller ignored the gesture. He straightened up and began pushing his fingers together as if tightening the black leather gloves stretched over obviously large hands.

"I have Mr. Avon," Steller said calmly and nodded toward the sedan. Glass looked, but couldn't see anyone in the vehicle.

"I knew that son of a bitch would show up again." Despite the angry words, Fine, too, sounded calm.

"Avon?" Glass thought aloud. "Wasn't that the guy who submarined the Anaconda buy-out by leaking the news a week ahead of schedule?"

"You're goddamn right." Glass was shocked when Fine thrust his face close to his. "The slimy shyster cost me over 130 million." Fine was hissing like a snake. Then in a sudden show of joviality he slapped Glass on the leg. "But what the hell. That was over three years ago. Let's go see how old Jack's been making out."

Steller opened the door and Fine climbed out. Glass followed, sensing that something strange was going on. He turned up his coat collar and looked out across the gloom of the Hudson. It was snowing lightly, but the weather didn't dampen Fine's suddenly improved spirits. They walked over to the sedan. "Whose car is this?" Fine asked.

"Avon was driving it," Steller answered.

Fine rubbed his hands together expectantly. "Well, get the boy out, Mr. Steller. I want to say hello."

Glass jumped backward as Steller brought one of his black booted feet up and kicked the trunk lid open with a loud bang. Glass felt as though he had entered some strange time warp where things happened beyond his control. Steller's foot had left a huge dent, and Glass figured the guy was a martial arts expert.

"Well, well," Fine said as he held out his hands in a mock gesture of welcome. "Jack Avon, as I live and breathe. What brings you to New York this time of year?"

Avon, a skinny, slight man in his mid-forties, crawled out of the trunk and held on to one of the sedan's fenders. He coughed a couple of times and spit. A trickle of blood was running from the corner of his mouth. Glass noticed that the man's eyes seemed to protrude from their sockets. At first he thought the exophthalmic eyes were caused by Avon's shock at being locked in the trunk, but after a minute or so, he realized they were just a physical feature.

"Come on," Fine said pleadingly. "Aren't you going to speak to me, Jack? After all, I made you a lot of money three years ago."

Avon made a weak attempt to brush some of the dirt from his wrinkled suit before attempting to speak. Glass thought he could see terror projected through the two protruding orbs that headlighted the man's face. "Hi, Oasis..." Avon seemed to choke, then continued. "I was going to look you up. As a matter of fact, I was on my way over to the Tower when—" He glanced at Steller.

Fine turned to Steller. "Where did you find him?"

"He was at the transatmo," Steller answered, referring to the city's dedicated airport for transatmospheric flights. "I had a tip that he would be coming in from Zealand."

"Very good." Fine turned to address Avon again. "I believed I'd see you again, Jack, and that's why I asked Mr. Steller to arrange a visit the next time you stumbled into town." Fine moved forward and brought his face within a few inches of Avon's. "I've always liked you, Jack," Fine said slowly, and, he reached up and patted Avon softly on the chest. "You have only one problem. You have an overactive tongue. Let's say—" Fine seemed to be searching for the right words "—your tongue has had a propensity to move in advance of my plans."

"But, Oasis," Avon whined, his face draining of what little color it had, "that was more than three years ago. It didn't hurt you bad—"

"No, I guess 130 million isn't such a bad loss to take and not even be able to write off, is it?" Fine looked over at Glass, who could feel a cold tremor dance up his spine. He didn't speak, but shook his head tentatively.

Fine turned his attention back to Avon, who was beginning to shiver. "The only thing you really did to me, Jack, was to deprive me of the one thing I don't have...which is more, just more." Fine smiled at his clever tautology and gave Avon another soft pat on the cheek before stepping back. "Mr. Steller, please terminate this conversation."

"No!" Avon pleaded hastily as he backed up and nearly fell when he banged into the bumper. Steller took two quick steps and grabbed the skinny body as though it were a rag. Glass could never forget what followed next—Steller literally tore the man apart, then impaled what was left of him on a steel foot peg, eight feet up a wooden light pole.

"I think he got the point," Fine had said and motioned for Glass, who had turned around to vomit, to get in the limo.

The memory of the grisly scene made Glass nauseated again. He wished he were any place but in Fine's office waiting for Steller to walk through the doors.

"You look a little pale, Alex," Fine said. "I believe my secretary is in by now. Do you want me to have her bring you some coffee, or a soft drink?"

Glass started to say something but was cut short by the intercom. Fine held up a hand and pressed the button. "Yes?"

A woman announced, "Mr. Steller."

"Send him in." Fine looked at Glass, who was now perspiring freely. "Look at you. You're sweating like a piece of pork."

Glass didn't respond. The doors to Fine's office opened electronically and Steller walked in. He wore a black jacket over a black turtleneck, black parachute pants tucked into thigh-high boots and leather gloves of the same color. Glass noticed that Steller's gloved hands seemed even larger than he remembered.

"Sit down, Mr. Steller." Fine gestured to the chair next to Glass. "You remember Alex Glass?" Steller was staring at Fine without answering or acknowledging Glass's presence, and Fine shrugged before asking, "You had a problem recovering the reactor plans?"

Steller ran gloved fingers through his short blond hair and answered, "No problem." He reached inside his jacket, pulled out a large sheaf of papers and tossed them on the desk. Glass caught a glimpse of a large handgun strapped to Steller's side.

"You mentioned a slight change of plans, something to do with the cop's family. What happened?" Fine asked with a slight degree of impatience in his voice.

"Very well," Steller spoke deliberately, almost like a machine. "Two CSU cops, midtowners, I think, took down the garbage collectors you sent to get these." He nodded at the plans on Fine's desk. "One of the cops took the plans home. I followed."

It suddenly dawned on Glass that Steller had to have been watchdogging the whole operation. "You mean you were following the two thugs we sent to Bowen Brothers?" Glass interrupted before he could restrain himself.

Steller turned and looked at Glass for a full ten seconds without blinking. "No, I mean the two thugs *you* sent," he corrected emphatically. Glass tried to swallow, but all of his spit had dried up. Steller turned back to Fine.

"I took out the cop's family with the Mag. Wanted it to look like a conventional hit." Fine nodded in approval as Steller continued. "He had a wife and daughter. Too bad they were home."

Fine shook his head in mock regret, but his face showed no sympathy. "What about the cop?" he asked. "How did you do him?"

"I gave him a taste of my boot and a couple of bullets—besides the one in the back." Steller looked at Glass who had a deadly stillness and pallor. "I left him swimming in a pool of his own blood. He had a look on his face much like your vice president's now."

"Wait a minute," Fine said, unable to keep the concern from his voice. "Wasn't the cop dead?"

"He was as good as—"

"You mean the goddamn cop wasn't dead when you left him?"

"He couldn't have lived long."

"That's just great!" Fine snapped, his face flushing with anger. "If he was living when you walked out the door, he lived too long!" Fine spit out the words as if he were filled with high-pressure steam.

Steller started to speak but didn't have an opportunity to finish.

"I don't want to hear it!" Fine yelled, which shocked Glass so badly that he nearly fell out of his chair. He couldn't believe Fine was talking in such a manner to a dangerous man like Steller. Glass glanced at the huge blond killer who calmly stared at the CEO.

"Now listen to me, both of you." Fine lowered his voice and sat down. He glanced at Glass, who shifted nervously. "We are going ahead with the New Pittsburgh plan. You—" he nodded toward Glass "—better get your ass in gear and review the insurance policies for that chunk of rock. I don't want some asshole lawyer screwing us on a technicality."

"As for you—" Fine paused to glare at Steller "—I want a confirmation on this cop."

"His name was Horn," Steller said.

Fine looked puzzled. "What?"

"The cop's name was Horn. It was on his mailbox," Steller said matter-of-factly.

"I don't give a good goddamn if his name was Jesus, for Christ's sake!" Fine hissed. "I want you to make sure his ass is a dead chunk of ice. Got it?"

His face still expressionless, Steller nodded.

Fine looked Glass over, then waved toward the door. "Dismissed." Steller also started to get up, but Fine motioned for him to remain.

As soon as Glass got into the hall, he headed straight for the men's rest room. Once inside, he barely made one of the stainless steel sinks before unloading his breakfast. He didn't hear the door open or the black boots walk across the marble tile.

He raised his head from the sink and froze in fear as Steller's face grinned at him from the mirror. The big man brought his gloved hands up and clapped the open palms on either side of Glass's head. It was like the crashing of cymbals; at least that was the last thought Glass had before his brain went dead.

AT HIS DESK, Fine smiled to himself. He knew Steller would find some creative way to dispose of Glass's body. He was glad he wouldn't have to worry about how much Glass knew. He had sensed a vein of morality in his vice president's makeup—or at least some cowardice—and knew the only way to get rid of it was to get rid of the man. The concerns of right and wrong weren't, after all, in Glass's charter.

Fine almost started to laugh aloud at his thoughts, but checked the sound in his throat and nearly choked when he noticed the woman who stood in front of his desk. "Mother," he gasped weakly. "How did you get in here?"

"I wanted to see if you botched this operation, Oasis." She sat down in a chair and crossed her long legs before she continued. "And once again, you have not disappointed me."

Fine stared at her and his blood ran cold. "I, er, things are on track." His voice was nervous and his palms felt wet and clammy.

Ashley Fine was well preserved for a woman in her mid-fifties. She was tall and well built, with a hint of toned muscles in her slender legs and long neck. Her body was an intriguing contrast to her face, which was showing its age a little more, although not ungracefully. Her eyes burned with intensity, and their startlingly green color was enhanced by her almost ethereal gray hair, which was pulled back sleekly, matching her elegant gray suit. Hanging on a platinum chain around her neck, looking like a third eye, was a thumb-sized, teardrop-shaped emerald. She wore black stockings and black heels that were almost too high for her look of conservative ease, yet they fit with her overall demeanor, which exuded self-confidence and a studied sensuality.

Fine moistened his lips and felt a tingling at the back of his neck. He often wondered if his mother had been a guiding force in his late father's life, too. Fine wasn't complaining, however. His mother's shrewd manipulation of their stock holdings after his father's death had allowed them to make the leveraged buy-out of Titus Steel.

There was something else about his mother that put Fine on edge. It was an odd sort of attraction to her as his mentor, somebody more powerful than he. Yet he didn't like to think he derived his power and place from the woman who had given him birth. Her association and involvement in his business operations had from the beginning been as close as though she were one with him, a companion more than a parent on the sidelines. Because of that, her sensuous attractiveness made Fine strangely nervous and created a dimension of intimacy into which he felt helplessly drawn.

Fine cleared his throat and avoided his mother's gaze. "Well, this problem with the plans was just a glitch. Nothing for you to worry about. Steller . . . ah . . . I have everything under control." He moved uncomfortably in his chair and thought, ironically, that he felt the way Glass must have when he and Steller were making him squirm and sweat.

"Sure you do, Oasis." Ashley Fine smiled, exposing even white teeth behind slightly colored lips.

Fine wondered how she could look so immaculate and in full possession of her senses at such an early hour. Then again, he could not remember ever seeing her when she wasn't dressed and made up to a tee.

"There's no problem," he said with authority as he lost a little of his nervousness. "Steller will take care of the cop—"

"I am well aware of Mr. Steller's capabilities," Ashley cut him off, the smile instantly disappearing from her face. "Need I remind you of the importance of executing this New Pittsburgh operation without . . . how shall I put it, outside interference?"

Fine held up a hand in agreement. "No, Mother."

Ashley stood and leaned forward, placing her hands on the desk. "Steller is only as good as the direction he receives." Her voice was low, almost soothing, and seemed to float to Fine on a cloud of her perfume. "You can't depend on him to make critical decisions."

Fine looked down at his hands while he formulated his reply. "No doubt I hadn't been specific enough when I told Steller to—"

"That's water under the bridge." She straightened and walked behind the desk to stand next to Oasis. Feeling more alert and aware, he watched her from the corner of his eye. He said nothing and didn't try to stop her when she pulled open the drawer of the desk where he kept his pills.

"Oasis . . ." Ashley's voice was strangely emotionless. "You shouldn't be taking these." She held up the large bottle of pills.

Fine was a little surprised when she put the amphetamines back in the drawer and closed it. He felt her move behind his chair and cradle his head briefly in her perfumed hands. "You really should take better care of your health, Oasis."

Fine experienced a floating sensation as she began to rub his temples. Her sure fingers moved lightly and soothingly, and Fine felt himself relax.

He exhaled softly. "You always could bring me to heel," he acknowledged admiringly. But there was no response and when he next turned around, she was gone. Her scent lingered on, and he wondered fleetingly if he could live without her at all, then came a darker thought—would he be better off with her gone?

CHAPTER THREE

HORN THOUGHT it was raining diamonds. It was beautiful, warm and wet. Through the sparkling curtain he could see Sharon and Julie laughing and running across the green grass. Horn got up from where he had been sitting and took up the chase, thinking all the while that a rained-out picnic had never been so much fun. Julie was giggling and jumping from puddle to puddle, while Sharon chased her with glee.

"Hey!" Horn yelled. "Wait for me!" He thought it odd that his voice came back to him in a strange echo. "Hey!" he yelled again and noticed his wife and daughter moving farther and farther away. He willed his legs to pick up the pace, but the harder he tried, the more slowly they moved. "Hey! Wait!" But Sharon and Julie continued to dance and play, growing more distant, seemingly oblivious to Horn's voice.

Great weights seemed to drag Horn's feet to a stop, and he watched Julie and Sharon fade into the rain. He looked around the park and was suddenly filled with an overwhelming sense of emptiness. He felt as though his chest were in a giant vise, and he began to weep. In a while Horn looked up from his sobbing and saw a lone figure coming toward him through the rain. There was something vaguely familiar in his walk, and Horn realized it was Riddle.

"Dan!" Horn's shoulders stopped heaving, and he was overcome with a sense of relief. "Man, am I glad to see you!"

"It's good to see you, partner." Riddle put a comforting hand on Horn's shoulder.

"Come on," Horn said as he made an attempt to move. "We've got to go find Sharon and Julie."

A pain-filled look washed over Riddle's face. "No, buddy," he said softly, "you gotta come with me."

"No!" Horn's voice echoed loudly in his ear. "I've got to find Sharon and Julie. This park isn't the place...."

Horn felt a tug on his arm and realized that Riddle was trying to hold him back. "Let go!" Horn shouted, but his voice sounded as if it emerged from a well. "I've got to get Sharon...."

Suddenly Riddle's pull on his arm became more pronounced, and the rain gave way to stark, white light. Riddle's voice became clearer and seemed to turn a key inside Horn's head. "Welcome back to the land of the living, partner. Damn, I thought we'd lost you."

Horn's eyes adjusted slowly to the bright light, and Riddle's face came into focus. He could see a border of chrome rails, a tangle of tubes running from his arm up to inverted bottles suspended above him, and he heard the soft hum of machinery. Horn grasped that he was in the hospital. At the same time the reality of what had taken place in his home grabbed his heart and threatened to crush it.

He let out a mournful cry that made Riddle jump away from the bed a couple of steps. A nurse quickly entered the room and moved to the side of the bed. "Nice to see you awake," she remarked as she went about checking the IV. "Are you in pain?"

Horn stifled a groan and turned his head away. The nurse tactfully refrained from saying anything else to Horn. "I'll follow up with the doctor," she said to Riddle. "He'll probably want to prescribe a sedative...besides an analgesic. It will make him drowsy."

"Give me ten minutes first. I need to talk to him."

The nurse looked at Horn before glancing at her watch. "Very well, but don't tire him out." She left Riddle and Horn alone.

"Listen, partner—" Riddle patted Horn on the shoulder "—you damn near died on me." Horn kept his head turned away and remained quiet, and Riddle tried hard to swallow the lump in his throat before carrying on. "I've always shot straight with you, Max, and I'm not going to pull any punches now. The bastards got Sharon and Julie.... I'm sorry."

Riddle was a little surprised to hear Horn's low response. "I know. But there was just one."

"What?" Riddle had heard what Horn said, but in his surprise the word popped out of his mouth before he could stop himself.

Without turning his head Horn restated, "There was only one guy, Dan, just one."

Riddle suddenly felt very uncomfortable. "Listen, buddy," he rattled off as he shifted his weight from one foot to the other. "The doctor's going to be here in a couple of minutes and give you some, ah, medicine. How about I come back later tonight and see how you're doing?"

"How long have I been out?" Horn demanded, ignoring Riddle's question.

"Seven days."

Horn turned his head toward his partner and realized he was seeing through only one eye. "What the hell, Dan? Only one of my eyes is working."

"Don't worry," Riddle hastened to reassure him. "You can't see out of your right eye because it's swollen shut. You got about sixteen stitches on your cheek."

Horn remembered the boot moving toward his face like a swinging ax. In a sudden flood he also recalled the rest of the scene in the hallway. He tried to move his limbs. His left arm and leg seemed to function, but attempts to move his right arm and leg resulted in a foreign sort of twitching beneath the sheets, followed by a mild shocking sensation running up and down his spine. "What the hell is going on, Dan?" Horn felt a wave of helpless panic wash through his chest.

Riddle cleared his throat. "They removed a slug from near your spine that damn near paralyzed you. A .44 took off your right arm and most of the shoulder... The guy must have let you have it point-blank."

"What about my goddamn leg?" Horn's voice was hoarse and almost pleading.

"Your knee was blown away." Riddle leaned over the rail of the bed and looked into his partner's eye. "They said it was *just gone...*."

Horn racked his brain, but couldn't remember his leg getting zapped. "Is it that bad?" he asked.

"They had to mod the whole knee. They saved the lower leg and foot. At least those will be almost normal."

Horn twisted his head around enough to see the lump under the sheet that should have been his right arm. "Shoulder and arm, too?"

"Yeah," Riddle said.

Horn willed his right arm to move, and an uncontrolled twitching made the sheets bounce up and down. He tried the same thing with his leg and heard the rails bang as it flopped around. Like a goddamn fish out of water, he thought.

"Let me see the arm, Dan." Horn gazed fixedly at the sheet.

Riddle started to say something but checked it. He leaned over and pulled the sheet away from Horn's arm, revealing flesh-colored plastic. "Goddamn toy arm," Horn breathed.

"They're making them better than they used to," Riddle said, immediately regretting his words.

"Bullshit," Horn snapped, emotion filling his voice. "You remember that uptown cop who lost his legs in the subway?" Riddle didn't answer. "That poor bastard looked like a drunken puppet walking down the street."

"Take it easy," Riddle said in an attempt to console Horn. "The state has made significant improvements in the electromech—"

"Give it a rest," Horn cut his partner off. "I know all about the goddamn state mod program for trauma cases."

"Hold on a minute—"

"No, you hold on a minute, Dan. You're not going to have to move around like some goddamned gimp—I am." A sad sort of half laugh escaped Horn's lips. "They may as well give me a peg leg and hook, for Christ's sake."

Riddle squared his shoulders and stepped away from the bed. "I'm going to take off now, but I'll see you later tonight. I'm sorry about Sharon and Julie."

A black curtain fell over Horn. He'd been so caught up in his self-pity that he'd momentarily forgotten his true loss. A smarting filled his eye and constricted his throat. "I'm sorry, partner," he mumbled.

"Forget it," Dan said, waving an arm. "I'll see you tonight."

Without thinking, Horn attempted to raise his right arm in order to wave, and the lump under the sheets jumped spasmodically. He was glad when the nurse finally came in and stuck the laser needle into his right hip.

During the weeks that followed, Horn went through the motions of physical therapy and trauma counseling. His heart wasn't in it. He was released from the hospital on the assumption he'd have ongoing outpatient therapy, but Horn wasn't a good patient in or out of the hospital. Especially after the memorial service for Sharon and Julie, he often skipped his therapy sessions, preferring to sit alone in his apartment, drinking and staring at the darkness.

Riddle could see that his partner was in a long downhill slide. He'd tried to snap him out of it several times, but nothing seemed to work. He tried to talk Horn into taking a desk job that had been set up with the division chief, but Horn sloughed it off as "cop charity."

Riddle was nearly at the end of his rope. For more than eight weeks he'd tried unsuccessfully to get Horn back on track, any kind of track. He was taken aback when Horn unexpectedly disclosed his intentions.

"You're going to do what?" Riddle raised his voice in surprise. The two men were sitting in Horn's kitchen, which was literally inundated with trash. Beer cans filled the sink. Empty whiskey bottles overflowed the garbage can. A half-empty bottle sat in front of Horn, who was drinking from a dirty coffee cup. Dark circles outlined his eyes, and the fresh pink scar across his cheek looked like a furrow in the two weeks' worth of beard.

"I'm taking a slot on New Pittsburgh. I saw the opening on the net," Horn answered, referring to the limited-access hot line for openings in the police department.

"You've got to be shittin' me!" Riddle said with disgusted surprise. "Why the hell would you want to go there? That's where they send the rookie screwups and washed-out boozers."

"Look at this crap," Horn said. He picked up the cup of whiskey with his right hand in a jerking motion that sloshed whiskey onto the table. "I hate it." He grabbed the cup with his left hand and downed what was left of the amber liquid.

"What's that got to do with you wanting to play security guard on some burned-out mining colony?" Riddle scowled ferociously as he added, "In space, for God's sake!"

"Maybe I just need a new start," Horn answered weakly, then almost laughed at the shallowness of his own statement. He wondered if he would ever get over the nightmare deaths of his family. And the face of the grinning blond specter that had left him for dead seemed to be burned into his mind with a branding iron.

"But there are a lot of other options, partner," Riddle offered. "I guess I don't understand this New Pitts—" He stopped in midsentence. "Wait a second!" His eyes narrowed, and he stared suspiciously, almost knowingly at Horn.

"What's the matter?" Horn poured more whiskey into the cup and gulped down a mouthful. A trickle of booze ran from one corner of his mouth, and he wiped it with the sleeve of his bathrobe.

"Wait a second," Riddle repeated. He seemed to be searching his memory for something.

"Aw, screw you," Horn said drunkenly as he staggered to his feet. He grabbed the bottle of whiskey and shuffled over to the counter, which was covered with dirty dishes and food wrappers. "Where's my goddamn pills?" He jerked open a drawer and fished around, finally pulling out a bottle of generic painkillers. He managed to open it and dump a couple of the capsules into his mouth. He tried to raise the whiskey bottle to his lips with his right hand, but it began to jerk around, and the liquid dribbled down the front of his robe.

"Look at you!" Riddle said, momentarily forgetting that he was trying to remember something. "I doubt if they'd send you up in a garbage scow, let alone a goddamn shuttle. The shape you're in, you'd die before you got out of orbit."

"Why don't you go mother somebody else?" Horn grabbed the bottle with his left hand and raised it to his lips. He suddenly choked, spitting whiskey and pills across the dirty floor. "Jesus!" he said after gagging a couple of seconds. "That was an interesting jolt." He returned the bottle to his lips and downed what was left of its contents.

"Yeah, just hold it a minute," Riddle said, as though the memory he had been searching for had suddenly become clear.

"Blow it out your ass." Horn stopped and belched for greater effect. "You been saying 'wait a second, wait a minute' for the past goddamn hour. You're giving me a ten-ton headache." He turned toward the sink, scooped out several handfuls of dirty dishes and turned on the water. "Excuse me while I shower." He leaned over and stuck his head under the stream.

"Yup, I remember now," Riddle crowed triumphantly. "New Pittsburgh."

"What?" Horn yelled. "I can't hear what you're saying."

"I said," Riddle shouted over the sound of the running water, "the plans—the goddamn plans those punks ripped off were for the smelter reactor on New Pittsburgh!"

There was a metallic thud as Horn suddenly raised his head and banged it into the faucet. "Son of a bitch!" he yelled painfully and fumbled for the knob. He managed to get the water turned off and spun around to face Riddle.

Water dripped from his matted hair and he raised the tail of his robe to dry it. "You keep your face out of my business, Riddle," Horn said in a sober, mean voice as he rubbed his hair with the dirty terry cloth.

Riddle could see the fake pink flesh of Horn's modified knee. The real flesh, above and below the high-impact-plastic covering of the artificial joint, was still bruised in shades of dark purple and wine-red. In spite of what Horn had gone through, the rest of his body remained hard and lean.

Riddle felt an intense stab of sorrow for his partner, but it didn't keep him from honing in on his suspicions. "That's the real reason you want to go to New Pittsburgh, isn't it?" he asked.

"You're full of shit." Horn sat down and stared at Riddle in a deadpan manner.

Unblinking, Riddle returned the look. "You think there's a connection between those plans and what happened to you and your family."

"At least . . ." Horn paused a couple of seconds before completing the sentence. "I *hope* there is. Now you listen to me. Some punk tried to off me in the tube the other day when I was coming back from therapy."

"Why didn't you—"

"Don't worry about it, goddammit." Horn seemed a little irritated. "I took care of him, but that's not the point. The guy had been tailing me for about a week. He wasn't hard to nail once he got up enough courage to make his move."

"What has that got to do with the plans?" Riddle seemed anxious to hear Horn's logic.

Horn held up a hand. "Hold on. Anyway, the tail was kind enough to describe the guy who put him onto me."

"Yeah?" Riddle leaned forward in his chair.

"A big blond bastard with a nose that's been rearranged about forty times." Horn got up from the table and walked over to the sink. He picked up a glass and filled it with water. "Want something to drink?" He held the glass toward Riddle, who glanced at the heap of dirty dishes before shaking his head. Horn continued. "The son of a bitch that came after the plans and killed my wife and daughter has figured out that he didn't finish the job. He should have left me dead, instead of *for* dead."

"What about the punk on the subway?" Riddle asked, more out of curiosity than anything else.

"Oh, the clumsy asshole fell in front of the midtown express." Horn chuckled strangely. "I guess a 9 mm in the back of the head made him a little dizzy."

"Shit." Riddle sounded mildly concerned. "Didn't you report it?"

"Hell, no," Horn answered. "Those lazy bastards uptown laughed when I asked them to check out the connection between the plans and the hit on my home, remember? They said the double theft of the plans was, to quote them, 'a coincidental duality, interesting but without merit in terms of conducting a major investigation.'" Horn turned and spit into the sink.

"Yeah," Riddle commented, "not much face time to be had on a case like yours."

"Thing is," Horn stated matter-of-factly. "I'm going to find out who and why. I've got nothing else to do."

"What about your career?" Riddle asked.

"My career as a cop?" Horn laughed. "Look at this." He let his robe drop away from his shoulders, revealing the smooth plastic of his right shoulder and arm. He reached out, his motion strobelike and shaky, to pick up the telemonitor from the table. It slipped out of his electromechanical hand twice before he was able to manage a

substantial grip. "See? This thing is about two steps behind my brain, and it's the same with the leg. You think I'm
ever going to get back on a CSU with this kind of junk?"

"I see." Riddle had the wily look in his eyes that showed
when he was circumventing or ignoring regulations. "How
much money have you got, Max?"

"What?" Riddle's question caught him completely off
guard. "How much money? My wallet's over there." He
pointed to a table near the door. "Take as many credits as
you need."

"No." Riddle shook his head. "How much money do
you have cumulative, in total?"

Horn couldn't figure out why Riddle would ask such a
question. "Why the hell do you want to know?"

Riddle's voice became dead serious. "Because, if you're
really going to pull this New Pittsburgh jaunt, then you're
going to need some help."

"I'm going to go solo," Horn said.

"You dumb ass." Horn was a little taken aback by Riddle's language and the tone of his voice. "That's not the
kind of help I'm talking about. Now, how much goddamn
money have you got?"

"I've got over a hundred grand." He hung his head, then
looked up with the bleakest look in his eyes. "Sharon and
Julie's insurance, you know."

"Probably cost you about half that, but if you insist on
chasing down this mystery, it'll be worth it. May even wind
up saving your butt," Riddle said, chuckling.

"I still don't know what the hell you're talking about."
Though Horn shrugged, he couldn't help sounding curious.

"Well," Riddle ventured cautiously, "I have a friend
who has a friend who can get those worthless state mods of
yours supertuned."

"Huh?" Horn's eyes lit up suddenly, which made Riddle take particular notice. It was the first sign of vitality he'd seen in his partner's eyes. "For real?"

"Sure, the guy's a friend of Rollie G.," Riddle answered, referring to one of his regular informants.

Horn had heard stories about an underground group of technocratic doctors—techno-docs in street terms—who would replace the substandard, detuned state body modifications with enhanced modifications, for a price. The practice was considered a first-degree felony for those caught performing what was called an E-mod operation, and a third-degree felony for anyone receiving one of the outlawed mods.

"Do you think the stories about guys getting supertuned, turning into...you know—" Horn broke off as though searching for the correct word. "What am I trying to say, Dan?"

"You mean turning into flaming assholes?" Riddle grinned, and Max let out a brief guffaw. "No, really—" Riddle stopped to resume a serious expression again "—I've seen a couple of guys over the years who got tuned up. The strength was damn near uncontrollable. The problem with those guys, as well as others I've heard about, is that it went to their heads." Riddle caught Horn's eyes with his own. "I heard one guy say it felt godlike."

"What happened to him?" Horn asked.

"He forgot his skull wasn't modified, and some rookie blue suit blew his head apart with a damn .22 water hose." Riddle shrugged, then eyed Horn speculatively. "You interested?"

"Yeah," Horn answered.

"Well," Riddle said as he got to his feet, "you sleep on it a couple of days. If you want to give it a shot, give me a call and I'll set it up."

"You forgot one thing, Dan." Horn said.

"What's that?" Riddle asked as he reached for the doorknob.

Horn patted his partner on the shoulder. "I don't sleep."

CHAPTER FOUR

THERE WAS NO DOUBT in Horn's mind even before Riddle had left his apartment, but he waited until the next day before calling him. "I'm ready," he announced simply.

"You still look like hell," Riddle said, squinting into the LCD screen of the telemonitor. "What are you ready for? To die?"

Horn could see Riddle trying to suppress a smile. "No, Mother." Horn chuckled and gave his partner the bird. "I'm ready to up the status of this tired old body."

Riddle was encouraged. It was good to hear Horn kid around. "In anticipation of your decision, I contacted Rollie G.," Riddle said. "We're supposed to meet him tomorrow night at a joint in the Bronx. In the meantime, get some rest and get cleaned up."

"Get cleaned up?" Horn continued to joke. "To go to the Bronx?"

"Get your credits together, too." Riddle figured they would have to fork over payment as well as some type of agent's fee to Rollie.

"Fifty grand?" Horn asked, remembering their previous conversation.

"Yeah. I hope whoever Rollie hooks up with takes electrocash."

"Anything else?"

"No. If I think of anything, I'll call." Riddle paused a couple of seconds. "I'll pick you up tomorrow night about seven."

"See you." Horn reached over and clicked off the telemonitor. He almost felt good.

Riddle rang Horn from the Buick when he was ten blocks away. Horn was waiting by the curb and got into the car, wearing a faded green fatigue jacket Riddle had never seen before. He started to ask about it, but checked himself when he noticed the faded combat patches and realized it must have been Horn's father's.

"Where are we supposed to meet Rollie?" Horn asked as Riddle pulled away from the curb.

"Ned Edge's," Riddle said as he jockeyed the Buick into traffic.

"Ned Edge's?" Horn thought out loud. "You don't mean Ned Edge's Limber-Up Lounge, do you?"

"Yeah. The one and only."

"I thought they closed the place down."

"Which time?" Riddle said with a laugh. "The place is an institution."

"That's what I understand." Horn grunted. "An institution for every wacko in the city."

Ned Edge's Limber-Up Lounge was infamous. Located in the remains of the long-abandoned Bronx Zoo, it was the gathering place for drug dealers, prostitutes, weapons peddlers and any other street hustlers imaginable. The name of the place fit, for it was where the desperate limbered up, made their deals, passed their information and tried to get an edge on the other scramblers, string heads and needle racers.

When the zoo went broke, Ned Edge, a jazz musician of local fame in Spanish Harlem, moved in and purchased what had been the ape house. It was huge, having once housed more than a hundred primates. The common complaint was that the place still smelled of urine.

It was almost 10:00 p.m. when the two cops pulled up in front of Ned's. Although it was early, the place was packed. Dozens of people milled about on the sidewalk near the huge front door over which a red-and-white neon sign proclaimed: Ned Edge's Limbo Lounge and Jazz Hall.

Riddle parked next to a fire hydrant and, although they hadn't spotted another cop since they crossed the George Washington Bridge, he reached into the glove box and stuck the official vehicle ID on the dash. "Afraid you're going to get a ticket?" Horn chided.

"Hold on," Riddle said, turning away from the crowd on the sidewalk. He reached into his jacket, pulled out a dull black Composite Arms .44 Automag and ejected the 10-shell clip. He gave it a quick look, then shoved it back into the butt of the weapon. Riddle glanced over his shoulder as he charged the big handgun and pushed it back into the holster beneath his jacket. "You carrying a piece?" he asked Horn.

"Just my old laser niner."

Riddle locked up the Buick, and the two cops walked toward the entrance to Ned's. They hadn't gone six feet before two slinky-looking women stepped out of the crowd and into their path. "I know it's early, guys, but would you like to get the evening started right?" Horn looked over the one who had spoken. She was good-looking: long legs, long blond hair and an athletic, yet generous body that was straining to break out of the silver wraparound minidress. She looked like a strange, sexy bullet.

"You hunting werewolves tonight?" Horn asked, and the blonde smiled, parting her pouty, sensuous lips and revealing a mouthful of perfect teeth.

"How about you, sweetie?" Riddle asked the other hooker, a shorter but also beautiful blonde. "You always dress to kill?"

"Come on, Danny," the tall one said. "What brings the cops into bonzo land tonight?" She looked at Horn, and before Riddle could answer her question she asked another. "Who's your friend? He a cop, too?" There was a glint of pure animal sex in her eyes as she smiled at Horn.

Horn felt as though she had reached down and squeezed an intimate part of his body. He looked at Riddle and asked, "You know the ladies, Dan?"

"Yeah," Riddle answered, as if revealing a secret. He introduced Horn to Robin Silver, the long-legged silver bullet, and Desirée Oldham, the more petite man-killer.

"You still didn't answer my question," Robin said. "What are you doing up here?"

"Supposed to meet Rollie G." Riddle glanced briefly around the crowd. "You seen him?"

The smiles immediately faded from the women's faces. "Rollie G.?" Desirée said disgustedly. "Why do you want to meet with that jerk?"

"Don't worry, sweet one," Riddle said, smiling. "I don't want to date the guy. I just want to talk to him."

"He's in there." Robin shrugged nonchalantly toward the door, setting two orbs into motion in the confines of her dress.

"Thanks, babe." Riddle nodded at Horn, and they started toward the door.

"Hey!" The two cops turned back when Robin called after them. "Why don't you come looking for us sometime?" She smiled seductively, while Desirée gave them the classic pose: hand on the extended hip, the split red skirt showing leg to the waist.

"Yeah," Desirée added, shifting her weight to the other foot. "Maybe we'll give you a freebie."

"Sure, that'll be the day," Riddle laughed good-naturedly.

"I'm shocked at you, partner," Horn said as they paused near the massive steel doors of the club, which seemed to vibrate in time with the music coming from inside.

Riddle was grinning. "What do you mean?"

"I didn't know what kind of company you kept," Horn said with a conspiratorial wink at his partner.

"You got a lot to learn, rookie," Riddle said, shoving the doors open. "Let's go have a brew with old Rollie G." Horn followed him into the din.

Ned Edge considered himself one of the avant-garde leaders of jazz music in the twenty-first century. He made it a practice to book innovative bands, whether or not they had talent. Indeed, he saw himself as the pioneer of punk jazz, limbo jazz, slide metal jazz and BD motor-driven jazz. Because his club was filled to capacity every night, Ned believed he had established a following that bordered on cult status. He didn't realize that the majority of the street life wasting hours in his place were simply chasing desperate dreams down dead-end streets. Also the booze was cheap.

There was a huge stage in the center of the club that had once been an elevated platform for the apes to lounge on. An oval bar was built around it. The stage was bathed in blue and white spotlights shining through the smoky haze. The only other lights in the place were a few candles scattered on the tables. An area of about two hundred square yards was set aside next to the bar for dancing.

Ned weighed in at close to three hundred pounds, all of it packed on a frame that didn't exceed five feet by much. He loved his club and liked to roam around the bar acting like a big shot. He had slicked-back jet-black hair, and his beard had stripes of silver in it that were actually aluminum spray paint—a carryover from his punk jazz period. Wraparound mirrored shades and island print shirts were part of his trademark. About one night a week one of his bouncers would help him onto the stage, and he'd play two and a half hours of solo free form on his alto sax, which had been modified with a fuel control valve from a gasoline turbine. When he'd first start to play, the crowd would get real quiet, as though they were about to witness something historic, but after about ten minutes of old Ned puffing his cheeks like a blowfish, the noise would return to its usual riotous level. Ned would continue blowing away, oblivious to the crowd, the lights, everything but his playing.

But it wasn't Ned who was gracing the stage when Riddle and Horn entered the place. It was a band from Queens called the Dave Raven Review, which consisted of two trumpet players and a drummer who had a setup driven by an electric motor. The actual striking of the snare, bass and cymbals was programmed to be random. The drums' operator controlled the speed at which they were struck by twisting a rheostat...twisting it, naturally, in time with the music.

As the two cops took a seat at an empty table, Horn figured the drums were hitting about a thousand revolutions per minute. He watched a few minutes and noticed that the electric motor was beginning to smoke. He glanced at the rheostat man, who was fiddling with the control device. The limp-haired, skinny musician looked over at his drum set just in time to watch and hear it self-destruct in a crescendo. Both trumpet players stopped blowing and watched the death throes of the drum set in obvious bewilderment. It flopped around a couple of seconds after the motor finally froze, before settling into a sad heap of junk. The crowd went wild, and the Dave Raven Review got their first standing ovation.

Horn and Riddle ordered beer from a tired-looking waitress. When she brought the lukewarm brew, Riddle handed her a ten-dollar disposable credit and asked her to send Ned over to their table. "Ned? Who's Ned?" the washed-out-looking woman questioned.

"He's the owner of this dump, sweetheart." Riddle pointed at the obese proprietor, who was waddling around behind the bar. "See? He's the short fat guy with the racing stripes in his beard."

"Oh, yeah," the waitress said without looking around. "You mean the round horny one." She walked back toward the bar in a winding path through the crowded tables.

Horn picked up the foaming glass of beer with his right hand, which was so unsteady that some of the brew slopped over onto the table. He muttered angrily under his breath and grabbed the glass with his left hand. He noticed Riddle watching him and wanted to divert attention from the sloppy functions of his appendage. He didn't need to be pitied. "So, do you see your buddy, Rollie G., anywhere?"

"No, and I've been looking for the little toad, too." Riddle glanced at his watch then craned his neck around, peering into the hazy shadows. "Old Rollie always has to be fashionably late. I remember the time over on the West—"

Riddle's reminiscing was cut short when Ned slapped a pudgy hand on the cop's shoulder. "Hey, Riddle, Riddle," the huge man chortled as he turned a chair around and straddled it. "You just come in out of the rain, or what?"

"This is my partner, Max Horn," Riddle said. Horn reached across the table with his good hand and slapped Ned's fat paw.

"Yeah, Horn," Ned grunted then turned back to Riddle. "How about that goddamn Dave?"

"Who?" Riddle looked puzzled.

Ned almost looked hurt. "Dave, Dave Raven. The band."

"Oh, yeah." Riddle shook his head. "That was some finish there, Ned."

"Yeah, that bastard knows how to bring down the house." Ned shook his head as if amazed, then asked, "What can I do for you?"

"I'm looking for Rollie G. He was supposed to meet me here more than an hour ago. You seen him?"

"Yeah, the little chimp is here." Ned turned his head to one side and spit on the floor. "He's back in the corner doing string with some other flake. Want me to send him over?"

"I'd appreciate it."

Ned got to his feet and ambled off through the heaving mass of humanity, shaking hands and demanding to know if people were having a good time. From some of the looks Ned got, Horn figured most people didn't realize that he owned the place.

Riddle ordered himself and Horn another round of beer, and they watched the crowd. "Here he comes." Riddle indicated a man who stood out even in that assortment of oddities.

Rollie walked up to their table among the jostling crowd as though he were tuned in with radar. "Hiya, Dan." He spoke quickly, two or three times faster than a typical New Yorker. "This your friend with the bad bod?" Rollie emitted a high-pitched stuttering cackle every so often, as though he were punctuating his sentences with them.

Horn looked over the skinny little man. He had dirty, sand-colored hair that was combed straight back and his face was deeply pitted with acne scars. A clownish plaid sport coat hung on his shoulders like a rag, covering a wine-stained gray turtleneck. Round, black sunglasses called Blindmans covered his eyes, and when he smiled, those in his presence felt compelled to look away in embarrassment at the less than pretty sight.

"Yeah," Riddle answered, "this is Horn."

Rollie nodded to Horn as he sat down. "How about some wine, Dan?" He moved his head around constantly in a jerky manner and tapped his fingers on the table in time to the weird light-speed music that was obviously playing in his head.

Riddle raised a hand and ordered a glass of red wine for the informer. He then turned toward Rollie and said, "Man, what have you been doing, gas track? Your mind seems to be running at flood level." Riddle knew Rollie was addicted to stimulants and rarely saw the little beggar when he wasn't blown out of his brain.

Rollie cackled again. "No, not track," he said, pulling a little plastic box out of his inside jacket pocket. It looked like a roll of dental floss, but having seen Rollie's teeth, Horn knew it wasn't. "I been doing string, man." He pulled a foot of white string out of the container and snapped it off with his teeth. He then rolled it into a little ball, popped it into his mouth and worked it around for a couple of seconds before he cleared his throat and coughed. He leaned over the table and appeared to gently blow his nose into the palm of his hand. When he lifted his head, the end of the string was hanging out of one of his nostrils. "Ta-da," he said conspiratorially. "Want some?"

"Ah, no thanks," Riddle answered.

Horn shook his head and almost gagged as he watched Rollie grab the end of the string and slowly pull it out of his nose. "Ahh..." he said, tossing it to the floor. "That's some fast ride." He stuffed the roll back into his coat and wiped his runny nose on the sleeve of his jacket. "Great stuff."

"No doubt," Riddle scoffed. "Now let's get down to business. You got my friend Horn here lined up with a mod doctor?"

"Only one of the best." Rollie's eyes glinted as his mouth kicked into high gear. "The cat's name is Dr. August. Used to be a rocket scientist, for a supersecret, space-based military way station, designed for the light wand, the laser trapper..." Rollie's speech suddenly made no sense, and his words ran together. For a couple of seconds Horn thought the guy had started speaking some foreign language.

"Hey!" Riddle leaned over and slapped Rollie on the cheek. "You ain't on Mars—come back here."

"Huh?" Rollie shook his head and looked around as though he had just emerged from a dream. "Wow!" he said. "Man, was that clean."

"Have you got Horn set up with this August guy?" Riddle repeated.

"Ah, yeah. As a matter of fact—" Rollie paused to look at his wrist, and Horn noticed he wore no watch "—you can go over there anytime within the next three days."

Riddle figured they had another day before the window closed. "How do we make contact?" he asked.

Rollie seemed a little more coherent and pulled a piece of folded graph paper out of one of his pockets. "I got a map," he said, unfolding it, and Horn moved the slow-burning candle closer.

"See this building here?" Rollie stabbed his finger onto the page near the Bronx Expressway. "That's August's crib. I told him you would use the code word . . ." Rollie seemed to be straining to remember. "Light wand, yeah, that's it."

Riddle grunted dubiously through his nose. "You gotta be full of shit, Rollie. I guess it hasn't penetrated that out-of-control comet you call a brain that I haven't paid you yet. Remember our discussion of a finder's fee?"

Rollie got a pained look on his face. "Oh, yeah," he said, "I guess you'll probably want me to take you and do the intros, huh?"

"I guess." Riddle looked at Horn, who just shrugged. "What do you think, partner?" he asked. "How credible do you think Mr. Speed Racer here is? Still want to take a chance?"

Horn looked at the druggie, who flashed him a big smile. "Hell," he said, turning away from the sight, "I've got nothing better to do."

"I suspected you were going to say that." Riddle looked at Rollie speculatively. "Yeah, you're going to have to take us tonight."

"Shit." Rollie grinned. "I knew you were going to say that." He pushed his chair away from the table. "Gimme my creds, and I'll take you."

"Give the man two hundred credits, Horn," Riddle said.

"Wait a second. You said a thousand."

"You'll get the other eight hundred when we meet Dr. August," Riddle answered. "Fair enough?"

"What the hell . . ." Rollie picked up the two-hundred-dollar credit disk that Horn had tossed on the table, then stood up. "You guys meet me out front . . . I gotta go take a piss."

Horn was a little surprised when Riddle answered, "Sure, go ahead, Rollie."

"Let's go," Riddle said as soon as Rollie had disappeared. Horn followed his partner out to the car. "Ha!" Riddle went on as he quickly unlocked the doors and fired up the big rotary. "I can read that little son of a bitch like a comic book."

Horn was jerked back in the seat as Riddle gunned away from the curb, tires smoking, causing the hangers-out in front of the bar to turn their heads. Riddle fired the Buick down the alley and slid to a stop next to a lone door marked Zoo Personnel Only. He grinned at Horn before stepping out and opening the rear door of the sedan.

Not ten seconds later the back door of Ned's burst open, and Rollie G. stumbled out looking as if he'd been shot out of a nuclear bazooka. "Hi, Rollie," Riddle said, grabbing him by the neck and shoving him headfirst into the back seat. He told Horn to cuff him to the door handle before slamming the door.

Riddle got behind the wheel then twisted around to face Rollie. "Now, are you ready to take us to meet August?"

"Ah, sure, man . . ." Rollie was bouncing around in the seat like a fast dribble.

"You got a rat in your shorts?" Riddle was purposely letting himself get a little hyped up. "What's your goddamn problem, Rollie?"

"I, ah, don't remember."

"Don't remember what?"

"How to get to August's," Rollie answered.

"Listen, you asshole!" Riddle lunged over the back seat and grabbed Rollie by the lapels, then banged his head against the window three or four times. He reached into the little informer's pocket, pulled out the piece of graph paper and stuffed it into his mouth. "Chew on it!" Riddle grabbed Rollie's head and jaw, moving them in a mock chewing fashion. "This'll help your memory."

Riddle released his grip and Rollie immediately spit out the paper with a gasp. "You bastard!" he said, almost choking, and grabbed his sunglasses. "You almost broke my Blindmans!"

"I'm going to break your neck by kicking you in the ass," Riddle barked in the most disgusted, tough-guy voice he could come up with.

"All right, all right, take it easy." Rollie held up his uncuffed hand. "I'll take you there, but don't blame my ass if something goes wrong." Rollie had become strangely serious.

"What do you mean?" Horn asked out of curiosity.

Rollie looked at Horn, surprised the cop had spoken. "I mean the neighborhood ain't exactly your normal, all-American family type."

"You mean it's pretty rough?" Horn wondered about Rollie's sudden mood change.

"I mean it's like a space shot into hell." Rollie turned his head and stared out the window.

"Bullshit," Riddle said. He started the engine and stepped on the gas.

CHAPTER FIVE

RIDDLE DROVE the beat-up Buick through the maze of streets in the South Bronx. Occasionally Rollie G. would speak up about a change in direction or tell Riddle to slow down so he could see the street signs, which were few and far between. The going was slow, for many of the streets had become impassable. They were strewn with trash, abandoned cars and the remnants of crumbling buildings.

New York City had long ago abandoned the South Bronx, giving it up to the gangs and pockets of poor minorities. It was a matter of money: there wasn't enough of it to keep the place going. The sewer system, water lines and power stations were, for the most part, defunct. Over the years, the city fathers had ignored the South Bronx. It was like ignoring cancer. There was little to be found in the inner city wasteland . . . unless, of course, one knew where to look.

"Take these freaking cuffs off me." Rollie slapped Horn on the shoulder with his free hand. "Don't want to be tied to this goddamn hunk of metal, not in this kill zone."

Without saying anything, Horn turned and, with some difficulty, pressed the release sequence on the cuff's digital combo. "Thanks," Rollie said, rubbing his wrist. He then reached in his coat and pulled out the string. Horn turned away as the little addict started coughing it up. "See this place up here on the right?" Rollie directed his question to Riddle between spells of gagging.

Riddle maneuvered the Buick around a gutted taxi that blocked most of the street. "Yeah, I see it," Riddle answered. "Isn't that the old Crotona Municipal Building?"

"How the hell do I know?" Rollie was cooking from the string. "Today it's Dr. August's crib. Pull up to that door over there." He pointed to a big steel overhead next to the remains of a concrete loading dock.

Riddle stopped the car and clambered out. Horn followed, giving their surroundings quick sweeping glances. He sensed danger.

The sky was just beginning to show the first gray streaks of the spring morning. It was cold, and their breath fogged out of their mouths and hung in the chilled air like clouds. "Get out here," Riddle said, turning toward Rollie, who hadn't moved from his spot in the back seat. "Come on." Riddle walked over and opened the back door. "Get your thin ass out here and earn your credits."

"It smells like someone's torching tires," Horn commented as he looked up and down the seemingly empty street. Buildings, mostly burned out and falling down, lined both sides of the potholed avenue. The one they had stopped in front of was obviously maintained to a certain degree; the maintenance consisted of reinforced steel bars strapped across boarded-up windows and razor wire covering the perimeter of the three-story roof. There was a big skull and crossbones painted in white on the faded overhead door. Beneath that international sign of danger, someone had written Dogs Rule, in red spray paint.

"Yeah, it smells like burning rubber." Rollie got out of the car, rubbing his arms in an effort to warm up. "It also smells like someone tried to piss out the fire." He cackled loudly, and his inane laughter echoed down the desolate street eerily.

Riddle looked at Rollie. "Well?"

"Well, what?" Rollie suddenly looked apprehensive.

"Where's August?" Horn asked.

"He's in there." Rollie nodded at the skull and cross-bones.

"So get his ass out here," Riddle ordered impatiently.

"Oh, all right." Rollie climbed up on the rubble of the loading dock and glanced up and down the street. He then gazed at the door with a puzzled look spreading across his stubble-covered face. "No buzzer," he said more to himself than anyone else.

"What?" Riddle asked.

"I said no goddamn buzzer," Rollie said over his shoulder. "He told me to buzz—"

"Shit!" Riddle said disgustedly and spit into the street. "Knock, for Christ's sake."

"Oh." Rollie moved closer and banged on the steel door with one of his puny fists.

"Harder!" Riddle yelled.

Rollie banged the door with both fists, the sound floating off through the still morning air like that of a kettle-drum. "Dr. August!" Rollie yelped at the top of his lungs. "The cat I was telling you about is here!"

Horn was beginning to wonder if Rollie was for real, when a voice caused all three of them to turn around and face the street.

"What's with all the goddamn racket?" Six huge soot-covered men stood in a group, their crude weapons hanging off their bodies like ornaments on trees. The one speaking was obviously the leader. "You done woke up me and the rest of the Dogs. Now we's hungry." The guy scratched at the top of his massive head, which was covered with matted hair.

"Looks like we's got ourselves a car," one of the men said, walking over to the Buick. He kept an antique-looking shotgun trained on the three.

"Watch your ass, Gene," the leader said. "That sombitch could be rigged."

Horn looked over the weapons, noting they were in a sorry state of repair. There were a couple of old M-21 military automatics, but they were scarred and wrapped with duct tape. He wondered if they would fire at all, let alone fire accurately.

"Listen, we're cops," Riddle said, moving slowly to Horn's left. Horn knew the routine. Riddle was splitting the gang's concentration and would soon create some sort of diversion that would allow Horn to go for his weapon.

"I'm not a cop!" Rollie objected in a high-pitched voice, sounding like a screeching bird.

"He's a cop. Don't believe him," Riddle said calmly.

"Riddle, you son of a bitch!" Rollie was astounded as well as angry. "I ain't no cop. Why are you telling these ass—I mean guys—that I am?"

"Hey, shut the fuck up 'fore I blow yous away," the head Dog snapped. "What the hell is yous punks doin' here at Doc's place, anyways?"

Head Dog's reference to "Doc's place" made Horn think that maybe Rollie hadn't been giving them the runaround, after all.

"We're, ah, looking for Doc...you know him?" Rollie started to step down from the loading dock, when one of his pointed-toed shoes caught on an exposed section of re-bar. "Haaa!" he screamed and fell face forward down the six-foot pile of jagged concrete chunks.

The gang members were startled and jumped back a couple of steps. It was all the diversion Riddle and Horn needed. They both drew their handguns and crouched in the classic police stance. Horn managed to get his 9 mm under control after several seconds and at least had the barrel pointed in the general direction of the Dogs. "All right, assholes, drop those BB guns!" Riddle ordered, moving the big .44 in an arc.

While glancing at his partner, Horn noticed that Gene had stopped checking out the car and was taking aim at Riddle with what looked like an old target pistol. Horn jerked the 9 mm around and squeezed the trigger just as the red beam of the laser sight tracked wildly to the middle of Gene's broad chest. The sound of the big handgun was deafening and made the Dogs crouch as if a jet had just broken the sound barrier over their heads. The 9 mm chunk of lead hit Gene square in the chest and plowed through his heart. He was thrown over the hood of the car and into the street.

Horn swung the automatic back to cover the rest of them, expecting that they would attempt a countermove. He was wondering if he could manage another shot as accurate as his last when one particularly heavy guy dragged his old shotgun pistol up and pointed it in Horn's general direction. Riddle's .44 barked, and the gunman folded forward.

"Who's next?" Riddle yelled, sweeping the pistol from man to man. "Drop that junk and raise your hands where I can get a good look at them."

The clatter of weapons hitting concrete filled the air as the four remaining Dogs slowly raised their hands. "What now?" the leader asked. "We ain't seen no cops here in three, maybe six years. What are ya goin' to do, arrest us?" The big man let out a loud belly laugh. His followers snickered tentatively.

"Nah, I left my ticket book back on the island." Riddle appeared relaxed, yet he never dropped his bead for a second. Horn was impressed. "Why don't you guys take your two buddies—" Riddle nodded toward the downed Dogs "—and get the hell out of here?"

"You mean that?" Head Dog asked suspiciously.

"Yeah, he means it," Horn said. "But hurry the hell up before he changes his mind."

"We'll just take the clothes," the leader said, moving toward Gene's crumpled form. "We's leave the body for real dogs."

"The hell you will!" A loud voice coming from behind and above startled Horn. He swung around, looked up and saw that a small slot had been opened in one of the boarded-over windows. "Take them goddamn bodies with you," the unseen speaker ordered. "Take 'em and throw 'em in the river."

"Shit, Doc." Head Dog was looking up at the slot in the window. "The river's three or four miles away." He was almost whining.

"Just get that carrion away from my door," the doctor insisted.

"You got it," the leader said, and motioned for the other Dogs to grab their fallen comrades.

"Go ahead and take your weapons," Horn said.

"Are you nuts?" Riddle asked, glancing at Horn.

"They're going to need them," Horn answered. "Anyway, I don't think these guys are any real threat to us."

As Horn watched the four gang members drag their two dead troopers away, the steel overhead door began to open, making him and Riddle swing their handguns toward the creaking sound. Horn could see a pair of combat boots followed by the drab green of an old Nomex flight suit. The door ground all the way open, revealing the entire five-foot-five-inch form. "You must be Dr. August," Horn said.

"I hope so," the man answered, and ran a hand through his shoulder-length, thinning white hair. August was built like a fireplug. His barrel chest filled the upper portion of the flight suit, stretching the material like the head of a drum. He had a beaklike nose and crystal-blue eyes that flashed beneath heavy silver-white eyebrows. "Where's the little grease stain that brought you here?" he snapped.

"Huh?" Riddle said and turned around. He had forgotten about Rollie G., who was stretched out on a broken chunk of concrete, moaning in pain.

Horn walked over to help pull Rollie onto the smoother section of the dock. He was still holding his 9 mm in his left hand, and without thinking, grabbed Rollie under the arm with his modified hand. Riddle started to pull at the same time, but the weak grip of the underpowered electro-mechanical device caused Horn to release his grip on the skinny arm. Rollie spun around suddenly, still held by Riddle, and struck one of his knees on the sharp end of a section of steel rebar.

"Goddamn!" Horn looked down disgustedly at his hand, which twitched involuntarily. Rollie screamed in pain as Riddle dragged him onto the surviving portion of the dock.

"I see that you are the one who seeks my services." August nodded at Horn, who continued staring in frustration at his appendage. "Don't worry. I can turn that piece of analog technological embarrassment into a hard-wired, digital dynamo. I can make a goddamn photon reduction valve look like a nozzle on a water hose."

Horn looked up without a word and slid the 9 mm back into the shoulder holster.

"You see," August continued enthusiastically, "the problem with that plastic state junk they scabbed onto your body is twofold: first of all, the servos and actuators are slow and underpowered.''

Riddle chuckled and moved closer to hear August's discourse, leaving Rollie wiping his bloody nose on the sleeve of his jacket.

''The second problem with that useless pink crap is that it's multiplexed into the nervous system through the actual nerve endings in the appendage that's modified. It sucks.'' He held out his hand in a gesture that implied ''what can I say?'' and continued. ''It creates a lag between the time your brain tells the limb, or whatever, to move and the time of the response. As a result, you jerk around like a frigging spas—I tell you, it's sad to see any kind of technology employed in such a stupid manner.''

Horn had gotten carried away by the doctor's account and was left hanging when it suddenly ended. ''What can you do to, ah, fix it?'' Horn asked, holding up his right arm.

August smiled. ''You'll have to come in. I'll explain it all to you there. First, we need to get your car inside, too. It won't last long out here in the...elements.'' He turned to the inside of the building and yelled, ''Winder! Front and center, boy!''

A figure appeared from the shadows and went up to August. He wasn't a boy, but could have been mistaken for one. His short, muscular body was no more than four and a half feet tall, and he made August look like a giant. ''Yes, Doctor,'' Winder reported eagerly.

''You can put that away.'' August nodded at the strange-looking weapon Winder held in his gloved hands. ''These men are here to do some business. We need to get their vehicle inside because they'll be staying a while.''

''Sure thing, boss.'' Winder stepped back into the shadows and moments later came out dragging two long planks.

Riddle understood the intention. He got into the Buick and pulled it around to align it with the door. Winder positioned the planks to bridge the caved-in part of the ramp, and Riddle drove up and into the building's garage area. Horn could tell it wasn't the first time the maneuver had been performed.

"Shall we?" August inquired, indicating the interior of the building to Horn, while Winder pulled in the makeshift ramps.

Horn looked over at Rollie, who was lying on his back, either sleeping, passed out or dead. "Hey, Rollie!" he yelled. "Let's go!" Rollie didn't move so Horn walked over, bent down and placed his fingers on the pencil-thin neck. He felt a rapid pulse.

"Is he okay?" August asked casually.

"Drugged up," Horn said, knowing that no fatal injuries had been sustained.

"Winder!" August motioned the dwarf toward Rollie's horizontal frame. "Drag that zombie into the garage and lay him out on that pile of rags. We'll check him in an hour or so and see if he'll outlive this high."

"Fair enough," Horn said as he straightened and followed Dr. August into the garage. Winder dragged Rollie in by the ankles, then closed the door.

"Let's go upstairs and talk some business," August suggested. Horn and Riddle followed the techno-doc through the junk-filled garage. They went on a wide flight of stairs and stepped into a well-lighted room that covered the entire second floor.

At one end was a massive conglomeration of tables and stands, which were overflowing with parts, test equipment, tools, computer terminals, scopes, cylindrical tanks, manuals and hundreds of other items that could only be generically described as technological garp. There were also many crates and custom shipping containers, some of which, Horn noticed, bore yellow, radioactive-material warning labels. Right in the center of the haphazard techno junkyard, surrounded by several high-intensity lamps, was an operating table. Directly over it, suspended from a complicated system of pulleys and cables, was a bell-shaped glass dome. When lowered, it was obviously intended to provide a sterile operating environment.

Riddle was looking around in disbelief and couldn't help commenting, "That looks like a mortician's slab in the middle of a satellite salvage."

August grunted a halfhearted laugh. "It does, doesn't it?" he said. "Come over here, gentlemen. We can discuss the business at hand."

Horn didn't feel too comfortable with the facilities, but he and Riddle followed the older man over to the other end of the room, which served as a living area. There was an ancient run-down couch, a couple of mismatched chairs, a cot covered with ratty blankets and a card table with a hot plate. Must be the kitchen, Horn thought, noticing a number of cardboard boxes scattered around overflowing with empty cans.

Riddle walked over and stared at the mess. Most of the empty cans were labeled Grandma Lucy's Leek Soup. "Is this all you eat?" Riddle asked, picking up one of the cans and turning toward August, who had flopped on the sofa.

But their host ignored the question. "You guys have a seat and let's talk business. I hope to hell you didn't come up here to waste my time."

Riddle sat on the other end of the couch, almost disappearing into the dirty brown cushions. Horn lifted a stack of science and electronic magazines from a chair and sat down facing August. He peeled off his jacket, removed the shoulder holster and took off the turtleneck.

"Take off the glove," August said as he got up to walk over to Horn. "You know, as many times as I've seen this pink shit—" he ran a hand over Horn's modified shoulder and down the arm "—it never fails to make me sick to my stomach. Where else?"

Horn rolled up his right pant leg, exposing the modified knee. "Looks like a goddamn reject from a department store mannequin." August bent over and tapped the round plastic plate that had replaced the kneecap. "Ever try running with this piece of junk?" he asked.

"I can barely walk on it," Horn responded wryly.

August had evidently seen enough and he returned to the sofa. "Well, son, you're a cop, right?" He waited for Horn to nod, then went on with his piece. "You ain't going to be busting much crime with those kitchen appliances for an arm and a knee." August leaned over and pulled a pipe and tobacco pouch from one of his leg pockets. He filled the bowl and tamped the tobacco down with the end of a disposable lighter before torching it off. The rich smell wafted across to Horn, who started to relax.

"I've got some parts. Just got a new shipment last week." August's voice was low as he leaned forward and squinted at Horn through the blue smoke curling up from his pipe. "I can turn you into something that you'll never get used to, and you'll never want to." He leaned back on the couch.

"What about the lag?" Horn asked. "I'm sure you can make the devices, uh, stronger, but what about the lag time from the brain to the servo?"

"Yup, that's really the trick," August answered knowingly. "You see, you can get any other back street mod house in the city to bolt some goddamn thousand-foot drum and bracket onto your ass, and sure, you'll be able to knock down a wall or some other bullshit, but you'll move like a diesel backhoe. Won't help you dodge bullets, that's for sure.''

"What makes *you* different?'' Riddle threw in the question as the doctor sucked on his pipe.

"I'll tell you. Like I said before, the state multiplexes your nervous system into the electromechanical loops down the trunk from the spine. They then have to use firmware to serially decode your nerve impulses into signals that can be processed in order to drive the servos, actuators and other shit, which is mostly...well, like I said before, kitchen appliances. Stuff all of that junk under a thin coating of baby pink plastic that couldn't stop a mosquito bite, let alone a bullet, and what have you got? You." He jerked his thumb at Horn's arm and then his knee.

Riddle started to say something, but August waved his pipe at him. "Let me answer your question. Other than some secret meddling in the military, there's one other mod house in the world that does the kind of work I do. Believe it or not," August said with mild amusement as he cocked his bushy eyebrow at them, "that place is in Italy. Anyway," he went on, suddenly serious again, "what I'll do is hard-wire some of the best electromechanical stuff in the world straight into your spine."

"What does that do?" Horn asked, wanting to hear the rest of Doc's sales pitch.

"Main thing is, it gets rid of all that goddamn time-consuming firmware," August answered. "I bet you got over ten thousand lines of code in those archaic memory modules just to drive your limbs around in that slow-motion circle jerk. What I do is let your brain directly drive your limbs. All your operational software is right up here." August touched his temple with the stem of his pipe. "What this does is give you instantaneous movement. In a few cases I've even seen anticipatory movement."

"What do you do about the skin?"

"Oh, you mean the pink stuff? In your case, I just got a section of skin from that Air Force satellite killer that went down over India last summer."

Riddle, who had been quietly listening, startled visibly when August turned his head and yelled, "Hey, Winder! Bring me a piece of that SDI-14." Within ten seconds his assistant was standing at his side holding a piece of dull, dark green material.

The doctor took the material from Winder and handed it to Horn. "Here, take a look at this."

"What is it?" Horn asked, turning over the ultrathin piece of metal in his hands. He couldn't believe how light it was.

"It's titanium."

"I thought titanium was shiny, like the YF-44," Riddle interjected, referring to the latest fighter aircraft capable of transatmospheric flight.

"It is," August explained. "But this is combat titanium, designed to withstand bullets and lasers as well as high temperatures. It's got a ceramic composite base that enhances the natural strength of the exotic metal."

Horn leaned back in his chair. "How much to do both my mods?" he asked.

"Well, that's the other trick, isn't it?" August smiled delightedly. "It'll cost you seventy-five thousand credits."

"Seventy-five!" Riddle exclaimed. "Why, that little freak Rollie said—" But Horn shook his head, and Riddle abruptly stopped.

August hadn't been bothered, though. "I've gotten in some new material since last talking with your drug-crazed little agent. And what I've got in mind for you is well worth seventy-five thousand credits. As a matter of fact—" the doctor half closed his eyes and smiled "—I'd call it a god-damn bargain."

In anticipation of some kind of financial glitch, Horn had brought every credit he could access. He had well over a hundred thousand. "All right," he said, feeling as though he were giving away nothing, instead of most of his life savings. "It's a deal. When can we do it?"

"When can you pay?"

"Now."

"Then we can proceed." The doctor flashed an una-bashed grin. "As they used to say, let's see the color of your coin."

Horn picked up his jacket and pulled out three twenty-five thousand credit wafers. August looked at the little playing card-sized devices incredulously. "What the hell are those?" he asked. "I told your little monkey man delivery boy that I took blue slip or gold. What's this shit?"

Horn looked at Riddle, who just shrugged his shoulders. "What's the problem?" he asked the doctor, who appeared a little irritated.

"If you want me to take that electronic crap it'll cost an extra ten thou—" August began curtly.

"Done." Horn pulled another wafer out of his jacket and handed all four to August.

"Winder!" the doctor called out. "Bring that bloody credit machine." Winder was by his side almost instantly, holding a shoe-box-sized silver apparatus that had an al-phanumeric keypad and a digital LED readout. "I'll have to run this through my sister's account in Brussels," he said, sticking one of the wafers into a slot and punching in a series of codes. "Keeps my ID free of hindrances. Know what I mean?"

August finished transferring the last credit and tossed the spent wafer on the floor. "Winder, get the table and my electron glasses fired up." He stood and motioned for Horn and Riddle to follow. "Let me show you one of the actuators I'll use in your mod."

They walked over to where Winder was fiddling with the valve on a tank of liquid hydrogen. August lifted the lid of a big wooden crate that was half full of fantastic pieces of electronic gear and electromechanical devices. "Ah, here we are." August pulled out a small, precision-machined gold-colored actuator the size of an egg. "This is better than mil standard," he said. "This is nuke-hardened space war junk."

"Tell them what it is," Winder said as he adjusted the flood lamps.

"This crate full of parts here—" August nodded and grinned like a kid showing off his toys "—is what's left of the 2005 Long Shot probe recovered by the Russians. It ought to be in the Smithsonian."

"Whaddaya mean, boss?" Winder said. "We stole that crate right off the Smithsonian's loading dock."

"Winder, you loggerhead." August looked at his assistant, who cringed and ducked his head sheepishly. "Will you just concentrate on prepping for the mod, please?"

"There's one more thing..." August turned and looked into Horn's eyes. "It's only fair to warn you that I've seen some modifications go a little haywire."

"What do you mean?" Horn asked.

"Stray electrical impulse, bad reaction to certain chemicals, sneak circuit in the processor, any number of things and the mod may function independently of the subject's will."

"Did any of yours malfunction?"

"Just one." August shook his head ruefully. "I supertuned a transpilot's leg one time. To make a short story even shorter, he apparently had a malfunction in the aircraft oxygen system that gave him hypoxia. The signals from his brain got weird as a result, and so did his leg."

"Must have gotten stuck on one of the rudder pedals and lost control," Riddle suggested.

"No," August said. "He jammed his leg completely through the fuselage and outer skin of the aircraft, which caused a decompression that crushed the machine like a paper sack."

"How the hell did they know that?" Riddle demanded.

"They found the in-flight image recorder. They also found Jake's modified leg. It and the hardened recorder were about the only things they did find."

"I'll take my chances," Horn said, and looked right at August.

"Good. Then let's get started." August shuffled around, then stood stock-still and glared at Riddle. "You have to go downstairs and wait. Check on your friend or something—I just don't want you around during the process." At Riddle's uncertain look, Horn nodded reassuringly.

"How long will it take?" Riddle asked.

"Ten or twelve hours, at least. Get some food from here."

"Will you put me under?" Horn asked.

"Only when I tap into your spine." August smiled reassuringly at Horn before turning to Riddle and waving his hands like an old woman shooing out her cat. "Go on, git."

SEVENTEEN HOURS LATER, Riddle lay snoring in the back seat of the Buick. He was having a dream about a group of women cavorting in a blue sea, while he lay on the beach with no other purpose in life but to watch. The women were all young, slender and beautiful. Their fluid movements were hypnotic, and the longer he watched, the more Riddle could feel his own body moving back and forth. Gently at first, but the longer it lasted, the more pronounced and faster the motion got.

In his dream state Riddle didn't understand what was going on. The movement had progressed to a definite shaking, and a sound that was like two pieces of iron being slammed together began to pierce his brain. Riddle was scared and realized the swimming women were gone. Everything was dark, and he could barely make out a vague round shape. He suddenly figured out that he was in the back seat of the Buick, staring at the dome light. But the motion he had experienced hadn't stopped, and the metal banging was louder.

Riddle managed to get up and stumble out of the car. He fell flat on his face on the cold concrete of the garage floor. For a second he had thought an earthquake had struck, but realized that the floor wasn't moving. He turned his head sideways and couldn't believe what he saw. Horn was slowly lowering the Buick with his right hand. He was grinning from ear to ear, which for some reason scared Riddle.

"Watch this, partner," Horn crowed, and he began to flex his modified arm back and forth so quickly that it became a nearly invisible blur. Riddle could feel the breeze it generated.

Riddle realized that Horn was naked, and he could see the green titanium of the newly supertuned knee. Recovering from his fright, he said, "Holy shit, Horn, is the knee the same?"

"Let's check it out." Horn crouched and suddenly took off like a rocket. Riddle looked up and watched his partner swing from the steel girder rafters that were a good twenty feet off the floor.

"Jesus, Horn," Riddle breathed with amazement. "I didn't think it would be like—"

"Superhuman?" Dr. August had materialized stood next to Riddle, his hands on his hips and the pipe hanging out of one side of his mouth. He looked wrung out and worn.

"Yeah, superhuman," Riddle repeated.

"Come on down here," August ordered.

Horn released his grip and fell to the floor like a stone. He groaned as he hit the concrete, and wound up in a sitting position, rubbing his right ankle and leg below the modified knee.

"Whoa, what a stupid stunt," August scoffed. "It's a wonder you didn't hurt your back when you lifted the goddamn car. Don't waste my work doing bullshit stunts like that. You have to build up your body around the mods in order to at least keep up with their minimum capability." He pulled the pipe out of his mouth. "The trick is to let the modifications be the leading edge of your body."

Horn got to his feet and dusted off his bare skin. He had quickly returned to an all-business mode. "I understand, Doc." Turning to Riddle, he said, "If Rollie's not dead, throw him in the back seat of the car. If he is, then into the trunk with him. I'm going upstairs for my clothes. We're hauling ass in ten minutes."

"What's the hurry?" Riddle demanded.

"I want to catch the next shuttle to New Pittsburgh. My orders should be ready as soon as the precinct opens. What time is it?"

Riddle checked his watch. "Three a.m."

"Check on Rollie, will ya?" Horn asked.

"Sure," Riddle said, getting to his feet and walking toward the back of the garage, where Winder had deposited Rollie.

August followed Horn upstairs and watched him dress. "You're that cop that got all blown to hell, aren't you?" he asked as Horn finished lacing his military-style jump boots.

"How did you know that?" Horn asked. "Did Rollie mention it?"

"Nah, I saw it in the paper."

"Yeah, I'm him. Why you want to know?"

"I figured that was why you wanted to get your mods supertuned." August started loading his pipe. "Figured you had a legitimate reason, that's all."

Horn strapped the shoulder holster on and slipped into the fatigue jacket. He looked into August's bloodshot eyes for ten seconds or so before nodding his head slightly. "Thanks, Doc." He turned and clattered down the stairs.

Riddle was in the process of shoving Rollie's limp body into the back of the Buick. He slammed the door and said, "I'm afraid he's still alive, but he's not awake enough to navigate us out of here."

"Don't worry," Horn answered as he climbed behind the wheel. "I remember how to get back."

"Hey, Winder!" Riddle yelled. "Door and ramp please!" He was a little surprised Horn had gotten behind the wheel. "Sure you don't want me to drive?"

Horn shook his head as he cranked the big rotary to life. Winder had opened the door and was just putting down the last plank. Horn stepped on the gas and blasted out of the garage, and the little man had to jump out of the way. Riddle looked over his shoulder and could see Winder waving goodbye with his middle finger.

Horn drove around for ten minutes or so until he located the dilapidated Bronx Expressway. When he picked up speed to start up the on ramp, he noticed a jet-black Essex four-door behind them. It closed the gap and turned on its twin rows of fog burners.

"Looks like someone's in a hurry." Horn reached up and flipped the deflector on the rearview mirror.

"What the hell?" Riddle twisted around in his seat and stared as the black car accelerated to within a foot of the Buick's bumper.

"There's his buddy," Horn reported calmly and watched an old Mercedes van pull onto the freeway from the shoulder.

"Shit, Horn, this doesn't look ... ah, normal."

Horn guffawed. "No, it sure as hell doesn't. At least not at four in the morning on the Bronx Expressway."

As Horn closed in on the van, the Essex slammed on its brakes and dropped back. The rear door of the old Mercedes burst open, and Horn caught a glimpse of a guy holding on to the handles of what appeared to be a multi-barreled weapon. Within a split second, giant red splotches of light erupted from the barrels and the windshield came apart before Horn's face.

Horn cranked the wheel hard over, sliding the Buick around 180 degrees in a cloud of tire smoke. He slammed down the foot feed and headed straight for the Essex, which was now lined up for a head-on, its lights shining like the seeker on a AIM-19 missile.

"You okay?" Horn yelled, and glanced at Riddle, who was brushing shattered glass off his face. "Get your auto-loader!" he ordered before his partner could answer his question.

Riddle pulled the 12 gauge from the bracket under the dash and charged the chamber. He laid the barrel out over the hood and lined it up with the Essex's headlights, which were less than one hundred yards away. Horn pulled out his 9 mm and cocked it.

The Essex came at them like a runaway train. Horn cut loose with the 9 mm and could hear the amplified bass booming as Riddle blasted away. At the last moment the Essex swerved to the Buick's left and went into a 360. The driver finally got the machine under control and spun it around just as the van blew by, having taken up the chase.

"We got the van and the sedan behind us now," Riddle yelled over the roar of the wind coming through the front of the car.

"Try to slow them down!" Horn said as he whipped the Buick down the same ramp he'd used to access the expressway. Riddle climbed out through the shield's hole and turned on the dash facing backward. Horn heard his partner's shotgun bark and from behind heard rifle fire being returned. He grabbed Riddle's pants and pulled him back into the car just as he whipped the wheel around and slid the Buick onto a side street.

"They still back there?" Horn asked as he slowed down.

"No...wait!" Riddle panted, craning his head around. "There's the van, but I don't see the car."

Horn spun the Buick around and brought it to a dead stop. "Let's take the van out while it's one-on-one," he said.

"Sure," Riddle replied, as he opened the door. "I'm gonna get a shooting platform here."

"What the hell are you doing?" Horn asked.

Riddle was standing on the rocker panel with his right arm hooked over the top of the open door. "Go, Horn! Those bastards are rolling!"

The van was less than two hundred yards away and closing fast. Horn slammed the Buick into gear and jammed his foot down, burning rubber for twenty yards. Muzzle-flashes kept coming from the sides of the van.

Horn got his 9 mm ready and was about to tell Riddle to open up when he looked to his right. His eyes locked onto the Essex, which was burning out of a side alley like a cruise missile. Horn's reaction caused him to jerk the wheel to the left, but the Essex's driver had calculated his angle of attack accurately. The black torpedo crashed into the right side of the Buick, slamming shut the door Riddle had been hanging out of.

Horn watched in horror as Riddle's headless body flopped in from the window and sat down. Both of the cop's arms were severed above the elbows, and blood was spraying everywhere. "Dan!" Horn let out a shriek of anguish and gritted his teeth.

A bright flash of light suddenly filled the inside of the car, and Horn was vaguely aware that something had banged into his left shoulder. His senses snapped into focus, and he realized that the Buick was moving down the street in a fender lock with the Essex. He knew the light that had just flashed by had to have been the van.

A cold calm curtain fell on Horn's mind as he did a one-handed change of the clip in the 9 mm. He aimed the weapon straight where Riddle's head should have been and squeezed off three quick rounds into the driver's window of the Essex. Even over the noise, Horn heard a yelping scream as the Essex cut hard left, driving the Buick onto rubble-strewn sidewalk. Both vehicles ground to a smoking stop next to the broken-down doors of an abandoned laundromat.

Horn crawled out and dived onto the roof of the Essex. He swung his right arm down and smashed out the rear window effortlessly, then stuck his head and shoulders into the opening. Horn jammed the barrel of the 9 mm to the back of some guy's head and pulled the trigger, creating an explosion of blood, brains and bone inside the vehicle.

Someone cut loose with a bloodcurdling scream. Horn tracked the red beam of the laser right to the source of the cry, pulled the trigger and sent a copper-jacketed slug straight into a long-haired punk's mouth. The punk's ad vanced Uzi cooked off six rounds into the side of the already dead driver.

Horn paused to make sure there were only three occupants in the Essex. He jumped down and pulled Riddle out of the Buick, deposited his body on the hood and crawled back into the front seat. Through the bullet-riddled back window Horn could see the headlights of the van coming up the street. He lay down in his partner's blood, concealing the 9 mm in the small of his back.

Horn heard the van come to a crunching halt on the glass-strewn street. Covering his face with his left forearm, he waited. He heard the doors open and a voice broke the stillness. "Wow, look at this shit. Hey, Rudy, get a load of this—"

"Shut up! Check out that goddamn sedan. See if anyone's alive in there."

Footsteps were approaching the car, then Horn's closed eyelids fluttered violently as a drugged-out voice from the back seat stuttered, "Hey, where . . . what the hell's going on?"

Horn had forgotten about Rollie and he started to whisper something but all hell broke loose. Horn heard Rollie grunt as dozens of bullets slammed into his skinny body.

"I got him! Yeah, look, Rudy!" Horn eased up toward the edge of the window as the gunner chattered excitedly. "He was hidin' in the back seat, but I nailed the son of a bitch."

"Quit your crowing," the man called Rudy instructed. "Get your lame ass over there and check out the rest of the car."

"All right, take it easy." Horn listened to the footsteps walk casually up to the rear of the window. "Yeah, the bastard's dead."

"How about the front seat?" Rudy was obviously not into checking out free fire zones himself.

Horn tensed as the guy crawled up on the trunk lid and then on the roof. "There's a guy spread out on the hood. What a mess."

"Is he dead?" Rudy asked.

"He ain't got no head. I think he's dead."

"No shit." Rudy sounded even more pissed. "You're a goddamn genius, Leon. Check out the front seat."

Horn heard Leon grunt as he leaned down to peer into the car. As soon as his face came into view, Horn shot his right hand out like a striking cobra and grabbed the man's bushy hair. He jerked hard and flipped him down onto the hood on top of Riddle's body. He kept his grip on the greasy hair and scrambled through the blood-smeared opening.

Horn grabbed the barrel of the automatic rifle Leon had been carrying and jerked it out of the guy's hands. He tossed it into the car and glanced around, trying to locate Rudy. There was movement near the back of the car and Horn squeezed off a couple of rounds from the 9 mm as he slid off the hood, dragging Leon with him.

"Watch out, Rudy!" Horn was surprised the guy had the guts to call out. He banged Leon's head into the Buick's front bumper a couple of times. It quieted him down.

Horn bent down and peered beneath the car. A man was crouched at the rear of the vehicle, and he appeared to be holding the big multibarreled machine gun that Horn had seen earlier.

The pencil beam of the laser was resting directly on the target's belt buckle when Horn squeezed the trigger. The supersonic piece of lead disemboweled the would-be assassin and knocked him rolling and screaming into the street.

"Anyone else?" Horn pulled Leon's face to within six inches of his own. The greaser shook his head, his dark eyes wild with fear. "Are you sure?" Horn asked, shaking the man for greater emphasis. Leon nodded, and Horn could feel the whole skinny body shaking through the sensors in his arm.

He dragged the man around to the van and cautiously checked it out. "I told you there wasn't no one else," Horn's captive said nervously.

"Who hired you?" Still holding Leon by the hair, Horn pushed him up to the side of the van and slammed his head into the metal a couple of times. "Come on, I don't have time for this." Horn stared into Leon's eyes. "Describe the guy who hired you bunch of killers."

"Big tall b-bastard." Leon stuttered a little in his haste to spill his guts. "Blond hair, looked like a Swedish rock star. No shit."

"Close enough." Horn pulled the guy's head away from the van, and then in one swift motion, slammed it back, right through the sheet metal panel. The skull shattered in Horn's grip as he forced it through the side of the Mercedes. He left the body hanging like a limp rag and backed away.

Horn looked down at the blood dripping from his dull green titanium fingers as bile rose in his throat. Shaking his fists, he leaned his head back and let out a howl, all anger and anguish, more animal than human. The sound echoed down the empty, cold streets like the voice of a lost ghost. Horn stood still for a long time, then turned and started toward Manhattan.

CHAPTER SIX

FINE LEANED BACK on the wooden bench and breathed in deep lungfuls of steam. He made a concentrated effort to relax, but while he managed to render his body inert, his mind raced nonstop somewhere on the edge of control. Even in the brief periods of sedated sleep, Fine could only manage to launch his mind for short plunges into the restful darkness. He figured he'd rest when he died.

A buzzer sounded, and he glanced at his watch. He'd been sitting in the steam bath for a total of fifteen minutes, but it seemed that he'd been there for fifteen hours. The whole New Pittsburgh scenario was running through his mind like a high-speed hallucination. There was something wrong with his plan, but Fine couldn't pin down what it was. He pushed open the door and walked into the dressing room, his skin puckering from the cold air and the cool marble floor.

Fine sat down on a bench next to a row of stainless steel lockers and ran a towel across his face. It was four in the morning, and he was alone in the small but luxuriously appointed executive spa, just one floor down from his penthouse office. Fine had been spending a lot of time in the spa lately, especially in the early-morning hours when most of his associates were still in bed. It was the only time he seemed to be able to slow his mind down to a speed that permitted something akin to rational objectivity.

While the planned sabotage of New Pittsburgh was by far the largest project Fine had undertaken since becoming CEO of Titus Steel, it was not necessarily the dirtiest. Elimination, as he liked to call it, had long been in his arsenal of corporate tools as a method to remove obstructions—organizational as well as temporal. New Pittsburgh's several thousand residents simply represented a change in scale for Fine's trade-off equations. And, as in all such business decisions, Fine made no major move unless it was underwritten by Ashley Fine.

Fine's use of murder for vengeance was a more recent bent in his role as a corporate executive. It was justified, in his mind, as a foolproof insurance policy that key players in bad deals wouldn't be around to repeat history. It was also his way of reimbursing Steller for services rendered. Fine wasn't bothered that his executive assistant took such pleasure and pride in his work. He even encouraged it.

The New Pittsburgh scheme was a must-win for Fine. Fine's position, as well as his reputation, had received a serious blow when the Anaconda takeover bid vaporized. The only way to get back the lost ground was to turn around the entire titanium market and lock it in a monopolistic Titus Steel grasp. Fine saw himself going down in history as another Iacocca or Donald Trump. The key, as he had set up the lock, was the destruction of the asteroid.

Fine had gone through the plan more than one hundred times on paper, more than a thousand times in his head and nearly as many times in discussions with his mother. He ran through it again, trying to pinpoint the ghost that was nagging his mind, warning him the plan had a weak link that was about to break.

Suddenly Fine's concentration was thrown offtrack. He sensed someone behind his back and turned. Steller was standing at the end of the bench, arms folded across his massive chest, staring at Fine without expression. Startled, Fine dropped his towel. He wondered how long Steller had been standing there.

"You scared the hell out of me," Fine gasped angrily.

"Sorry," Steller answered, glancing at his watch. "We had a meeting at five o'clock. The guards said you were down here."

Fine grabbed a robe hanging from one of the lockers and put it on. He looked at his watch before speaking. "Damn. Go on up to my office. I'll be there in ten minutes."

"I saw Mrs. Fine entering the building," Steller remarked almost casually. "Will she be in this meeting?"

"Yes, I invited her," Fine lied. "Now go on, I'll be up shortly."

After Steller left, Fine rubbed the towel across his sweating face and remembered how his mother's presence had come about. She had informed him she would be involved in any future decisions regarding the New Pittsburgh operation. She had also requested a daily status report on the cop, and Fine had willingly obliged.

He shrugged his damp body into his clothes and took the executive elevator up to his office. Steller and Ashley Fine were occupying chairs in front of his desk. They were at ease, and Fine wondered if they'd been talking. And, if they had, about what.

"We've got to get things rolling at New Pittsburgh." Fine was perched on the edge of his desk, and he leaned forward to emphasize his words. "Tokyo tite prices went a tenth today. We're going to get our margins cut to hell the longer we wait."

Steller wondered if Fine intended to impress him with the financial detail. He was sure Fine knew the only margin he cared about was the one between life and death. "I'm ready when you are," Steller answered. "Just tell me what you want done."

Fine stood up to stroll around, then chanced a sideways glance at his mother. As usual, she looked cool and collected. She wore a dark blue business suit, a white high-necked blouse and navy stockings. True to form, her heels were spikes. She caught his look and smiled at her son before speaking. "I'm just a bystander, Oasis. Please proceed."

Fine took refuge behind his desk and turned his attention to Steller. He knew what kind of a bystander Ashley Fine was.

"What have you done to eliminate the surviving policeman?"

The question made Steller wince slightly. "I hired two tails to—"

"I thought that was the goddamn mistake last time," Fine interrupted. "That idiot, Glass, sent amateurs to take out a pro."

"That's not the idea. They were just supposed to follow Horn."

"Horn?" Fine looked puzzled at the mention of the name, and Steller was pleased because it created a bit of a diversion from the CEO's impatience.

"Yeah," Steller answered. "I think I mentioned to you before, the cop's name is Horn. A jerked-down West Sider. Anyway, one of the punks figured he was going to impress me by taking Horn out. He wasn't quite able to get the job done."

"How so?" Fine leaned back in his chair and glanced at his mother, who was staring at Steller as an odd sort of fascination spread across her face.

"He ended up kissing the front end of a moving subway train." Steller paused and was surprised that his employer didn't take the opportunity to chew his ass. He knew he was the only known exception to Fine's policy that "nobody makes the same mistake *once*." Avon's and Glass's violations of the policy had certainly cost them.

"But I have plans for Officer Horn," he said aloud, and for the moment Fine seemed satisfied.

"Some coffee?" Fine offered.

He saw Steller nod, then looked up at Ashley and found her absorbed gaze on him. "Yes, thank you," she answered.

Fine buzzed the secretarial station and ordered a service of coffee, all the while wondering why his mother lingered. She preferred to have no knowledge of the more unpleasant side of their business dealings.

He now addressed his words to her in a flat, emotionless voice. "In two months, if all goes according to plan, New Pittsburgh will no longer be the loss leader of the corporation. It will be dust."

"What's the operative plan?" Steller asked.

Fine turned toward his mother. "Do you mind if such details are disclosed to Mr. Steller?"

"Go right ahead. Mr. Steller has our trust," she said while looking steadily at Fine.

Fine turned back to Steller. "We're going to cause the main smelting reactor to melt down. I've ordered one of the fuel pellets to be modified in the appropriate manner. When it is inserted in the core and they bring up the reactor, everything will function normally for at least forty-eight hours. Frank Wand, our security chief on that rock, will ensure nothing gets sidetracked."

"What about the cooperative agreement?" Steller prompted, referring to the agreement Titus Steel had with the city of New York whereby the police department supplied a contingent of officers to maintain a reasonable semblance of law and order in the mining colony.

"Don't worry about it, Steller. No threat from that quarter. You know who winds up pulling duty in the godforsaken place."

"Not exactly New York's finest," Steller answered.

Ashley was leaning toward Fine now, and he continued, pleased at her interest. "The trick will come when the contaminated fuel from our pellets hits the neon isotope cycling device. The cooling system and all the backups will shut down faster than the Russians shut down the Congo in '94."

The announcement buzzer rang once, interrupting Fine's speech. He waited until the secretary had deposited the coffee tray on the desk and left the room before he resumed. "Approximately one hour after the cooling systems have been taken out, the primary reactor will melt down." Fine smiled slightly at Steller, his eyes looking like the business ends of two bullets. "It should be spectacular."

"Will it take out the whole asteroid?"

"It will."

Steller leaned back in his chair. "You know, Oasis, there are more than fifteen thousand people in that mining colony."

"Don't tell me you're worried about a bunch of migrant space scum." The intercom buzzed again, and Fine pushed the button. "Yes?"

A woman answered, "There's a call on the private line for Mr. Steller, sir."

"Who is it?" Fine asked, looking over at Steller, who shrugged.

"His name is Teague, sir. Said it was urgent."

"Very well," Fine said with an edge of irritation. "Put him up on the wall monitor."

Immediately, the telemonitor image was projected onto the wall. A long-haired man with a large handlebar mustache began to speak. "Steller, we got a problem."

Teague was obviously at a remote telemonitoring station, as evidenced by the poor quality of the image which looked like an old celluloid newsreel. "You hear? We got a problem." Teague's voice was strained and high-pitched as he repeated the statement. One of his hands, in a fingerless glove, kept coming into the picture and twisting the handlebar.

"You already told me that," Steller snapped, knowing that something had gone wrong with the hit and that Fine—and worst of all, Fine's mother—were going to get a first-hand account of it. He knew he shouldn't have given Fine's private number to his front-line associates. "Just tell me what the goddamn problem is." Steller glanced at Fine, who was listening with surprising calm.

"Well," Teague began in a slightly quavering voice, "I tailed the boys from L.A. like you told me to, and they followed the two cops into the Bronx."

"Go on," Steller ordered, glancing again at Fine.

"The cops and some stoolie—I think his name is Ollie...or something like that..." Teague was tweaking the hell out of his mustache in an apparent attempt to aid his memory.

"It doesn't matter," Steller barked. "Go on. And get your goddamn hand away from your face."

Teague looked shocked, and his hand quickly dropped out of the picture. "Ah, sure, boss." Teague suddenly grinned weakly and held up both hands as if he were pushing something invisible. "But don't shoot the messenger, eh, boss?" He let out a funeral sort of laugh.

"Just tell me what went down," Steller said as calmly as he could.

"Yeah, well, we wound way up in the Bronx, and the L.A. boys did a setup for the cops." Teague paused and waited for a reaction.

"What the hell is wrong with you, Teague?" Steller was livid. "Are you going into a trance?"

"Sorry," Teague said almost thoughtfully. "I was just wondering how I could say this—"

"Just say it." Steller checked out Fine once again but saw no reaction. Ashley Fine was sipping her coffee.

"Well, okay." Teague's vocabulary was evidently limited. "The punks from L.A. got their asses ripped by the cop."

"You mean the *cops*—there were two of them," Steller corrected.

"No, they got one of the cops," Teague answered. "They didn't get the guy you wanted...ah, Horn. That's his name, right?"

Both Steller and Fine gave a little start in their chairs. "What happened to Rudy Law and his hitters?" Steller asked uneasily.

"They all got nailed. I watched almost the entire battle from the top of an abandoned building on the street where it happened." Teague seemed to relax a little, at least his lips did. "This Horn guy must be some kind of martial arts expert, besides being good with a piece. He nailed one of Rudy's guys with one hand, picked him up like a rag doll." Teague held up one of his hands in an apparent attempt to mimic what he'd seen.

"That's enough," Steller said, cutting him off. Teague looked disappointed. "See Walt tomorrow. He'll pay you."

Steller reached over and discontinued the connection before Teague could say anything else. His spine felt like ice. He looked at Fine and waited for the inevitable.

"I guess my biggest disappointment," Fine said, his voice booming around the room, "is that you indicated to me the cop was as good as dead. Not only is he not dead, but he's apparently leaving in his wake a trail of the incompetent gutter trash you've hired!"

Steller was a little shook up—not from the ass chewing that Fine was starting to give him, but from the knowledge that Horn was still walking the earth. "Let me make a call." Steller didn't give Fine a chance to give his permission but got up from his chair and went to a corner table. He picked up a hand-held telemonitor and entered a code, then had a brief conversation with someone.

When Steller returned to his chair, Fine raised his eyebrows. "What was that all about?"

"I've got one of my insiders at Horn's precinct checking on his whereabouts," Steller answered. "He's going to call me back in twenty minutes."

Fine leaned forward in his chair. "I don't want you farming out this job anymore! You got that? I want you to take this Horn out personally, and no ifs about it." He pointed a thin finger at Steller's face. "This cop is getting to be a real thorn…" His words trailed off, then he looked thoughtful. "A thorn," he murmured. "That's it!" he said, brightening momentarily.

"What do you mean?" Steller asked cautiously.

"The cop."

"What about it?" Steller looked perplexed. "That's what we were just talking about."

Fine looked at Steller. "That cop," he said slowly and deliberately, "is the unplanned-for contingency. He is the unpredictable element that can throw us. It's what's been eating away at my logic."

"I see," Steller said uncertainly.

Fine raised his eyebrows a fraction of an inch. "As long as the cop lives, I can't be one hundred percent certain the plan will work. The man's a wild card."

"I don't see how one cop can—" Steller cut off his sentence as Fine's eyes flickered rapidly.

"You don't understand, Mr. Steller. We—" Fine glanced down at his desk, then returned his gaze to Steller. "Well, actually, *you* killed this Horn's family. He's not going to stop searching for you until he finds you or dies. If it's not the latter, the New Pittsburgh plan could wind up seriously damaged."

"I will take care of Horn myself," Steller responded. "He will find me and his death. It should ease your mind."

Fine smiled benignly. "Well, that's really your job—to keep my mind free of these nagging details, isn't it?"

The intercom buzzed and Fine punched it on. "Yes?"

"There's another call for Mr. Steller on the private line," the secretary said.

Steller took the call, and Fine waited. "Good news, I hope?" Fine asked as Steller returned to his chair. "Tell me Horn was run down by a truck."

"No truck. I've just been told that Detective Horn has taken an assignment on the New Pittsburgh mining colony. He was scheduled to leave today or tomorrow, but that has been delayed a week so he can attend the funeral of his partner."

"Looks like you'll be going to New Pittsburgh," Fine said calmly.

"Unless I can make the hit before he leaves."

Fine compressed his lips. "This time, do what I tell you. Wait until you get to the asteroid. Do it up there. It'll hardly be noticed."

"Whatever you say," Steller answered.

Fine didn't like Steller's nonchalance. "He's beating the bushes, Mr. Steller. Don't underestimate him again." He let his words sink into Steller's mind a few moments before stating, "I'm scheduled to go to New Pittsburgh as soon as things have been set up for the deactivation. You can travel with me."

"Why are you going?" Steller asked.

"My lawyers say it will look good to the insurance underwriters. My presence will imply that I had no knowledge of the unsafe conditions of the reactor." Fine raised his eyebrows. "Anyway, you can make the trip with me. I'm sure you will find some innovative way for Horn to die."

Steller leaned back in his chair. "It will give me something to look forward to."

They heard the slight rattling of a china cup, and turned toward Ashley. Surprisingly she said, "I think you're right about one thing."

"Excuse me?" Fine asked.

"I said—" Ashley's voice was firm and carried an edge of irritation "—that you have one thing correctly perceived. The man Horn is the one variable that could cause the entire operation to fail. You are also correct that he must be eliminated. However," she said, turning toward Fine, who felt himself sink slightly in his chair, "Mr. Horn must be taken care of prior to his scheduled departure for the asteroid."

"It'll be easier once he's there. We own the damn thing," Fine said in a near-petulant voice.

Ashley's voice dropped, but there was command in her silky tones. "We've got too much at stake to allow this game to continue." She turned toward Steller. "Mr. Horn won't be a problem by the end of the week. I will see to it myself."

Fine jumped forward in his seat. "What do you mean by that?"

"Don't worry yourself about it." Uncrossing her elegant legs, she turned to Steller. "In twenty minutes be prepared to give me a briefing on Mr. Horn's whereabouts and schedule. Make certain your information is accurate."

Fine watched her walk out of his office, then looked incredulously at Steller. "What do you think she's going to do?"

Steller shrugged. "How the hell should I know?"

"Keep an eye on her. We don't need strange developments."

"Anything else?"

Fine turned his chair around and stared out the window. The sky was turning gunmetal gray over the eastern horizon. "I've got a bad feeling about this cop." Fine's voice was calm, almost resigned.

"In what way?" Steller asked.

"I can't explain," Fine answered, without turning around. "Just be prepared to go to New Pittsburgh."

CHAPTER SEVEN

HORN DIDN'T REMEMBER much of Riddle's memorial service. He'd been to cops' funerals before, and they were all the same. Bad. The fact that Riddle had been his partner made it that much worse. He went through the motions, staring blankly, repeating numbly what the priest said. It wasn't quite as black as Sharon and Julie's service, but then again, Horn thought, what's one step up from the bottom of hell?

Two days after Riddle's funeral, Horn walked into the Manhattan South precinct house to pick up his transfer orders. As he walked through the front doors of the dismal brownstone building, he caught himself thinking that he wasn't going to miss the place. He was hoping that some of the memories of his and Riddle's short career together would be left behind also.

Horn's thoughts were interrupted by the voice of the desk sergeant. "See the captain, Detective Horn. He has your orders."

Horn's knock on the smoked glass door was immediately followed by a sharp demand to enter. He walked into the sparsely furnished office of Captain Dick Kelso, commander of the Manhattan South precinct for the past eight years. "Sit down, Detective Horn," Kelso said, without looking up from the screen of his computer terminal. Horn sat down in the only unoccupied chair in the office.

"I've got your orders for New Pittsburgh." Kelso had suddenly punched off-line and swung around in his chair to face Horn. "The chief has signed them, but as you know, it's my prerogative to release them or not."

"Is there a problem?" Horn asked, already hating the bureaucratic bullshit he was having to go through. He just wanted to get out of New York City and see what was so special about an asteroidal mining colony that might possibly have a connection to the loss of everything he cared about.

"There might be," Kelso said. Wrinkles furrowed his forehead as he worked himself into an expression of seriousness. "Why are you so anxious to get this transfer?"

Horn almost laughed out loud. He figured Kelso was the kind of guy who would ask someone with a bullet in the guts if they wanted him to call a doctor. "Let's just say," Horn answered with a blank expression on his face, "that I need a change of scenery." He held up his right arm, then opened and closed his gloved hand in an exaggerated jerking motion. "Anyway, now that the state has done such an outstanding job of patching me back together, I'm ready to move on to bigger and better things." He let a hint of sarcasm enter his voice, almost enjoying his small pretense with the captain. He was a little surprised that he had some difficulty making his modified hand jerk around, as if the control were substandard. Since August's enhancements, there was no longer a reaction lag. He found the use of the modified components exhilarating, almost exciting.

"Well, there's just one hang-up," Kelso said, pulling a file stamped Private from his center drawer. He flipped open the folder. "The department shrink ran her program on you and you didn't come out with a real high score for stability."

"Well, you sure don't need to run one of those tests on her. She's about as stable as they come."

Kelso suddenly blurted out a laugh. Melody Locke, the department's psychiatrist, weighed nearly two hundred pounds and looked like a small mountain. Kelso leaned back in his chair and appeared to relax. "You may have lost your mind, but at least you haven't lost your sense of humor."

Horn smiled, but Kelso went back into his serious mode. He leaned over his desk and looked Horn in the eyes. "I don't give a damn what Locke's psycho profile says. What I really want to know is what were you and Riddle doing in the Bronx that got him and his stoolie whacked. Well?"

"You read my report," Horn said.

"I saw the report," Kelso said skeptically. "Internal Affairs saw the report. The goddamn janitor saw the report! And even he doesn't believe you guys were in no-man's-land because you had a hot tip on a 'big string deal' coming down. For Christ's sake, Horn, couldn't you do better than that?"

"Check it out," Horn answered. "Riddle's stoolie turned us on to it. Check out his body, he'd been sampling the shit all night. Probably had enough string in his nose to fly a kite."

"We did, and you're right." Kelso leaned back in his chair and folded his arms across his gut. He stared at Horn for almost a full minute before speaking. "Sorry about your wife and kid, Horn. Sorry about Dan, too." Horn didn't react, and Kelso waited a few seconds before figuring out that Horn wasn't going to respond. "Anyway," he went on as he pulled a manila envelope out of his desk drawer and tossed it across to Horn, "here's your transfer orders. I hope you know what the hell you're getting yourself into up there."

"Don't worry." Horn picked up the envelope and stood.

"Watch out for Roach," Kelso said, referring to Lieutenant Sam Roach, the commander of the New Pittsburgh police contingent.

"Why's that?"

"He was busted down from captain. Had an eye for quick cash when he should have had it on his job." Kelso shook his head. "Bastard's about a quart-a-day man, too."

"Well, thanks for the heads up." Without waiting for Kelso to speak again, Horn turned and walked out of the office and the station without a goodbye to anyone.

He returned to his apartment for the last time. He had already placed a limited number of items in storage. The rest of the things—furniture, clothes and so on—he'd donated to the NYPD Fund for the Homeless. He felt strange. He used to have a family, and this had been their home. At times he thought he heard Sharon's laughter echo from the walls and heard the quick patter of Julie's feet. Now he was leaving the place behind, and he knew a part of him was missing, too, forever. He picked up his single duffelbag and was about to walk out when he noticed the message light flashing on the telemonitor. "I thought I had this thing disconnected," he said aloud as he punched the replay button.

"Mr. Horn." Horn heard the voice before the face appeared on the screen. "You don't know me, but I think it important that we talk." The image behind the voice finally became manifest, and Horn found himself absorbed by the woman's beauty. "I have some information regarding your late partner that should probably be passed along only to you."

Horn couldn't imagine what a woman like that was doing calling him. He watched as she paused and appeared to overcome a slight embarrassment before continuing. "I'd considered approaching his superiors at the station, but it involves something rather personal....'' She smiled hesitantly. ''I guarantee it's nothing that will complicate your life.'' She looked away then back at him, the expression in her eyes warm and sincere. ''If you could be so kind as to see me, I'm certain it would only take ten or fifteen minutes.''

Horn looked at his watch. He had more than four hours to kill before he caught the shuttle that would take him to the cruiser on which he'd booked his passage to New Pittsburgh.

''My name is Ashley White,'' she continued, ''My number is 212/555-0802. Please call, Mr. Horn. I know that Dan thought a lot of you, and I'm certain you're the only one he would have wanted to...'' The woman's voice trailed off as she turned away from the screen, apparently to collect herself. She turned back toward Horn, who couldn't help but feel the same sort of sadness as he thought about Riddle.

''Excuse me,'' she said, after regaining her composure. ''He meant a great deal to me. Please call as soon as you find it convenient.''

Horn watched her image fade. He stared at the blank screen, and all he knew was that he wanted to see that face and hear that voice again. He immediately punched in the number and waited for her image to come up on the screen again. Before he could say anything, she broke into a deep smile and spoke. ''Mr. Horn, what a pleasant surprise. I was afraid you wouldn't call.''

''Your message referred to passing along some of Dan's...'' Horn's voice trailed off to give her the opportunity to finish the sentence.

''Yes, he confided in me about a number of things. However, there is something in particular that should probably be taken care of. I think you're the only one Dan would have wanted me to tell."

"I take it you don't want to discuss it over the monitor." Horn kept looking at her steadily, trying to put his finger on what he found so magnetic about her. It wasn't just her beauty—she possessed a mysterious poise that hinted at a woman who was fully aware of her sensuality.

"That's correct," she said, looking down almost shyly. "It is an extremely personal matter and I do not credit the telenet for its guarantee of privacy."

"I understand," Horn said. "Where would you like to meet?"

"If it's not too much of an inconvenience for you, I would prefer to meet here, at my apartment."

"Give me the address." Horn wrote down the address, which was in an exclusive area of Manhattan that had been overhauled by developers to provide another sanctuary for the wealthy. He looked up at the screen. "I'm actually on my way out of town. I could stop in say, twenty or thirty minutes."

"That will be fine. I look forward to seeing you in person." She smiled again, and Horn found himself returning the smile. He punched off the monitor and headed out the door.

After a quick stop at the landlord's to drop off the key, Horn hit the street and grabbed a cab. Twenty minutes later he was in front of a huge brownstone that had been renovated from the ground up. He walked up to a reception desk behind which a security guard was staring at a number of closed circuit monitors. "May I help you?" the man asked, still absorbed.

"Yeah," Horn said. "I'm here to see Ashley White."

"You must be Mr. Horn," the guard stated, still not looking up. "She's expecting you. Take the elevator at the end of the hall to the penthouse."

"Who else lives there?" Horn asked out of curiosity.

"Just Mrs. Ashley White Fine," the guard said.

"Okay to leave my bag here?"

The guard finally gave him an annoyed glance. "Just put it down. I'll take care of it."

Horn was impressed with the modern upgrade of the building. Everything inside was new and clean; polished wood, stainless steel and mirrored glass. He felt somewhat overcome when the large mahogany door opened and Ashley White invited him in. In life she was more beautiful and vibrant than on the telemonitor.

"Mr. Horn, please come in." She moved aside and Horn stepped into the luxurious apartment. "Follow me, please," she said, after shutting the door. She led Horn through a huge room with a safari decor. There was a zebra-skin rug on the highly polished marble floor and several big-game trophies hung on the walls.

"Nice place," Horn commented. "Are you the one who bagged these?" He gestured toward the stuffed heads.

"Not quite," the woman laughed, her voice low and friendly. She glanced back at Horn and smiled. "Memories of my late husband. In here," she said, opening a door and standing aside. "This is where I spend most of my time.

Horn walked into the room and stopped, his eyes drawn toward a wall that was one huge window, looking out across Manhattan. Horn had to admit that even through the smog, the view of the city at twilight was breathtaking.

"Still has some of its old magic, doesn't it?" the woman remarked as she crossed the room and perched on a stool set before a small oak bar in the corner. She leaned back against its edge and watched Horn.

"Yeah," he answered, turning. He was mildly surprised, that, except for the bar, the large room was a spa, designed for bodybuilding. There were two weight training benches, a rowing machine, three different bicycle exercisers and a large mat, obviously intended for calisthenics. At the back of the softly lit room, Horn saw double doors that led to a dressing room and shower area, complete with a large whirlpool and sauna. From hidden speakers, classical music played softly.

"Quite a setup you have here," Horn said, as he watched her stand and stroll behind the bar.

"What can I get you to drink?" she asked.

"Do you have any beer?" Horn walked across the smoke-gray carpet to the bar as she pulled a bottle of Galactica from a small refrigerator. She opened it and poured it into a tall glass.

She got herself a Perrier. "I'm glad you were able to come."

Horn looked at her closely. Going by her face and silver-gray hair, he guessed her to be in her late fifties. However, when he looked at her body, he could swear it belonged to a woman in her twenties. Even the conservative gray business suit and high-cut blouse revealed enough to tell Horn she hadn't been joking when she said she'd spent most of her time in the spa.

"I really am surprised that you and Dan knew each other." Horn sat on the black leather surface of one of the weight benches. He watched her emerge from behind the bar, sit down and cross her long legs, exposing a good portion of her well-shaped thighs. "I didn't think he..."

"He what? Could get involved with an older woman like me?" The playful glint in her eyes showed Horn that she was teasing.

Horn shook his head, as though in disbelief, then set his beer on the floor and pulled off his jacket. He was perspiring and realized it was quite hot in the room.

"Let me look after that." Ashley quickly left her chair to take his jacket. "Want me to hang that, too?" she asked, pointing at his shoulder holster. Horn shook his head, and hung his jacket on a coatrack near the door. "I keep it warm in here. Would you like to move to another room?"

"No, that's okay. I like the view."

"Why don't you take off your gloves, Mr. Horn?"

"Thanks, but I injured my hands recently and my doctor told me to keep them covered." Horn figured it was a pretty lame excuse, but better than none.

Ashley didn't return to her seat but stood in front of Horn, her arms crossed, staring at him. Horn couldn't turn his eyes away, he was so fascinated by her almost glowing green eyes and the contrast between her face and body. "Dan and I had a very special relationship." Her voice was low, almost husky. "He liked my body. Do you, Mr. Horn?"

Horn raised his eyebrows. He was mildly shocked by what the woman had just said. The cop part of his brain flashed a number of warnings that he was in a potentially dangerous situation.

Horn ignored the warnings. He felt he didn't deserve it, but he *was* alive, and figured the woman also might be looking for release, for a way to short-circuit the grief she was experiencing at the loss of Dan. He wondered if she had gotten him up to her penthouse on a trumped-up pretext just to seduce him. Something didn't fit, but Horn ignored it. Something stronger, from deep within him, sent an electrical tingling up his spine. He felt as though a dark brooding anxiety was on the verge of being relieved, or at least sidetracked for a while. He felt sweat bead his back between his shoulder blades.

"Your body is..." Horn was surprised at his voice; it sounded distant, separate. He was also surprised at what he was saying. "It's extraordinary."

Ashley smiled, only this time it was a knowing smile. It said, *I have you and you were easy*. Horn didn't care.

Without speaking Ashley pulled off her jacket and let it drop to the carpet. She unbuttoned her blouse, never taking her eyes off Horn, who stared in amazement at her lean, slightly muscular upper torso. She unhooked the lacy bra and let it fall to her feet. Her breasts were small and perfectly shaped, with large nipples standing erect. A little trickle of perspiration ran down between them, making a line to her navel. Her skin was deeply tanned. It sharply offset the conservative makeup and silver hair that framed her attractive face.

A powerful wave of desire washed over Horn as Ashley let her skirt fall to the floor, revealing an old-fashioned garter belt from which her sheer black stockings were suspended. She stepped out of the skirt, still wearing her heels. Horn noted that her upper thighs were as deeply tanned as her upper body.

"Do you want me to leave the stockings on?" she asked seductively. "Dan always liked them."

"Sure," Horn answered hoarsely. He noticed for the first time that the emerald pendant around Ashley's neck matched her eyes almost perfectly. In his bewitched state it fleetingly occurred to him she might have hypnotized him, but his body told him that his was a very normal masculine reaction.

Ashley unhooked her garter belt from the stockings and pulled it and her cream-colored panties down. She stepped out of them smoothly, then straightened and raised her arms over her head as if to stretch. Horn saw the muscles stand out across Ashley's shoulders and realized she was flexing instead of stretching. He watched as she brought her arms down and flexed, and the muscles across her flat stomach rippled and became distinct.

"Like the show?" she asked, bringing Horn out of his mesmerized state. Reaching up and behind her head, she removed a clip from her hair. She shook her head, and a silver cascade swirled around her shoulders.

"Yeah, a lot," Horn breathed as Ashley moved toward him. She pushed him backward until he was supine, and straddled him on the bench. He felt her loosen his clothes and couldn't help but gasp slightly as she held him possessively.

"I hope this is what you wanted," she whispered, leaning close to his face. Horn opened his mouth slightly and let her lips cover his. She went into a frenzy of kissing, and when he thought he needed to take a breath, she broke the kiss, then ran her tongue down the side of his face to his ear. "Just relax." Ashley breathed hard into his ear. Horn felt her lowering herself onto him. "I'll do all the work." She sucked in a long breath as he entered her. She surrounded him tightly, completely.

Horn tingled, as if an electric current were coursing through his veins. He watched as the woman pushed herself up into a sitting position, her hands on his chest. She leaned her head back and her eyes rolled back in her head as though she were on the verge of unconsciousness. Horn felt her flex her muscles sharply, and waves of nearly painful pleasure radiated through his body.

After several minutes of the exquisite exercising, Ashley started rotating her hips, slowly at first, and seemed to come out of her trancelike state. She gazed down at Horn and shook her hair, allowing it to fall down, nearly touching his face. The emerald pendant swung from her neck, swaying in front of Horn's eyes with the rhythm of her movements.

Horn's senses were nearly overloaded. Something wet struck his lips and a salty taste seeped into his mouth. He realized it was the sweat dripping off Ashley's face. He opened his mouth slightly and caught the next drop, which was tinged with a slight taste of perfume.

Horn half closed his eyes and allowed himself to absorb the exotic pleasure. For once he was free of all the darkness, the pain, the dark curtain of the seemingly endless funeral he'd been going through.

"I am ready for you now," Ashley whispered, then said, "Now." Taking his head in her hands, she pressed her lips to his hungrily. She began a stronger, more conventional motion with her hips, while tantalizing him with her tongue, her lips. Horn immediately felt himself achieve a point of no return and break loose. His body jerked sharply, his modified knee kicked down, and he felt Ashley fly forward. He immediately grabbed her waist and she emitted a loud half scream. Together, they bucked violently for nearly a minute before Horn gradually relaxed his grip as the sensation faded.

"That's quite a grip you have," Ashley gasped.

Damn, Horn thought, I could have crushed her ribs. He felt her roll off his sweat-soaked body, and she moved away lithely.

He lapsed into a highly relaxed state, and he was almost sleeping when Ashley's voice roused him. "On a scale of one to ten, Detective Horn, I'll have to give you a nine and a half."

Horn raised himself to a sitting position. He looked toward the bar and found himself staring stupidly into the barrel of a .38 instead of Ashley's green eyes. "I'd score it about a five," he said, his voice void of surprise.

Ashley was apparently surprised at Horn's lack of reaction. She lowered the barrel of the weapon slightly and gave him an irritated look. Slowly a smile crept onto her face, revealing her perfect teeth. "You must think it heroic to joke in the face of death." She raised the gun, aiming it at Horn's chest.

"What's this all about?" Horn asked soberly. "I've got the feeling it's got nothing to do with Dan."

"Looking down the barrel of a loaded weapon often makes one more perceptive, doesn't it, Detective Horn."

"What, then?" Horn repeated, his voice calm. "Why me?"

Ashley's green eyes were as cold as ice. "Let's just say that I'm like the black widow spider. I kill after it's over."

Horn felt the hair on the back of his neck suddenly bristling. There was a strange twitching in his E-mode, and a microsecond later Ashley squeezed the .38's trigger. Horn's right arm jerked up in a blur as the weapon went off, kicking the woman's arms into a short, upward arc. The slug slammed into the titanium forearm, then ricocheted into a full-length mirror, shattering it in an explosion of glass.

Horn didn't give her time to pull off another round. He rolled off the bench and lunged toward her, and his momentum, driven by his modified knee, sent him flying headfirst into Ashley's midsection.

The air whooshed out of her as the force of Horn's body drove her backward into the bar. Her head slammed into the rounded edge of the hardwood with a distinct thud. Her eyes rolled crazily in their sockets, and she blinked out like a dead star.

Horn pulled himself off the woman, who lay half-tangled between two bar stools. Instinctively, Horn stepped on her wrist before bending down and removing the .38, which was still clutched in her sweaty grip. He tossed it behind the bar, then placed two fingers on her wrist to check her pulse. He felt a faint throb, then slapped her face a couple of times to see if it would bring her to. It didn't.

Figuring it wouldn't pay to stick around and see who showed up, Horn got himself together, grabbed his jacket and headed for the door. He didn't think once about calling the cops.

CHAPTER EIGHT

HORN SPENT less than thirty minutes at the Ed Koch Memorial Transatmo before boarding a shuttle to the orbiting interplanetary cruiser that would take him to the New Pittsburgh titanium mining and smelting colony.

As the shuttle pulled into docking position, Horn got a good look at *Orion Arrow*, a Rickenbacker-class midrange cruiser that had been converted to a cargo scow. It was big and it was dirty. The ship's dull red color made it seem covered with rust, though Horn knew corrosion did not occur in space. The vessel was wedge-shaped, about two hundred yards long and seventy-five yards wide.

The pilothouse, also wedge-shaped, was located thirty yards out from the leading edge of the main fuselage, on a tubelike structure ten yards in diameter. *Orion Arrow* sported three gigantic level-four General Dynamics ion-propulsion engines capable of great thrusts of speed. From stem to stern the machine was covered with patches of gray and black carbon from countless retro burns and with thousands of dents and scrapes from being driven through meteor showers and clouds of space debris.

Horn boarded *Orion Arrow*, checked in with the cargo master, paid his credits for the trip and was assigned a berth. For many of the more than eighty passengers the trip was a connecting flight from other space-based mining and industrial colonies. The ship was soon under way, returning to New Pittsburgh after delivering its load of titanium.

The cargo this trip was water for the reactor cooling system, food, medical supplies and miscellaneous stores.

Horn squared away his gear and wandered around the ship for several hours, checking it out and trying to unwind. He ended up in the Bulkhead Bar, a crowded, low-ceilinged room the size of a small gym, which was located near the safety valves of the engine's reactors.

It wasn't hard for Horn to surmise that the Bulkhead was the only bar on the ship. He elbowed his way to the round aluminum bar at the center of the joint, from which whiskey and brew were dispensed. The bar was tended around the clock, most of the time by a big Australian named Red Zeke. He was called Red because of the color of the horseshoe-shaped strip of hair accenting his gleaming bald upper scalp. It hung down to his massive shoulders. Red was said to be able to clean and jerk more than four hundred pounds.

Horn ordered a beer and was surprised that it was served cold. "Somethin' wrong with the brew, mate?" Red asked, noticing Horn's mild reaction.

"No, just surprised to get beer this cold up here." Horn tilted back the mug with pleasure and quaffed another mouthful.

"Wouldn't serve warm brew to a goddamn mindless sodbuster. And I can tell by lookin' at ya that ya ain't one o' them, so here." Red held out his hand, which Horn shook. "Red Zeke's the name," he said.

"Horn."

"Headed to the Pitts, are ya?" Red asked, but before Horn could answer, the Australian excused himself to wait on a customer at the other side of the bar.

Leaning on the bar with one elbow, Horn turned around and watched the rough-looking crowd. The patrons were mostly migrant laborers, traveling from one tough, low-paying job to another. Some had families, but few had homes. Horn recognized himself in the bleak faces and the cockiness that stemmed from constant troubles. His family was gone and along with it all his hope. He thought he was looking into a mirror, down the road into his future.

The real difference between Horn and the dejected, lost souls with whom he was traveling was his debt. It was a debt of violence he owed to the specter who had wrenched away his loved ones, his life. Horn felt that he had no soul: it had died in a blood-splattered nightmare. What he did have was a void that could be filled only with vengeance, extreme and fully exacted. Horn intended to repay the debt with interest ... and New Pittsburgh was where he would make a start in that direction.

His thoughts were interrupted by a hand on his shoulder and a cheery voice. "Buy you a beer?" He swung around and faced a short stocky man who wore the flight suit and rank of the ship's captain. The gray-haired man grinned, exposing a mouthful of shiny gold teeth. As far as Horn could tell, not a one was the original enamel. "The name's Crossfield, Jack Crossfield, captain."

"Max Horn." After shaking hands, Horn accepted the beer.

"You're new to this kind of run," Crossfield said, stating a fact more than asking a question.

"That easy to tell?" Horn asked.

"Just look around you, mate," Crossfield said, without turning his head. "I've been hauling ass and cargo long enough to know the difference between a miner, a farmer and a..." He looked Horn up and down as if he were going to guess his weight. "Prisoner chaser. Going to the Pitts to pick someone up?"

Horn chuckled. "Something like that. I'm a cop. Been assigned to the colony for standard duty."

Crossfield let out a muted whistle. "What the hell did you do to get stiffed with this assignment?"

"And why did you get stiffed with flying this garbage truck?" Horn smiled, noticing that Crossfield's face was a crisscrossed mass of fine scars.

"Ha!" The captain slapped Horn on the shoulder, and suddenly the smile slipped from his face. He had hit Horn's right shoulder, and there was no mistaking the hollow thunk that was unlike the sound of flesh slapping flesh. Crossfield hesitated just a moment before the grin eased back onto his face. "You've got a point, Horn." He spoke as if nothing out of the ordinary had taken place. "I guess there's not much else for an old washed-out fighter pilot to do nowadays, except drive something like this hunk of junk." He slammed the bar. "Used to fly recce birds. Even did a tour down in Africa during the civil wars."

"Air Force?" Horn asked, draining the beer in his mug and gesturing at Red for two more.

"Contract pilot," Crossfield said, "but I flew anything the Air Force had. Probably still could. The goddamn drones ruined it for all of us." He shook his head. "Hey, thanks," he said as Red placed two full ones in the bar.

"Where is everybody?" Horn asked.

"What do you mean?" Crossfield looked puzzled.

"I've been walking around your ship for the past couple of hours, and I know more people were on board and boarding when I got on than what I saw a while ago," Horn explained.

"Oh, yeah. Well, you're right. There's a couple of hundred down on C deck. Those are the sleepers."

"Sleepers?" Horn asked curiously.

"Those are passengers we drug for the trip. They're mostly migrant workers who can't afford eight weeks of chow, so we put them to sleep. Only costs them twenty-five creds, fifteen for children. Sometimes—'' Crossfield looked around the bar ''—I wish most passengers were sleepers. After five or six weeks you'll see what I mean.''

"No doubt," Horn said. "What can you tell me about New Pittsburgh?"

Crossfield looked at his watch before answering. "Probably more than you really want to know, but right now, I've got to get back to the bridge and sign off on the engine trim to cruise mode. I just felt them make it."

"I didn't notice anything," Horn said.

Crossfield shrugged. "Tell you what, Horn. We got plenty of time. You can find out what I know about that god-awful rock you're headed for as long as you can keep Red in the mode of putting these on the bar." He tipped his mug at Horn before draining it.

"It's a deal."

"See you later, then." The captain turned and headed for the bridge.

Horn was glad that Crossfield was driving in space instead of New York City traffic. At least in space, the odds were that one for the road wouldn't get you in trouble.

The next several weeks were relatively uneventful. Horn spent most of his time in the spacecraft's gym, working on getting in shape. He remembered what Dr. August had said about developing his body to the point where it would support the mod enhancements, and he worked hard, especially on the right thigh, calf and foot. It felt a little strange to have his knee supertuned with everything above and below it capable of performing only at human level. Horn likened it to having power steering on a chariot.

Horn's shoulders needed little work in terms of getting the surviving muscles into good enough shape that they could at least withstand some of the things the mod was capable of doing. He had managed to keep his neck, back and pectoral muscles in pretty good condition through isometrics, which he had practiced on a regular basis as a way to release tension.

Horn's adaptation to his enhanced modifications progressed well, for the most part. Late one night, while pulling the overheads, he experienced a glitch in the workings of his right arm that unnerved him to the point of fear. He was pulling the weights with his right arm in order to work the muscles to which the titanium shoulder plates were attached. He had let his mind drift, immersed in the routine, when a flashback of the front door's exploding and throwing him helplessly down suddenly flooded his mind. Horn's right arm went briefly berserk and ripped the overhead weight racks cleanly off the steel bulkhead with a scream of twisted metal. It happened so fast that Horn could only react to the sound. He was barely able to roll out of the way as the four-inch steel bolts sheared and the four-hundred-pound apparatus fell to the floor.

Up to that time he had not exercised the mods to their full capability. He had used them, but never really tested them to see what they could do. The power exhibited when the weight rack was ripped off the wall didn't scare Horn; but the fact that it happened involuntarily did. He remembered August's warning about uncontrolled nerve impulses affecting the mod's operations and was reasonably certain that was what had happened. The rationale didn't make him less concerned, but Horn was certain one good thing had resulted from the manifestation of the glitch: it had ended his flashback, at least for the time being.

Orion Arrow had been moving through space for a little more than six weeks when Horn finally met up with Crossfield again. Naturally, it was in the Bulkhead Bar. "Not as crowded as a couple of weeks ago," Horn said as he greeted the captain.

"Usually gets like that about this point in the cruise." Crossfield thanked Red Zeke for the beer and continued his explanation to Horn. "Most of the workers have either gambled away or drunk up their credits by now. Once they get to the Pitts, it'll be easy for them to get a loan." Crossfield took a long pull on his mug before adding, "All they need for collateral is their sweat."

"You were going to give me the lowdown on New Pittsburgh," Horn said, pulling a ten-credit wafer from his pocket and placing it on the bar. "Keep them coming, Red." He waved at the big Aussie, who dropped his jaw in a grin and snapped an abbreviated sailor's salute.

"That's right." Crossfield wiped his mouth with the back of a hand. "Let me tell you about the place. It's bound to cheer you up." He smiled sarcastically.

Horn didn't say anything so Crossfield began. "If ever there was a place in the universe that could eat the soul right out of a man, it's got to be New Pittsburgh. I've been to lots of god-awful places, too. I used to think the drilling operation on Alpha 266 was bad. The goddamn wind and sand on that hell zone would shred the flesh right off your bones. Then there's the marble mines of Sierra 8. Six months there turns a man's back into a gnarled-up piece of driftwood." He glanced into Horn's eyes before tilting back the mug.

"Yeah," Crossfield continued introspectively, "I've hauled human flotsam to the outskirts of hell, but all those places put together look like a health resort for lawyers when compared to the Pitts." He held up his empty mug to Red and opened his mouth as if something he was going to say was extremely painful. Horn was expecting to hear some other descriptive figure of speech. "It really sucks," was all he said. Then, as though by way of explanation, he added, "I've met the guy who runs the place."

Horn was a little surprised at the captain's shift in gears. "So what's he like?"

"I guess he doesn't really run the place, but he owns it. His name is Fine, Oasis Fine, if I remember correctly. The guy was a Wall Street type out of New York. I picked up him and his crew on one of our normal runs when their little Lear business shuttle broke down."

"How did he take it?" Horn asked.

"He was an asshole," Crossfield replied. "I don't really remember a whole hell of a lot about the guy. I could tell he didn't like being on the same ship with a bunch of New Pitt slaves. He kept pretty much to himself. Except for his bodyguard, that is."

"Bodyguard?" Horn didn't think having a bodyguard was out of the ordinary, but he asked the question to keep Crossfield from spacing out on him.

"Yeah, big blond bastard." Crossfield rolled his head around as if he were trying to relieve a crick in his neck. "Looked like a cross between a snake and a goddamn albino gorilla with a crew cut."

Horn's blood turned into ice water, and he felt his heart nearly jump out of his chest. "As a matter of fact—" Crossfield looked down at Horn's gloved hands then up into his eyes "—the guy was like you in one way—he never took off his gloves."

The two men's conversation was cut short as one of the uniformed crew members interrupted. "Excuse me, sir, there's been some trouble."

"What's that?" Crossfield asked.

"A fight in the H cargo hold, a dispute over a card game. Anyway, we've got another dead passenger."

Horn noticed that neither Crossfield nor the crewman looked too concerned. "*Another* dead passenger?" Horn asked.

"Yeah." Crossfield looked at him. "This will make six . . . or is it seven? Hell, it's about normal for this trip." He looked at his watch and turned back to the crewman. "There's a garbage dump at 1800. Put him in the tube. Anyone know who did the guy?"

"No, sir."

"Okay," Crossfield said nonchalantly. "Go ahead and eject the body with the rest of the refuse."

"Aye, sir." He gave a sloppy salute before leaving the bar.

"Listen, Horn," Crossfield said, "I have to go to the head. Think I'll take a nap, too. See ya around."

"Sure thing," Horn called as he watched the captain stagger out.

Horn didn't have another session with Crossfield the rest of the trip. It really didn't matter, either. The description he'd given of the New Pittsburgh owner's bodyguard made Horn think he would find more than tite dust on the rock that ate men's souls.

CHAPTER NINE

HORN GOT A GOOD LOOK at the asteroid and the New Pittsburgh mining colony as *Orion Arrow* made her final approach before swinging around and docking with the dome. Red dust billowed up around the ship like massive clouds of rust as the vectored thrust settled the machine into position. Horn knew then why the spacecraft's color resembled something pulled from a scrap heap behind a long-abandoned machine shop.

The asteroid was a desolate place. It was about twice the size of the earth's moon and shaped like a fat disk of layered shale. Some old-timers said it looked like a giant turd drifting in space. The surface was rough, pitted with meteor craters and the scars from years of mining the plentiful rutile ore.

The asteroid proper was never given a name. Titus Steel had laid claim to the rock when it was found to be rich in the ore required to smelt titanium. The company had established the New Pittsburgh Mining Colony and Titanium Smelting Operation after it was determined that the asteroid's elliptical orbit had stabilized. No one ever knew exactly how the asteroid got there; its discovery coincided with the disruption of Saturn's rings by what was called the Apocalypse Meteor Shower of 2002.

Horn's initial impression of the domed mining colony was that Crossfield had been too kind in his description. The dome was ten miles in diameter, and more than five hundred feet high at the apex, which housed the drone and laser control station. It was transparent, originally designed for farming communities in hostile environments. The structure was nearly surrounded by thousands of huge piles of dirty red slag. Little roads formed by the tracked mining drones wove in and out of these piles in a random crazy-quilt pattern. Horn thought the whole area looked like a worn and dirty land mine in a war zone.

It wasn't hard to discern the location of the reactor and smelting operation. Huge tubes snaked out from one area of the dome, connecting a series of smelting vents that resembled smokestacks and rose more than one thousand feet into the hazy atmosphere. There were sixteen stacks branching out from what was considered the back of the dome. To one side of these were four massive cooling towers, which served as the radiator for the ancient reactor. While the cooling towers were only half as tall as the vent stacks, they were much wider, with a flare at the top that ringed an opening twenty-five yards in diameter.

Great clouds of steam rose from the cooling towers whenever the reactor was in operation, which was most of the time. When the smelter was fired up, the steam from the cooling towers mixed with the soot, smoke and waste being vented to form a smothering reddish-colored brew.

The mixture would blanket the dome, creating strange electrical storms and a hellish environment. Jagged fingers of blue-white lightning would snake out of the churning red mass of waste and run helter-skelter across the convex surface.

The workers called the highly acidic and toxic substance slag rain, slarr or the sauce. One of the few pastimes in New Pittsburgh was to get bombed on booze or some form of hallucinogenic drug and watch the "sauce cook." At one time there had even been tales of a hideous creature that roamed the asteroid in the slarr. There had been some basis for the tales though, and the creature turned out to be one of the surface mining drones that had a malfunction in its transponder.

Horn received a brief in-processing by the Titus Steel security team at the dock. The whole procedure amounted to little more than signing in. He was then directed to a representative of the Titus Steel Housing Authority. The man punched Horn's ID into a desktop terminal, then turned to a big map of the dome on the wall. He pointed to a section at the head of a system of streets that covered about a quarter of the dome's area and appeared to be laid out at random. "You have been assigned a stand-alone three-room bungalow." He handed Horn a bar-coded plastic card. "The address is on the key. Your records show your rent has been paid in advance for six months. Any questions?"

"Yeah," Horn said. "What's this area?" He pointed to another part of the map. There the streets were straight and wide, arranged in the conventional rectangular style of urban neighborhoods.

"Oh, that's the new residential quarter. I hope you didn't want housing there. You have to request it in advance." The little man, who looked like a ticket taker at a theater, seemed worried that Horn would be angry.

"Well, what's the area you've got me on the border of there?" Horn asked. "The street system looks like a maze built by a bunch of drunks."

"Let me explain," the man said. "That's the old section, built before Titus Steel introduced its modular housing for remote sites. Naturally, the rent isn't as high as it is in the new section." He waved his hand over the high-rent district, which also covered roughly a quarter of the dome's area.

"What's the rest of the map showing me?" Horn asked in tones of polite interest.

"This is the staging and shipping area for the finished tite. It also handles all transport activity associated with the colony. We're right here." He pointed to one of the main docks. "Now, this area here—" he ran a finger along a curved line that, in effect, segregated another quarter of the dome "—is where the reactor and smelter are located. It's sealed off from the rest of the dome by a twenty-foot rock wall lined with lead bricks. It's called the Hot Zone, for obvious reasons."

"How do they get anything in or out of there?"

"Through rad-protected ports. The ore goes in from the outside, so that's not a problem. The two openings in the wall on the inside are controlled by Titus Steel security." The man started fiddling around impatiently. "Listen, buddy. Ask anybody around, they'll tell you about the place. Right now, it's my break time."

"Sure," Horn said. "But, just one more thing."

"What is it?" the housing clerk demanded irritably.

"Transportation. How do I get to my place?" Horn shouldered his duffel bag.

The man pointed to a set of scarred metal doors. "Right out there is a stop for the ground shuttle. It comes by every ten minutes or so. You'll figure it out."

Horn turned and stalked out without saying another word. Right at the doors he turned back and saw the man check his wristwatch while punching in a number on the telemonitor. Horn shrugged. He was familiar with this kind of employee—fawning over important people and to all others showing a minimum of interest and courtesy. Bad lot, Horn thought, but he knew that there were far worse types on the rock.

New Pittsburgh's public transportation consisted of an old half-track, buslike vehicle that would have been more at home on a battlefield. Horn gave the driver a slip of paper with his address on it and asked the man to let him know when they were in the general vicinity. Taking a seat next to a window, he got his first ground-level view of the mining colony as the worn shuttle plodded through the dust-covered streets.

The place resembled an ancient movie set that was intended to portray an alien world. As they moved through the new sectors of the colony, Horn experienced a certain claustrophobia, and a sensation of being trapped. People shuffled everywhere, shoulder to shoulder, like ants on the dusty sidewalks. They were mostly mine workers, Horn guessed. Their bent backs and crude-looking protective garb made them resemble a tired army of prehistoric warriors marching off to battle.

Like the population, the buildings were jammed together. The modular architecture enabled them to be stacked, one on top of the other, often three and four levels high. They looked like a bunch of faded toy building blocks fronting the narrow streets. Horn noticed that most of the street-level structures were reserved for businesses, while the upper stories appeared to be living quarters.

The shops were not much different from those found in Horn's New York neighborhood, with a couple of exceptions unique to life on an asteroid. One worn sign that hung above a set of double doors read Emergency Radiation Treatment. A smaller sign affixed directly to one of the establishment's doors requested No Terminals Please. There was also a sign over a restaurant that caught Horn's eye: Earthstyle Bar and Grill. He wondered what asteroidstyle was like.

The shuttle finally broke out of the residential business sector and cut across an unmarked road at the edge of the ore staging area. Horn was somewhat surprised by the size of the dome now that his view wasn't restricted by the box-like buildings. A field of rutile stretched out to the edge of the dome, which hung far in the distance like a gauze curtain. The red ore was piled into small hills, around which tracked front-end loaders and scoop drones moved, carrying the ore in from the fields or down a maze of narrow roads to the smelter. Horn could see the massive wall surrounding the reactor and smelting ovens. It looked like the inverse of a huge, crudely built dam.

The bus made another pass through the new quarter, and Horn got a look at the Titus Steel corporate complex, which consisted of a half dozen three-story buildings huddled together. He turned to a gray-haired miner sitting across the aisle and pointed a thumb toward the out-of-place-looking steel-and-glass structure. "What the hell are those?" he asked.

At first the bearded, dust-covered miner just stared at Horn, as though he was surprised someone had spoken to him. After several seconds, he finally answered in a gravelly voice, "Titus Steel. Hospital, offices, shit like that."

Horn nodded and turned away as the shuttle pulled up to a stop.

"This is where you get off, buddy," the driver said, pointing at Horn in the mirror above the windshield. "The old section is a couple of blocks that way." He indicated a side street that wound out of sight.

Horn dragged his duffel bag to the door. The driver handed him the slip of paper with the address on it. "Here," he said, "Ribbon Row is the first street you cross."

"Thanks." Horn stepped into the street with his bag. Less than ten minutes later he was shoving the card key into the door of his new home.

It didn't take long for Horn to put away his gear in the old but clean bungalow. Like most of the houses in the district it was built out of the red rock of the asteroid itself. But the similarity ended with the material. In shape and style no two houses were the same. Some were round, some square, some multistory, some single-story and so on. The architecture reminded Horn of the rubble of the Egyptian pyramids.

The man at the housing authority had had his geography a little screwed up when he told Horn the bungalow was on the edge of the old section. The distance between was a good four blocks, if you could define blocks in the maze of mismatched streets. He didn't really mind. He guessed the action, if any was to be found, would be located somewhere in the part of New Pittsburgh that resembled a tumbledown mud village.

Horn didn't have to report to Sam Roach until the next day, so he took a walk to check out the neighborhood and look for a place to get a bite to eat and a cold beer.

After being propositioned four times in one block, Horn knew he had found the main drag for street life in New Pittsburgh. The street was named Ostereams Boulevard, after one of Titus Steel's past presidents, Jack Ostereams, who had developed the process of smelting titanium with a nuclear reactor.

The streets were crowded. Dust-covered mine workers, hookers and flashily dressed dealers in all kinds of consumer goods jostled elbow to elbow. There were two or three bars on every block, along with countless strip joints and porno shops. The businesses advertised their goods and services with an elaborate display of flashing neon. Horn couldn't help but feel he was walking down the midway of some alien carnival. He even saw a tattoo parlor, sporting a multicolored sign in the window that read:

Needle's clean
See what I mean
Your skin becomes
A Technicolor dream

After a couple of hours of ambling around, Horn stepped into a joint called Beach Head Bar and Grill. The place wasn't crowded, and he had his pick of several empty stools at the bar. He ordered a beer and something called an All-American Old-Time Burger before trying to engage the barmaid in a little conversation. He noticed that she hadn't said anything since he walked in; even when he ordered she'd remained silent. Horn figured her to be in her mid-thirties. She wasn't bad-looking, but her face was sad.

"You got a name?" Horn asked. He was slightly embarrassed when she simply stared at him from across the bar without answering. Then she walked over to him. With her face within six inches of his, she opened her mouth as wide a possible and pointed at it. All that was left of her tongue was a mass of scar tissue that looked like a shriveled-up piece of rawhide. Horn couldn't bring himself to do or say anything. He sat there, staring into the barmaid's mouth, wondering if she was ever going to shut it and move away.

"Go ahead, bub," a hoarse voice at one end of the bar remarked. "Rosie there is waitin' for a big French kiss!" A cackle of laughter followed, and Rosie finally shut her mouth and moved away.

Horn left the place wondering if every joint on the asteroid was like the Beach Head. Another half a block down from a place called Lostdreams he went into Ringo's Nightowl. The place was livelier than the Beach Head and appeared to cater to a more sociable clientele. There was a bandstand and dance floor at the back of the place, but nothing much was happening. Horn figured it was too early. He made his way to the long S-shaped bar where most of the crowd milled about, and ordered a beer. The bartender was tall and skinny, with wire-frame glasses and an obvious toupee on top of his bullet-shaped head. The wig was jet black and molded to look like a wave that was rolling across the top of the man's head, toward the back of his neck.

Horn sipped his beer and scoped out the crowd, getting a closer look at the asteroid's majority. Most were miner types—big, hard-core dirty men who still carried red dust on their shoulders and the tops of their boots. Most of them wore Kevlar-coated parachute pants that were advertised to last as long as real leather. Many had tank tops or a new version of the old combat vest, but hardly any of the men wore shirts. Horn felt a little out of place in his long-sleeved turtleneck and leather gloves.

"Hello, stranger. Buy a working girl a drink?" Horn turned toward the voice, and his eyes locked onto those of a sultry, good-looking lady of the night. She had long black hair that was combed to one side and hung over the front of her right shoulder, down to her slender waist. She was wearing a stark white blouse and a black leather miniskirt. Her silver-studded, high-heeled black boots went up to the thigh.

Horn knew that most of the woman's work was done horizontally, but he couldn't resist buying her a drink. He had almost forgotten how pleasant a woman's company could be. "My pleasure," he said. "What would you like?"

"Shooting Star," she said, running her tongue over her crimson lips.

Horn ordered the drink then turned back to face her. "My name is Horn," he said.

She smiled seductively before responding. "I'm Linda. You're not a miner, are you?"

"No," Horn answered, as he paid for the drink and handed it to her. "You're not a hired killer, are you?" He was casting for something to change the subject.

"Why?" she asked, moving closer until her breast brushed against Horn's arm. "Do I look like one?"

"You dress like one." Horn was actually enjoying himself, but his pleasure was suddenly cut short as an arm snaked between him and the woman, then shoved her back.

"What the hell—" Horn said, turning to find the arm's owner. It was a tall, muscular, sandy-haired guy in an old pin-striped two-piece suit. He wasn't wearing a shirt, and there was a whole swath of gold chains hanging around his neck.

"Oh, excuse me," the big guy said, forcing himself in front of Horn so their chests were inches apart.

The woman grabbed the man's arm and complained in anger and frustration. "Reggie! I can't even enjoy myself on this sweat stain without your ruining it!"

"Move away, Linda," Reggie said over his shoulder. "I'll do the talking and the thinking." He turned back to Horn and smiled, and his eyes twinkled in the dim light of the bar. "You're new here, aren't you, Slick?"

Horn looked at Reggie without answering. He couldn't help feeling a little irritated and hoped the man would notice and simply leave.

"Well, I don't mind you talking to Linda, even though she is my girl." Reggie touched the tips of his fingers to the wide lapels of his suit and shook his head in constant slow motion as he talked. "And she is a very special girl." Reggie had lowered his voice as though he were telling Horn some great secret.

"Get away from me, pal," Horn said calmly. "I'm not interested."

Reggie did a little shuffling jive with his feet and blew smoke into Horn's face. Horn thought the guy was trying to put a tough look on his face, when he said, "Listen, Slick, I'm gonna let you go, but I oughta rip your heart out...."

Horn turned toward the bar, ignoring Reggie, and ordered another beer. "Hey!" The pimp grabbed Horn's shirtsleeve. "I was talking to your lame ass, Slick."

"Get your hand off my shirt," Horn said without turning toward Reggie, who had worked his tough-guy routine into a near frenzy.

"Okay, maybe you ain't interested in the merchandise." Reggie leaned toward Horn and placed his left hand on the bar. He took a long drag on his smoke then blew the ashes off the burning coal. "See if this gives you something to remember, anyway."

Horn smelled burning fabric and knew that Reggie had stuck the end of the cigarette to his right arm. He didn't react. He continued ignoring the excited pimp and sipped at his beer.

After a second, Reggie was highly perplexed. He knew something wasn't working right. He twirled the cigarette around and shoved it deeper into the hole it had burned through the shirt sleeve. But still no reaction. He was at a loss. "Shit, what the hell's wrong with you, Slick?" He laughed halfheartedly in a high-pitched voice, raised his eyebrows in disbelief and stammered, "Ain't you got no nerves in your arm?"

Horn looked down at Reggie's hand on the bar. Each finger had a massive gold ring covered with what appeared to be diamonds. With minimal movement of his arm, Horn slowly raised his gloved right hand and placed it on top of Reggie's. He willed a slight squeeze.

Reggie's very intense expression suddenly became stone-like. He stared at the side of Horn's face in a manner that could only be described as stupid wonder. Sweat broke out on his forehead, and in a matter of seconds, little streams of it ran down his face and neck.

"Get your cigarette away from my arm," Horn said, and bumped up the intensity of his grip on Reggie's hand.

"It's away! It's away!" Reggie squealed in pain, tossing the cigarette to the floor and doing a little dance on his toes.

"Now get your ass away from me," Horn ordered, releasing his grip on the pimp's hand.

"Sure thing, sure thing, man. Anything you say." Reggie backed away a couple of steps, rubbing his throbbing hand and staring at Horn, his eyes wide with pain.

"Go on, beat it." Horn turned away and raised the beer to his lips.

The bartender walked over and wiped a rag across the bar in front of Horn. "Get you another beer, Mac?" he asked.

"Sure," Horn answered, before downing the rest of the drink and sliding the mug across the bar. Seconds later the bartender was setting a full one down in its place.

"Don't look now," he said in a near whisper as he fingered the credit wafer Horn had placed on the bar. "Your buddy's back, and he's got a tubular reinforcement."

Suddenly he ducked behind the bar, and Horn swung around, his right arm automatically rising into a blocking position. Reggie stood wild-eyed a couple of steps away and was swinging a three-foot section of steel pipe down from over his head like an ax. The blow, meant for the back of

Horn's head, struck the titanium forearm with such force that Horn felt the jolt in the soles of his feet.

Reggie staggered back a step and quivered as the reverse shock of the blow ran through his arms and chest. He thought he'd hit an anvil instead of a man's arm. "Goddamn!" he gasped hoarsely. "You're not human!"

Horn took a quick step forward and ripped the pipe out of Reggie's hand. He tossed it across the floor, and a couple of miners who had been watching the scene had to quickly dance out of its way. Horn's right hand automatically dropped to waist level, then ripped upward like a missile, heading for Reggie's face. He could feel his anger driving the modified arm and tried to check his blow. The back of the titanium hand slammed into Reggie's nose like a rocket sled, smashing it flat against his face. The pimp's head flew backward, followed by the rest of his body. Reggie landed on the floor a good ten feet from where the blow was struck. He didn't move.

"I hope I didn't kill the dumb bastard," Horn muttered under his breath as he walked over to Reggie's outstretched form. He pulled the glove off his left hand and placed two fingers on the pimp's neck. There was a faint pulse. Horn felt something like relief as he took stock of Reggie's face. It was a mess. He wondered what it would have looked like if he hadn't held back the swing.

Horn glanced around the bar. The patrons had stopped what they were doing and were staring at him. Horn rubbed the back of his hand as though it were in pain, thinking it was a weak ploy, but better than nothing at all. As if on cue, the entire audience turned back to their booze, women, cards or whatever they were turned into before Reggie launched his attack. The din in the bar immediately returned to its near riotous level, as though nothing out of the ordinary had happened.

The bartender peered over the bar. "Need a couple of pimp draggers!" he yelled, and waved a hand at a pair who were setting up equipment on the bandstand.

Horn returned to the bar and watched the two guys drag Reggie toward the back door. He felt a tap on his shoulder and turned around. Facing him was a short, fat balding man with a big, droopy mustache. The guy wore a rainbow-colored headband, and a small animal's bleached skull dangled from his left ear on a gold chain.

"The name's Ringo, Laslow Ringo. This is my place." The man held out his hand, which Horn shook. "Sorry about the trouble there—your next brew is on the house." He motioned to the bartender.

"The name's Horn. And that wasn't any trouble."

"You handled yourself pretty well for, er, a newcomer. What do you do, Mr. Horn?" Ringo looked Horn over. "I can see you don't work the mine."

"I'm a cop," Horn answered, "New York City PD."

Ringo tilted back his round head and laughed loudly. "New York City cop?" the bar's owner asked when he finally composed himself enough to speak. "I knew there were some of you cats on this rock, but you're the first one I've ever actually seen."

Horn raised his eyebrows. "You joking?"

"Hell, no, I'm not joking." Ringo laughed again, but not as heartily as before. "No offense, but the city of New York is making the joke. There's no law on this roid other than what the styros enforce."

"What are the styros?" Horn asked.

"Styros are Titus Steel Security goons," Ringo answered. "We call them styros because they've got Styrofoam for brains. They're strictly force oriented, but they leave you alone. Hardly ever come down here."

"What's their function?"

"They keep the mine and smelter going, that's all." Ringo pulled on a corner of his mustache. "They're kind of like truant officers—make sure the miners show up for work and recruit terminals when they need new ones."

"Terminals?"

"Man, you *are* new. How long you been on this chunk of spit?" Ringo waved at the bartender, then tipped his hand in front of his lips in a bring-me-a-drink gesture.

"Less than twenty-four," Horn answered.

"You got a lot to learn if you plan on sticking around." Ringo reached over the bar to take a glass of amber-colored liquid. "A terminal is a Hot Zone worker." He took a stiff belt of the booze. "You know what the Hot Zone is?"

Horn remembered his conversation with the housing clerk. "Yeah. It's the sealed area containing the reactor."

"And the smelting operation," Ringo added. "Anyway, a terminal is just that—he's terminal. Anyone working in the Hot Zone ain't going to be around for long."

"Why's that?" Horn asked.

Ringo chuckled. "Because the only place you'll find a higher rad level than the Zone is on the sun. Most of the terminals take the job knowing they're going to die within a short period of time."

Horn raised his eyebrows. "Why do they do it, then?"

"The majority have some sickness, anyway. One of the many wasting-away illnesses, AIDS, nerve dox, you name it. They're recruited that way." Ringo shook his head sadly, and moved his hand as if he were flashing a newspaper line. "Wanted, losers who'll be dying soon."

"What makes them take the job?" Horn asked. "I wouldn't think credits would be any incentive."

"Mainly drugs," Ringo answered. "Painkillers, designer drugs, stims...anything they want. Anything to take their minds off dying."

"Sounds pretty grim," Horn said.

"You should see the poor bastards go for it." Ringo shook his head again and gulped another two fingers' breadth from his glass. "They let 'em out of the Zone once a week to get their pay. They line up, get their dope, then the styros herd them back in. It's kind of sad." Ringo slapped Horn on the shoulder. "Buy you another brew, Mr. Horn?"

"No thanks," Horn said, placing the empty mug on the bar. "I've got to be going."

"Come back when you can hear the band," Ringo invited with a smile. "They're pretty damn good."

"Sure will." Nobody paid any attention when Horn walked out of the bar and headed toward his bungalow. The stroll cleared his head and sharpened his senses. As he fitted the plastic key card into the door's locking device, he became aware that someone was watching him. Whoever it was, he deduced, had probably been following him all night.

CHAPTER TEN

THE BUILDING THAT HOUSED the NYPD's field office looked not much better than an excavated bomb shelter. It was located in the dome's shipping and receiving area, next to one of the huge atmospheric exhaust ports that emitted a strong, low-frequency hum twenty-four hours a day.

Horn showed up at 9:00 a.m. and found the office unlocked and empty. He sat down in a chair and looked around the shabbily furnished room. There were two desks covered with papers, empty cups and overflowing ashtrays. A couple of calendars hung from the gray block walls, but the pages hadn't been turned for several months. Horn finally walked over to a lone computer terminal and tried to punch on-line. Nothing happened. The age-old CRT screen stared at Horn like a big dead eye.

One of the desks had a worn nameplate almost buried under a mass of files. Horn picked it up. Lieutenant Sam Roach was spelled out in block letters, and a little chrome-plated NYPD badge was affixed to one corner. Horn walked behind the desk and pulled open a drawer. It was filled with papers and a nearly empty quart bottle of Comrade brand vodka.

Horn closed the drawer as tired-sounding footsteps approached the office door. He stepped to one side of the desk and leaned against the wall. A man Horn assumed was Sam Roach entered the room. "Who the hell are you?" he asked, obviously surprised to find someone there.

"Detective Horn, Max Horn. You should have been expecting me." He watched Roach shrug and look bleary-eyed at his watch before sitting down behind his desk.

Roach was dark-complexioned, with beady brown eyes that constantly shifted from side to side. His longish black hair was combed straight back and hung down over the collar of his rumpled blue, standard-issue jumpsuit. While Roach wasn't exactly fat, his gut stuck out as though he'd swallowed a cannonball. "Where's your goddamn uniform, Detective?" He pulled a file from a mess of papers stacked in a sagging plastic tray.

"I work plainclothes," Horn answered. "Check it out." He nodded to the file, assuming it was his. "I'm authorized."

Roach thumbed through the file. "I see here that you were in a CSU. Don't think that crap carries any weight on this rock. I don't want no hotshot pissin' on every cigarette butt someone throws down."

Horn looked around the office, and it dawned on him then that there weren't any other New York cops. He and Roach were the only ones. His mistake. He had just assumed there would be at least a couple of other detectives. "Wait a minute. You and I are the only NYPD cops on this roid?" Horn gestured at Roach then toward himself.

Roach laughed derisively, exposing a mouthful of gapped teeth that looked as if they'd been filed down. "Who else were you expecting?"

When Horn answered his question with a shrug, Roach motioned to a chair in front of his desk. "Sit down, Horn. I'm gonna tell you how we do things on this orbiting dog turd."

Horn sat and listened to the lieutenant's orientation. Its main thrust was "Stay out of the way and don't make waves." From what Roach was saying, Laslow Ringo had been telling the truth. Titus Steel Security ran the mining colony and didn't want any outside meddling. The NYPD office was a token only; it existed as a courtesy extended by the corporation. Roach ended his lecture by saying, "If Titus Steel Security wants our help, they'll ask for it. Any questions?" The look on Roach's face suggested he wasn't expecting any.

"Well, here then." He tossed a brown case folded across the desk. "Run over to the maintenance area and see if you can help Titus out. One of the drone tenders got killed— most likely an accident."

Horn opened the folder, which contained an FYI copy of a Titus Steel Security interoffice memo that was a single paragraph long. It read:

A migrant drone tender, ID'd as a 1, Frank Barker, was found dead this morning in the ore compartment of a scoop drone. It is suspected that subject 1 died from an overdose of some unknown substance. Records show no permanent address or relatives. No foul play is indicated.

"Is this it?" Horn made sure there was nothing else in the file. "It's dated a week ago."

"Just go over there and check it out." Roach rubbed his temples. "I need to close that case. If you don't find anything, come back in the morning and I'll give you something else."

Horn knew it was useless, but he went over to the maintenance yard anyway. He figured it would at least give him an opportunity to become better acquainted with the dome's geography. He asked a few workers if they knew Frank Barker. Every person he asked denied ever having heard the name. Horn wasn't surprised.

That evening, after getting a bite to eat at a place called the Steel Fork, Horn headed back down to Ringo's Night-owl. He wanted to find out if Laslow had connections with anyone at Titus Steel's local business office. The bar owner seemed to know the business of the asteroid pretty well, and Horn figured a stack of credit wafers could go a long way in terms of greasing him, as well as his sources of information. Horn had to find out why the New Pittsburgh smelting reactor was so important, and asking a Titus Steel employee seemed to be the simplest approach.

As Horn walked toward Ringo's, he wondered if anyone would recall his little unwilling production number from the night before. He certainly did, but what stood out in his mind was the exhilaration he'd felt at wielding such power. It had taken every bit of his willpower to check the swing his mod had intended to be a deathblow.

Horn knew that the E-mods had changed his attitude about dangerous situations. He now seemed to be seeking them out instead of trying to avoid them. He considered his E-mods to be tools, a cop's weapons. The reason he was modified was in itself enough justification to make danger a part of his life. In any case, Horn figured that sooner or later he would turn over the rock under which the king snake was hiding. It would then be only fitting that his mods be used to execute the viper.

Ringo's was jumping as Horn walked through the door. It was later than when he'd been there the night before and the band, a group called Ground Zero, was tuned up. It was hot in the process of beating the hell out of a medley of old Rude Ranger tunes. The dance floor was full, looking as if a small riot were under way, as couples bumped into one another and bounced their sweating bodies to the hard-driving music.

Horn elbowed his way up to the bar and ordered a beer. He thought he was hearing things as a soft feminine voice said, "Hello, stranger, buy a girl a drink?" Horn turned around, expecting to see Linda. Instead, his eyes fell upon an attractive blonde, who was startlingly familiar. He knew he had seen her before, but couldn't come up with the time or place.

It wasn't hard to tell the woman was a hooker, but she was a damn good-looking one. Horn couldn't keep his eyes off her. She was wearing a low-cut dress made from a slinky silver material that clung to her supple body like a coat of paint. "You don't remember me?" she asked in a manner that told Horn she was teasing. "I remember you, Detective Horn."

Horn grinned as he suddenly remembered. "Robin Silver," he said in as casual a voice as he could come up with. "You look stunning tonight."

Robin half closed her silver-tinted eyelids and smiled seductively. "Thank you. You want to sit down or dance first?"

Horn saw an empty booth near the back door. "Let me buy you that drink first." He led her over to the booth and sat down opposite her. She immediately got up and moved around, sliding in next to him. The smell of her perfume filled Horn's nostrils as his heart pumped into overdrive. He ordered drinks before thinking of something halfway coherent to say to the woman. "You come here often?"

"Don't you ever get a little tired of saying that?" she asked playfully.

"I'm tired of it already." Horn smiled and paid the waitress who had brought their drinks.

"When did you get here?" Robin asked and then added before Horn could speak, "I guess I didn't realize they had

New York cops on this place. Are you here on vacation?"
She laughed, exposing her perfect white teeth.

"Ain't it the place for it," Horn laughed. "Isn't this Six
Flags over Hell?"

Robin sipped her drink, then took a cigarette out of her
purse. Horn picked up a book of matches from the ashtray and lit it for her. Taking a long drag, she tilted her head
back slightly and blew the smoke upward. "When did you
get here?" She looked into his eyes as if she were truly interested.

"A couple of days ago," he answered. "What's the kick
around here? Who runs the place?" Horn figured Robin
was as good a source of information as Laslow, if not better.

"It's hard to say. No one person actually seems to run the
place. Any scams going are done by independents." Robin
took another sip of her drink.

"Why is that?" Horn asked.

"I don't really know. I think Titus Steel keeps it that way
so crime doesn't disrupt the work force. It's kind of like
they're saying do whatever you want to, but make sure
you're on the job in the morning. They sure don't go out of
their way to hassle you."

"You want to dance?" Horn surprised himself when he
asked.

"Sure." Without hesitating Robin slipped from the
booth and waited for Horn to get out. He led her to the
dance floor, which was swarming like an anthill. Horn had
never considered himself to be much of a dancer, but in a
place like Ringo's, he really didn't have to worry. Anyone
who hadn't known that the gyrating crowd was supposed
to be dancing would likely have assumed they were engaged in some form of full-body-contact martial arts ex-
hibition.

Horn found that he was actually enjoying himself. Ground Zero was really getting into a version of the classic "Uptown Blues," and Horn was moving smoothly to the beat. His E-mods seemed to pick up the vibrations and take the lead for the rest of his body. At first it startled him, but he gave in and followed, moving in the mathematical progressions inherent in the song.

Robin had never taken her eyes off Horn's. He finally noticed and gave in to her seductions. He decided on the dance floor that he had to have her, he had to get lost inside her perfumed magic. She seemed to have understood his intentions, and moved closer, working her body next to his in the rhythm of the music.

Horn and Robin had danced their way toward the back of the floor near the bandstand. The music was loud, but not totally overbearing. She leaned toward him and said something that Horn couldn't make out. "What?" he asked, and lowered his head. He could feel her warm breath wash over his ear; it sent a small electrical current down the back of his neck to the lower part of the spine.

"Whatever happened to Dan?" she asked, raising her voice over the din of the music.

As her words entered his ears, Horn felt another kind of electrical charge flash in his head. As though on a screen, he could see Riddle as he hung out the door of the Buick, blasting away...the Essex coming out of nowhere, smoking in like a hell-shot missile...Horn whipping the wheel and sliding into a shearing, rocking crash...

"Riddle!" Horn shouted in a frenzy at the top of his lungs. Even with the music as loud as it was, several couples stopped dancing and turned toward the horrific wail. The sudden outburst and look of sheer terror on Horn's face caused Robin to move back several steps.

Horn felt his right arm jerk hard in an uncontrolled spasm. He fought the image from his mind and forced himself to relax. Robin stepped toward him again and placed a hand on his arm as the other couples resumed their dancing. "Are you okay?" she asked.

"Yeah, I'm fine," Horn said. "Let's go back to the booth. I should have told you I'm not much of a dancer."

As soon as they sat down, Horn ordered a round of drinks. "Listen," he said as he lit Robin's cigarette, "I'm sorry about that incident."

"No probs," Robin said. "I guess I just don't understand what made you do it."

"It was Dan," Horn answered. "He's dead. You asking about him kinda caught me off guard."

"I'm sorry," Robin said contritely and squeezed his hand.

"If you don't mind," Horn said as he slid out of the booth, "I'll take a rain check on the dance, at least what was left of it."

"As long as you won't forget." She flashed him a promising goodbye smile.

Horn strode toward the front door, and Robin watched for a few seconds before following. She stopped him on the sidewalk in front of the club. "Wait a minute," she said, putting a hand on his arm. She rummaged in her purse for a scrap of paper and scribbled something on it. "Here's my address and com, code." She handed the paper to him. "Let me see you again."

"Sure," Horn said and watched her swinging walk as she turned away.

THE NEXT MORNING Horn reported for duty again. He had spent the night tossing and turning and felt tired and rumpled, but the lieutenant was a mess as well. Horn could smell the booze wafting across the desk as Roach spoke. "Nothing on that drone tender, huh? Well, I can close that one out." He took the folder from Horn and tossed it in a basket already overflowing with papers. "I guess—" Roach's next sentence was cut off as a loud, hacking cough erupted from his throat. He shoved his chair away from the desk and bent over. Horn watched his face turn bright red and wondered if he was going to pass out. Roach grabbed a wastebasket and coughed into it a couple of more times before gagging himself into the dry heaves.

"Goddamn flu," he sputtered, finally lifting his head and wiping his mouth with the back of his hand. He shoved the wastebasket away, lit a cigarette and went into another paroxysm. After twenty or thirty seconds he managed to bring it under control.

"You should take something for that," Horn said and could hardly keep the sarcasm out of his voice.

Roach cleared his throat and pulled another file from the mess in front of him. "Listen. Here's something that should keep you, ah, busy for a while." He tossed the file to Horn. "Titus Security found a dead woman a week ago. She'd been raped and then beaten to death. Sounds routine, I know. No doubt a bunch of miners did it—the body was in the old section." Roach paused to take a drag on his smoke. Horn watched the nicotine-varnished fingers shake as Roach removed the butt from his mouth. "Anyway, the woman had a roommate."

"Male?" Horn asked.

"No. She was living with some divorced nurse and her kid. It's all there in the report."

Horn got up to leave. He figured it wasn't going to do him any good hanging around watching Roach cough up his lungs. "I'll check it out."

"Do me a favor, Detective," Roach said, a pained look spread across his face.

"What's that?" Horn asked, turning the doorknob.

"Make it last a while. I don't need to see you every day of the week." He winked and Horn felt the skin on the back of his neck begin to crawl. "Know what I mean?"

Horn nodded and left the man to his coughing. He paused on the sidewalk and read the file, noting that the victim had worked in the Titus Steel accounting department. More interesting was the estimated time of death: around noon on a Wednesday. Horn thought it odd she'd got raped and beaten to death in the middle of a work week, and wound up behind an abandoned warehouse on the other side of the colony. Thoughtfully Horn repeated Roach's words aloud. "Sounds routine."

The address in the file led Horn to an apartment in a nice modular fourplex near the Titus Steel administrative support complex. According to the report, the dead woman's roommate was named Lydia Kline. Horn pressed the buzzer on the door, and a few seconds later it opened a couple of inches. A woman said, "Yes, who is it?"

"I hate to bother you, Ms Kline," Horn said and flashed his shield. "But I'm Detective Horn with the New York City Police Department field office here." He let her take a good look at his badge.

"What do you want?" she asked through the crack.

"I'd like to ask you a few questions about Alice Stenhaus. She was your roommate, wasn't she?" Horn was curious to see the face that went with the voice. Before Lydia could answer his question, he asked another. "May I come in, please?"

The door slowly swung open, and Horn was a little startled by the looks of the woman. She had flowing blond hair tied loosely in a bun. Her white nurse's uniform, a low-cut, thigh-length cotton dress, was almost translucent. It accented her tan skin and clung tightly to her upper body and hips. Her long, white-stockinged legs were muscular, but not out of proportion.

Her wide blue eyes examined him quickly. "I didn't realize that the New York police had anyone here. Anyway, I've already told the company's security people all I know." She seemed nervous and ran her tongue across her lips.

"I appreciate that, Ms Kline." Horn went into his cop routine with an ease that surprised him. "I've got nothing against the Titus Steel Security Department, but unfortunately they are not trained investigators, at least not in criminal matters. Especially rape and murder." Horn let the words hang heavily in the air before asking, "May I come in now?"

"Yes, I'm sorry," she said and backed away from the door. Horn followed her into a simply furnished living room and sat on a worn couch. "Excuse me a second," she said to Horn and then called out, "Zack, come in here, please."

Horn felt mildly sad as he looked about the room. Though some posters and colored throw pillows indicated an attempt had been made to make it cozy, it resembled a cheap motel more than it did a home. The place was an odd contrast to the woman, who at least on the surface appeared to have the potential to make something worthwhile out of her life. Then Horn recognized the dark humor his absurd thoughts had provoked. What use was potential on a bleak rock in space like New Pittsburgh?

Horn's attention was turned toward the door to another room as a sandy-haired, freckle-faced boy came into the living room.

"Zack," Lydia said, gesturing toward Horn, "this is Police Officer—" She paused and glanced at Horn. "I'm sorry, what did you say your name is?"

"Horn, Detective Horn."

"I'm sorry," she said again and turned toward the kid, who couldn't have been more than seven years old. "Detective Horn wants to ask me some questions about Alice. Why don't you go down to the playground for—" She looked at Horn again. "How long?"

"Oh, a half hour or less should be plenty of time to ask the questions I have."

"Okay, sweetheart?" she said to Zack.

"Sure, Mom." Zack was out the door in a flash of dungarees and sweatshirt.

Lydia sat on the edge of a chair opposite the couch where she had invited Horn to sit and folded her hands in her lap.

Horn removed his notebook and pen from his jacket pocket and placed them on the coffee table along with the file folder. "How long had you known Alice?" he asked.

"A little more than two years. But I already told the investigators all of this."

"Please," Horn said, "I understand what you've been going through and I'm sure this isn't the easiest thing for you to talk about...."

"How the hell would you know?" Lydia suddenly snapped, her voice on the verge of cracking. "Alice was like a sister to me. Do you really think you understand what it's like to have someone you care for raped and murdered? And to fear that it may happen to you?" Short, choking sobs erupted from her throat, and she buried her face in her hands.

Horn winced and leaned back on the couch. He watched the woman cry. A numb sort of empathy spread through his chest and made his heart beat hollowly. "I'm really sorry," he said, taking a handkerchief out of his pocket and handing it to her. "I'm sure I couldn't begin to understand." His voice sounded strangely tired.

Lydia took the handkerchief and wiped her eyes. Her sobs diminished to the point where she could talk. "I shouldn't have said that. It's just been a bad—"

"Never mind," Horn interrupted softly. Lydia looked as if she was going to start weeping again. "If you'll just bear with me, I'll try to make this as painless as possible. I'd like to catch whoever did this to Alice before it happens to someone else."

"Go ahead. I'm all right now." Lydia looked at Horn, her eyes red and watery.

Horn opened the folder and paused a second as he read. "Alice worked for Titus Steel, in the accounting department, correct?" He looked up at Lydia, who nodded.

"Yes," she answered. "Alice worked in the production finance section. I think that's what she called it."

"Did she work normal business hours?"

"Yes, eight to five," Lydia said in a steadier voice. "She didn't work odd shifts like me."

"According to this report—" Horn looked at a page in the folder again "—Alice was found to have died around noon last Wednesday." He returned his eyes to Lydia before asking, "Was she here the night before? Tuesday night?"

"Yes," Lydia answered. "I was working days then. We both left for work at the same time that Wednesday."

"Let me try to phrase my next question in a manner that won't sound offensive...." Horn seemed to be searching for the right words. "Did Alice have an active social life?" he finally asked.

"You mean, did she like to party?" Lydia interpreted Horn's question.

"That's basically what I meant."

"No," Lydia answered flatly. "Alice took the transfer to this place to get away from a bad marriage. She wanted to get her life together. Sure, she dated a number of guys, but no one steady, and hardly ever on weekdays. I think she got a kick out of staying home and helping me take care of Zack." Lydia turned her head and stared into space. "As I said, she had become like family."

"Did the security officials think it was odd that Alice was found in the old section of the colony on a weekday and that she'd died at such an odd hour?" Horn asked, hoping Lydia wouldn't start weeping again.

"They never brought it up," she said, turning her head back toward Horn.

"Did Alice spend much time in the old section at all?"

"She wouldn't go there," Lydia answered. "And as a matter of fact, I can't remember her ever mentioning that she'd been there."

"Do you think that's odd?" Horn watched Lydia's eyes closely as he asked the question.

"What? That she never went to the old area?"

"No," Horn answered. "That she was found down there when she should have been in her office."

"I never thought about it," Lydia answered quickly. "But now that you mention it, I suppose it is odd."

Horn saw something in Lydia's eyes that said she sure as hell considered it was odd and she had thought about it a lot. The dark circles under her eyes and the worried gaze attested to it. He also saw the razor-edged glimmer of fear. He repeated his earlier question. "And the security investigators never asked what Alice might have been doing down there?"

"I said they didn't," Lydia snapped.

Horn said nothing for a minute. It wasn't hard to tell that Lydia was holding something back. "Just a couple of other details. Can you tell me just what she did, exactly?"

"Production finance, and beyond that I don't know." Lydia shook her head. "I think she said she forecast the production revenue."

"Just for New Pittsburgh?"

Lydia looked puzzled. "Yes. What else would she do it for?

"I mean," Horn explained, "did her forecasts include any operations other than those that take place on the roid?"

"I don't think so. This is what Alice called a separate cost center. She used to try to get me interested in her work. Said I could make more money crunching numbers than sawing bones." Lydia smiled sadly.

"Was Alice under any pressure at work?"

"She was lately," Lydia answered. "They were going through a special reappraisal, she said, trying to make the place look like it was making money."

Horn gave her a keen glance. "Alice told you that?" He thought it unusual that the two women would have discussed the overall financial picture of New Pittsburgh.

"Sure," Lydia answered. "But it's common knowledge that Titus Steel is thinking about shutting down the operation and laying everyone off. At least that's been the rumor for the past six months."

"What was the pressure Alice was under? Was it the schedule for getting this reappraisal done, or what?" Horn got the feeling that whatever Lydia was keeping to herself was connected with Alice's job. Her response to his dual question seemed to confirm his suspicions.

Lydia stood up, wringing the handkerchief in her hands. "Listen, mister, I mean Detective—"

"Horn." He knew what was coming next.

"I've told you everything I know. Now I have to make Zack's lunch and get ready for work. I start swing shift today." When she finished, she gave him a quick glance and handed him the wadded-up handkerchief.

"No problem," Horn said, gathering up the folder and notebook as he stood. "But I'd like to tell you one thing before I leave.

"To be very blunt—" Horn paused to give the words more weight because he wanted to give her something to think about before he left. If his guess was right, it might loosen her tongue later. "I think writing off Alice's death the way Titus Steel Security obviously wants to is either stupid or intentional."

"What do you mean?" Concern flashed in Lydia's eyes.

"I mean," Horn said as he watched for a reaction, "there could be some connection between Alice's job and her death."

Lydia winced. The look on her face told Horn that he had hit the nail on the head. "I don't know what you're talking about." Lydia had tried to sound firm, and she walked to the door and opened it. "And I really have to get busy."

Horn wrote his bungalow's com code on a blank sheet in the notebook and tore it out. At the door he handed it to her. "Think about it. Call me if you remember anything that might help me." Horn caught the scent of her perfume and surprised himself a little when he added, "Call me if you just need a friend."

Lydia looked Horn searchingly in the eyes but didn't answer. He heard the door shut behind him and figured he would give her a couple of days to call before he got back in touch.

The way the styros and Roach had treated Alice's death made Horn wonder how many other deaths on the asteroid had been explained away so nonchalantly. Something else about Alice's case made him more curious. He was sure that Lydia thought there was a connection between the woman's murder and her job. Horn would just have to get her to verbalize what her eyes had already told him.

CHAPTER ELEVEN

STELLER IGNORED the view of New York through the window wall and instead watched his boss rub his temples. It was 4:00 a.m., not an unusual time for the CEO to call a meeting, especially with Steller. "I want an update on the New Pittsburgh situation. I understand you've been in touch with Wand," Fine said from behind the expanse of his mahogany desk.

"I've been in touch with him on a daily basis, ever since the cop, Horn, got there. For all it's worth, he's head of security there." Steller winced, knowing that Horn's continued existence was a sensitive subject around Fine, especially with his mother still in the hospital recovering from her failed attempt to dust the cop. Sure enough, the CEO did not let the opportunity to remind Steller slip by.

"No doubt about it, Detective Horn could become a very serious stumbling block. I believe I made that point during our last meeting. Now, what has he been up to?" Fine pressed his hands on his burning eyes wearily.

"According to Wand's reports," Steller began, "Horn has taken an interest in the roommate of Alice Stenhaus, the accountant who was questioning some of the numbers."

"She is the one who has been taken care of, isn't she?" With the tips of his fingers Fine began massaging his temples in a circular motion.

"Correct," Steller answered. "That's why I need to leave immediately for the asteroid."

"What?" Fine opened his eyes and frowned. "What's the urgency?"

Steller wondered if Fine had been listening to him. "Horn is the problem. If he's talking to the Stenhaus woman's roommate, he may start connecting the dots. I need to get up there and take the guy out before he complicates matters further."

Fine felt as though he was losing control of the situation. "You know, Steller, if you had done your job right the first time, Horn wouldn't be on New Pittsburgh now, threatening our plans."

Steller took a deep breath. He had expected the rebuke and wasn't surprised by it. "I agree that things have gone far enough. I mean to put a stop to Horn's meddling."

"Why the hell haven't you told Wand to take Horn out?"

"I considered it," Steller answered, "but that might draw too much attention. I don't want a mob of New York cops breathing down our necks because one of their brothers in blue got wasted. Horn's death has to look like an accident, or it has to take place just before the rock cooks off. Either way, we're running out of time and must do something about him."

"I'll give you that much," Fine agreed absentmindedly, but he didn't seem to have his mind tuned in to the conversation. "You want some coffee?"

Steller shrugged. "Sure."

It was still at least two hours before any of the secretarial staff showed up. Fine buzzed the guard station and told the duty officer to get coffee delivered. "Make it quick," he snapped.

Fine propped his highly polished dress boots on his desk. "Tell me about the Stenhaus woman's roommate," he said.

"She's a nurse in the infirmary, divorced, has a kid— that's about it." Steller shrugged.

Fine seemed lost in contemplation for a while, and Steller didn't break the silence until the buzzer interrupted. Fine shook his head, punched on and asked, "What is it?"

"Coffee, sir."

"Enter," Fine ordered.

The two men watched as the guard carried a tray into the office and deposited it on a corner of the desk. Fine waved him out impatiently, and as the door closed behind the guard, poured coffee for himself and Steller. "Is Horn screwing her?" Fine asked casually.

"Hard to say, but I don't think he's spent that much time with her." Steller tilted his head to one side. "Although Wand's incompetents probably don't know how many times he's seen her, or even what the hell he's been doing on a regular basis. The last report said he'd visited her at least once. Wand can't seem to keep a tail on the guy with any consistency."

"What do you expect from a group of mismatched department store detectives?" A short laugh broke from the CEO's lips. "You can't exactly get PhDs to sign up for a stint in the environment we're talking about."

"True." Steller nodded. "But it's not only that." The blond assassin seemed to be coming to some sort of realization.

"Then what is it?" Fine was genuinely curious because Steller rarely mused aloud.

"Horn seems to have some special edge. He's come out against heavy odds a few times."

Like a whirlpool, Fine's thought process returned to Horn's potential to torpedo his well-laid plans. He didn't know how that could be achieved by the cop, but he instinctively knew it was possible. He was ready to clutch at straws. "We should take out the woman just to be safe," he announced.

"Easy enough," Steller responded. "What about the kid?"

"What kid?" Fine looked puzzled.

"I told you she had a kid."

"Well, get rid of it, too, if it gets in the way. Otherwise, it'll get it soon enough when the whole rock goes."

"As I said earlier, the first priority is taking care of Horn," Steller said, swirling the coffee around in the bottom of his cup. "I can take the woman out, too, but there really shouldn't be any need if the cop is eliminated."

"Have Wand deal with her," Fine answered quickly. "Surely he can't screw that up. After all, he managed the other one."

"If Wand takes her out, Horn is really going to know he's tapped a live wire. Especially if she's told him anything." Steller wondered why Fine hadn't thought about that himself.

As Steller's objection registered in his mind, Fine realized the folly of his suggestion. He felt embarrassed for a half a second. "You're absolutely correct," he acknowledged.

"Then I may proceed?"

"Not so fast." Fine drummed on the table, then stood up to pace around it. "I want to make sure we've got our act together before moving. Some of us know personally how overconfidence can leave a task undone."

Steller caught the barb directed at him but ignored it. "Everything is set. The modified fuel pellet is waiting, in orbit, on one of our Lear Needles. Wand has a terminal set up to load the pellet into one of the auxiliary rods that will remain in standby mode until you arrive. All you have to do then—" Steller held up his hands in a nothing-to-it gesture "—is trip in the aux loaders and watch the thing go down like a four-credit whore. It'll come off the way you planned before. The only difference is that I'll be there a week before you arrive, to set the thing up and eliminate Detective Horn."

"That's what you really want, isn't it?" Fine said as he stood right before Steller and gazed at him.

"I don't get your meaning."

"You think Horn may be a challenge, even for *your* talents. At least you hope he is. Isn't that correct?"

Steller shrugged as though the answer should have been obvious, but made no comment either way.

Fine lowered his voice. "I don't mind you using the cop as some sort of personal performance exercise, but this time you damn well better get the job done."

Seated again, Fine resumed driving his point home. "I have a great deal hanging on the successful execution of this plan." He leaned back in his chair and stared at Steller through pupils the size of pinpoints. "If the plan doesn't go down the way we set it up, then you and I may as well stay on New Pittsburgh and bust ore the rest of our lives."

"Don't worry," Steller said, as a spike of doubt drove into his thoughts. There was something about Horn that bothered the usually confident assassin. The punk in the subway—well, that was certainly a case of sending a boy to do a man's job. Then there was Rudy and his Los Angeles specialists who "always" got the job done, even though it was messy. They relied on overwhelming firepower to ensure the odds were in their favor, but it hadn't worked with Horn. As for Steller himself— He had left the cop for dead, left him lying in a pool of his own blood, but he hadn't died. Steller knew there could be no more mistakes.

"When are you leaving?" Fine's voice brought Steller out of his thoughts.

"This afternoon. You should plan to leave this time next week." Steller paused a second, then added, "You may want to leave a couple of days early."

"Why's that?" Fine asked.

"I reserved the new bird. It's a little faster. I'll dock on the roid in two days less than five weeks."

"Do one thing before you leave," Fine said.

"What's that?"

"Get in touch with our satellite people in Costa Rica and have them jam every police band transmission from New Pittsburgh."

"I've already taken care of that," Steller said. "However, I've instructed Costa Rica to monitor, and interrupt only if something other than what's been transmitted over the past year or so goes through."

"What is that supposed to mean?" Fine looked confused.

"It means that I've had the links monitored since Horn got there, and nothing has changed. Roach sends and receives the same dull crap, week after week. Horn is more or less incognito. It appears he's been soloing it ever since he got there."

"That's good," Fine said. "If we don't have to jam the frequencies, it won't draw attention, even though I doubt if anyone at the NYPD would notice if we shut them down."

"If that's all, then, I'll be heading out." Steller stood, obviously waiting for Fine's permission to leave.

"Okay," Fine said almost hesitantly. "But remember, you have an ultimatum. The cop has to go. He's too unstable a variable."

"The sooner I'm there, the sooner he drops from the equation," Steller said calmly.

"I mean it, Mr. Steller." Fine leaned across the desk to emphasize the point. "No more failures."

Steller didn't answer and Fine leaned back in his chair. He swung it toward the huge windows and gazed at the eastern horizon, which had turned a deep shade of gray. "Have a good trip, Mr. Steller," Fine said, without turning around.

"I hope your mother gets better," Steller said. He could have sworn the hairs on the back of Fine's neck bristled as the words reached his ears. Steller smiled with self-satisfaction. Yes, he thought. Women, one way or another, were the weak spot.

LYDIA KLINE CLEANED UP the last details required to file away the leftover remnants of Alice Stenhaus's life. Lydia found it a painful task to go through her former roommate's belongings and pack them into boxes. She didn't know whether Alice had any living relatives. If she did, she had never mentioned them. Lydia had been told by the Titus Steel benefits representative to set the belongings outside the door at an appointed day and time. The company would take care of the rest. So much for Alice Stenhaus.

It took Lydia nearly an hour to clear out the closet in what had been Alice's bedroom. When she got to the single chest of drawers, she began to rush. It wasn't because she was in a hurry. Each article of clothing Lydia folded and stuffed into a box reminded her of Alice. Pictures of Alice wearing the red pullover...the green skirt...the blue jumpsuit flashed through her mind. She jerked open the top drawer as fresh tears filled her eyes.

"Damn!" Lydia exclaimed as the drawer came completely out of the dresser and swung down. It struck her leg as the handle slipped from her hand. Panties, bras and stockings fell onto the carpeted floor as she jumped back to prevent the drawer from landing on her feet. "Damn," she repeated with somewhat less consternation, wiping the tears from her eyes with balled-up hands.

She knelt and started to right the drawer, which had landed upside down atop the scattered lingerie. Her eyes fell on a yellow envelope taped to the underside. At first she surmised it was a packing or quality control slip that had come with the furniture from the factory at one time, but she quickly realized it wasn't. Printed across the top, in block letters, was Titus Steel Interoffice Correspondence. Thinking it odd to find anything from Alice's employer in such a place, Lydia opened the envelope and removed a single photocopied sheet of paper headed: Company Private—Destroy after Reading.

The interoffice memo was addressed to J.I. Durant, Head of Titus Steel's New Pittsburgh operations. Under Durant's name was the subject of the memo: Unscheduled Reappraisal. Lydia sat down on the bed and went through the short memo, her curiosity changing into a puzzled fear as she read:

The third quarter reappraisal failed to show a reversal of the downward trend in revenue. As you know, the New Pittsburgh operation has fallen into a negative margin position with no obvious means of recovery. The board's intent is to offer up the operation at the end of this financial year. The purpose of this special reappraisal is to provide input for a prospectus being prepared for purposes of the sale. You are hereby directed to immediately execute the indicated action and/or include the following in your revenue and profit calculations:

1) Accelerate the depreciation of all remaining capital.

2) Accrue all revenue projected through the first quarter of FY15 in the last quarter of current FY.

3) Freeze all hiring and cancel all open requisitions.

4) Discontinue paid overtime.

5) Utilize grades 1 and 2 ore only in the smelting process.

It is imperative that our current financial picture and projections reflect a healthy operation. Your plan need hold this picture only temporarily. Will explain in more detail at our next one-on-one.

The memo was signed by T. Strach, Titus Steel controller, and countersigned by the CEO, O. Fine.

Lydia got up and walked into the kitchen. She had suspected from Alice's manner and things she'd said that she was in some kind of trouble at work, or had discovered something there she shouldn't have. The memo was certainly connected one way or another. Alice had probably thought she could use it as insurance or leverage in the future to save her job. She had told Lydia on more than one occasion that she could wind up getting fired for doing what her supervisor had directed her to. "I'm doing damn funny things with the numbers. Anything to make them look good," were the words she had used. But Alice hadn't got fired: she'd got murdered.

Lydia walked to her refrigerator and pulled a slip of paper from beneath a shamrock-shaped magnet. The black ink scrawl read simply: Horn 060751.

CHAPTER TWELVE

THE CHAIN REACTION LOUNGE was a deadfall squatting smack in the middle of the seediest section of the rubble-strewn area around the Hot Zone known as the Ring. It was the only building still standing in an entire block of a street with the name Dogwood; someone had obscured part of the name, leaving only the word *Dog*. The name was apt, for packs of starving, mangy mongrels roamed the area, preying on winos, string addicts or anything else they were hungry enough to attack. Horn figured the animals were like the people he'd found on the roid: after a period of time they lost their domestic tendencies somewhere in the tite dust.

It was getting near dusk when Horn walked up to the torch-lit entrance. He pulled the 9 mm from beneath his leather jacket and made sure a round was in the chamber. He pushed on the ax-scarred door and walked inside, feeling as though he were entering the anteroom to hell.

The inside was dark, lit only by a few candles placed in bottles on the long bar and tables. The air smelled of rotgut brew, sweat, smoke, vomit and, occasionally, blood. The joint was packed as usual, for it was the meeting place of string dealers, prostitutes, leg breakers, pimps and other lost souls who called the Ring home. The dim, smoky room was a place where deals were made, where jobs were planned and oftentimes where lives were laid to waste. Killing over disagreements, even minor ones, wasn't illegal: the law in the Ring was that there was no law. Styros avoided the lounge like the plague.

Horn found a place at the bar, ordered and was promptly served a big mug of foaming, foul-smelling brew. He reached into his pocket and smacked down a five-credit wafer in front of the fat, sweating bartender.

There was a commotion behind his back, and Horn turned around. Two guys who looked like miners were fighting over a worn skin magazine. Both had knives in their grimy hands, the glinting blades matching the blood-thirsty look in their eyes.

One of the snipes was sporting a red silky jacket that had had Save the Whales stitched on the back. The wording had been altered to read "Screw the Whales." The other guy, who had taken a pretty deep slash across the forehead, was dancing in circles around Red Jacket chanting "Bowwow, bowwow" and tossing his six-inch blade from one hand to the other.

Pretty soon Fat Man came around from behind the bar and coldcocked Bowwow with an ax handle. Horn watched as Red Jacket started to jump on the downed guy, but the huge bartender stepped in his way. He held up the blade and laughed. "Get out of my way you stupid sea cow—" His threat was cut short as Fat Man pulled a 9 mm automatic from his back pocket and shot Red Jacket between the eyes, blowing blood and pulpy brain tissue all over a couple of guys sitting at a table across the room. They brushed themselves off with a slightly injured air.

Three or four customers got up from their drinking to drag the bodies out the door. "Drag 'em down the street a ways," Fat Man barked. "I don't want the dogs makin' a mess in front of the goddamn door."

"He's pretty quick for a blue-ribbon hog, ain't he?"

Horn looked down the bar at the guy who had made the comment. A huge man who resembled a benign Buddha with greasy shoulder-length hair and a deteriorating set of teeth smiled and winked at Horn. Without acknowledging the guy's attempt to be friendly, Horn shifted his eyes away, then glanced at his watch. He was curious why Robin Silver had picked the Chain for their meeting. He also wondered what she wanted to talk about. She had left a message at his bungalow two days earlier that she had information he would find interesting. He took a sip of his beer and watched the bartender sweep cigarette butts off the table-tops onto the dirt floor.

A shadow filled the doorway, and Horn's wandering vision locked onto Robin Silver's figure as she entered the door. As usual, she was dressed to kill. Her shapely buttocks were barely covered with a black sharkskin skirt. She had on a see-through halter top made from thousands of tiny, multicolor beads. At her slightest movement the beads would shift and her cone-shaped breasts would flash in and out of sight, changing colors like two warheads being shot through a rainbow.

"Buy me a drink?" Robin's sultry voice was pleasing to Horn's ears. He had liked the hooker's flirtatious manner ever since he met her back in New York. As she slid onto the seat beside him, her skirt rode up to expose lacy red panties.

"What'll it be?" Horn said, turning and holding up a finger to the bartender.

"Vodka tonic," Robin answered. She took a cigarette from her handbag and lit it. "I haven't seen you for a couple of weeks. Where have you been hiding?"

"Kind of hard to hide, wouldn't you say?" Horn gave her a friendly, wolfish grin after ordering her drink. He had talked to her a couple of times since their first meeting at

Ringo's and had filled her in a little on his official role on the asteroid. Horn figured she could be an invaluable source of information. He admitted to himself he was attracted to the woman, but after their dance at Ringo's, he had decided not to get involved for fun and games. However, Robin's presence never failed to stir some primal bent in him. Her body, her perfume, her smile and the look in her eyes told him a tantalizing story.... He could at least enjoy her in his fantasies.

"I hate the Ring," she said, taking her drink from the bartender who shuffled away after giving her a longing look. "It's the worst scene in the world. Usually I don't come down here."

"Then why did you want to meet at this place?"

"It was picked by a guy who said he has some information for you." Robin motioned toward a booth. "Could we sit over there?"

"Sure." They quickly relocated to the greater privacy of the booth, and when they were seated, Horn asked, "What's the guy going to tell me?"

"I don't know the details," Robin answered. "But he knows a terminal who has been with Frank Wand, the local head of Titus Steel Security."

Horn raised his eyebrows. "Recently?"

"Yes," Robin replied. "They meet when all the terminals come out of the Zone to get their ration of drugs."

"What do you think's going on?" Horn asked.

Robin shrugged. "I don't really know. Targa can probably give you the skinny on that. What time is it?" She looked over at Horn's wrist.

Horn looked at his watch. "Quarter to six," he answered.

"The little beggar should be here in fifteen or twenty minutes," Robin said, as she lit another cigarette. "You'll have to give him some credits."

"Just who is Targa?"

"He's a sawed-off little string dealer who would sell his soul if he thought he could cheat whoever was buying." Robin drained her glass. Horn signaled two more to the bartender. "What's with the gloves?" Robin asked. "You're always wearing gloves, even when it's hot."

Horn pulled the glove from his left hand, "It's the piano," he said, smiling. "I want to protect my hands, got a big concert coming up."

Robin laughed heartily. "That's good, Horn. Let me guess, you're going to solo with the New Pittsburgh Symphony."

"What's Targa's connection with the terminals?" Horn asked, getting the conversation back on track and off the subject of his hands.

"He deals to them." Robin took a deep drag on her smoke. "Those burn spots eat more dope than the styros pass out—wouldn't you?"

"Who knows?" Horn picked up his fresh mug of brew and took a healthy swallow. "How does Targa make connection?"

"Some say he knows a way in and out of the Zone," Robin answered.

"I thought that place was poison." Horn seemed to be thinking aloud. "I thought it fried your brain."

"It does," Robin said. "But it's radiation, you know. You can take it for a while, but not for a long while. On short trips I'm sure there's more danger from the terminals than the rads."

"No doubt. I've heard some stories."

"If you ever hear a working girl say, 'I'd rather do it with a terminal,' don't believe her." Robin chuckled. "There was supposedly a hooker who was dragged into the Zone. Story goes that she was in there four days and four nights. When they finally got her out, they ran some tests and discovered that her brain had been destroyed. She assaulted some intern in the infirmary and wound up getting a Titus Steel Security bullet through the head."

"Sounds pretty grim."

"Yeah." Robin shook her head. "Her body was a mass of rad burns and claw marks."

Horn was about to say something, but Robin shot him a warning glance. "There's Targa," she said.

He stood inside the doorway, letting his eyes adjust to the dim light in the bar. He was built like a tank—short, thick and muscular, with a square jaw. His bare arms hung out of a sleeveless leather vest, and his gleaming bald head sported an eagle's claw tattoo that appeared to have his skull in a death grip. Little drops of red blood ran down from the points where each talon gripped his head. He spotted Robin and walked over to the booth.

"Hi, Targa. This is the friend I was telling you about. His name is Horn." Robin gestured across the table.

"Targa," the man said in a raspy voice. Robin moved over and he sat down. Horn thought there was something screwy about the man's eyes, but in a second realized that Targa was wearing mirror-finish contact lenses. It was either that, or his eyeballs were highly polished steel bearings.

"How about a drink, Targa?" Horn suggested, waving at the bartender.

"Beer," Targa said with a grunt. He pulled a thin cigar from his vest pocket and lit it, using a lighter stuck in the wristband of one of his fingerless gloves.

Horn noticed that every bit of Targa's exposed flesh was a bright red, like sunburn. He also noticed a radiation dosimeter pinned to his vest. It was at the highest saturation reading. "That thing work?" Horn asked, pointing to the device.

Targa looked down at it and laughed. "Yeah, it works. Been showing red every since I been wearing it. Guess I'll worry about it when the plastic melts." He took a puff on the cigar and blew a perfect smoke ring as Horn paid the bartender for the new round of drinks.

"Robin tells me you know a terminal who's been getting pretty friendly with Frank Wand."

Targa took another drag on the cigar and inhaled deeply. He took a huge swallow of beer before exhaling and then seemed to lock up. Horn watched him hold the pose for twenty or thirty seconds, looking like a bizarre red frog that froze just before croaking. Targa finally released his breath in the form of a loud belch and a cloud of smoke.

"Good beer," he said, holding up the mug. "Thanks." He took another gulp and wiped his mouth with the back of his hand. "Yeah, I deal...ah, do business with a terminal who has been getting close to Wand." Targa took a long drag of the smoke again. "Robin tells me you're a cop. That true?"

"Yeah, I'm a cop," Horn answered. "But I'm not busy handing out traffic tickets and tanking drunks." Targa grinned appreciatively, his teeth looking like some sort of combat bumper for a battering ram. "This terminal, can I meet him?" Horn asked.

"Well, that's a problem, since the guy lives in the HZ."

"How many credits' worth of a problem is it?" Horn asked, making the tank man smile again.

"Half a hundred will get you a guided tour into hell." Targa leaned across the table, his words sounding as though they were being filtered through gravel. "May wind up meeting the devil himself."

"It's a deal," Horn said, not wanting to haggle over the price. "What's the guy's name?"

"Krak," Targa answered. "All the flamers in the HZ got weird names like that. Krak's got a big jagged scar that runs down the center of his forehead like a crack." He held the edge of his hand between his eyes. "That's probably how the zomb got his name."

"Zomb?" Horn looked puzzled.

"Yeah, zomb. You know, zombie." Targa's voice was rasping away into nothing. He took a swallow of beer and cleared his throat. "All the bastards in the Zone are zombs, but you gotta watch 'em. Every now and then they sort of snap out of it and get a little, ah, edgy."

"What do you mean?" Horn asked.

"They start looking for somebody to burn. I guess they want to get rid of their frustrations." Targa grinned. "It's especially bad if they come out of their trance right after a blast of string or some other kind of shit."

"I know where I'll spend the fifty." Targa turned toward Robin and winked, causing one of the eagle talons to dip down and touch his cheek. "Most of the women I've been with call me King Gripper." His laughter sounded like sandpaper being rubbed on a sensitive microphone.

Robin said in an aside to Horn, "See why I want to get back to the Bronx?"

Horn took a fifty-credit wafer from his jacket pocket and tossed it to Targa. "When do we meet Krak?" he asked.

"How about we head over there now? It's dark."

Horn looked toward the door. He couldn't get used to the measurement of time on New Pittsburgh. While the twenty-four hour clock was utilized, each hour was approximately one and a half earth hours. It had taken Horn two weeks to adjust the speed of his watch. "You hanging around here?" he asked Robin.

"No," she answered. "I'm going back to Ringo's. I told you, the Ring has a tendency to make my skin crawl."

"Want me to walk you out?" Horn asked, as he stood.

"No, thanks," Robin answered. "I can take care of myself."

Targa slid out of the booth and stood up. "You got a weapon?" he asked Horn, then without waiting for the answer, he added, "You might need one." Targa slapped his thigh with a huge paw and led the way out of the bar.

Targa took Horn to the gutted remains of a long-abandoned warehouse, which was located less than a quarter of a mile from the Chain Reaction Lounge. The massive wall surrounding the Hot Zone was a scant ten yards behind the structure. Horn heard, as well as felt, the humming vibration of the ancient reactor. He could see the rust-colored clouds of slarr churning outside the dome, which meant the smelter was going full tilt.

"Looks like rad shit in a blender, don't it?" Targa slapped Horn on the back. "Follow me." He bent and disappeared through a hole in the side of the warehouse. Horn had to get down on his knees to make it through the opening.

Once inside, Horn stood and looked around. The place was covered with a deep, smooth layer of red dust. Half of the building had collapsed, and debris lay scattered everywhere. Targa walked over to the remains of an old tracked mining drone and pulled off the pitted engine cover. "Come on," he said, and disappeared into the hole.

Targa led Horn down a ladder that seemed to go on forever. Occasionally, he would look up and ask Horn if he was doing okay. When he did, what little light there was reflected off Targa's mirrored contacts, making him look demonic. The farther down they went, the louder the humming got. Horn was beginning to think that Targa's earlier reference to hell wasn't too far off the mark. Horn went to place his boot onto another rung and was suddenly bombarded by Targa's curses. He'd stepped right on top of the eagle's claw.

"Goddammit!" the tank man yelled out. "Watch what the hell you're doing." Horn moved back up a rung, feeling his way in the darkness. "Hold on a second." Targa was breathing hard. "I gotta get this trapdoor unlatched. What a bastard!"

Horn heard a loud metallic click, and a wave of orange light flooded the shaft. The humming increased tenfold as a blast of hot air shot upward through the grim tube like steam in a boiler pipe. Horn looked down and watched Targa disappear into a gauzelike haze. He moved down quickly and swung through the same opening.

"Welcome to hell," Targa said, dusting off his pants.

Horn shaded his eyes with one hand and looked around. They were in a large hallway that seemingly stretched into infinity. Pipes hung from the ceiling and walls, running in a maze befitting a plumber's hallucination. More than two inches of fine red dust covered the floor; a lesser amount coated other surfaces, including the mercury vapor lights that hung from the ceiling and cast everything in an eerie orange glow.

Targa reached up and pulled the door shut. "I forgot to mention my one stipulation concerning our business arrangement," he said, turning toward Horn.

"What's that?" Horn dropped his hand, his eyes having adjusted to the light.

"This." He jerked a thumb upward, pointing at the trap door. "You gotta forget about it as soon as we leave here."

"No problem," Horn said. "It doesn't seem to be the kind of place I'd want to make a habit of visiting."

"Good." Targa spat into the dust. "Follow me then. Krak works down here in the rod room."

Horn walked down the hall after Targa, who was leaving a little cloud of dust in his wake. The low-resonance humming got progressively louder, and Targa finally stopped at a door and pressed the announce button on the cipher box. There was a big red-and-white warning sign on the door: Fuel Rod Prep—No Admittance Without Protective Clothing.

"Wait a second," Horn said, as someone on the other side of the door buzzed open the electronic locking mechanism. "What about the warning on this sign?"

"You gotta be shittin' me." Targa grunted a laugh and pulled open the reinforced steel door. "Come on, ya candy-ass cop."

Horn followed Targa, figuring he could survive at least one venture into the high-rad area. The room was large, resembling a warehouse. There were fifty or sixty fuel rods laid out on racks down a center aisle, which occupied most of the space. A big crane, set on rails, ran overhead. It was apparently used to move the rods in and out of the three chutes at the far end of the room. They were marked Incoming Only, Outgoing Only and Reactor Transfer Only.

About twenty terminals were shuffling around in the room. Horn noticed that not one was wearing protective clothing, not even gloves. Most of them were in the process of removing or replacing the fuel pellets in the dull gray, lead-covered rods. From a distance Horn thought they looked like normal humans except for two anomalies: they moved in slow motion, and in varying degrees they were all missing patches of hair from their scalps.

Horn didn't have to wait long before he was able to get his first close-up look at one of the Hot Zone's permanent residents. "What da hell ya want now, Targa?" Both men turned at the sound of the voice. Horn was a little shocked at how big and ugly the terminal was. He knew instantly that it was Krak addressing them. The massive, grotesque scar running down the middle of the guy's forehead looked as though it had been carved with an industrial meat saw.

"I gotta guy here who wants to interview ya, Krak." Targa nodded toward Horn. "Works for a newspaper or some kind of shit."

What the hell is he trying to pull? Horn thought to himself, as he glared at Targa. "Ah, actually, I'm with the city," he muttered, addressing Krak.

"City?" Krak grunted. "What da hell ya mean?"

Horn finally thought of something. It was weak, but it was something. "I work for the, ah, health department. The New York City Health Department."

Krak stared malevolently at Horn. It was obvious that the high rad levels had taken their toll on Krak's mind. The terminal moved his huge, nearly seven-foot frame a step closer, and Horn could feel the heat radiating from the giant body.

"Take it easy, pal." Horn held up his hands in an I-don't-want-any-trouble gesture. "Titus Steel Security asked us in here to see if we could make any recommendations for improving the working conditions."

Krak had bent over slightly as he listened to the speech. He kept on looking at Horn's face for a full ten seconds after he'd stopped talking. Then suddenly, as though a switch in his head had been tripped, Krak leaned his head back and laughed as though he'd just heard the funniest joke in the galaxy. The rest of the terminals stopped what they were doing and slowly turned their patchy heads toward the sound.

"You make a joke, right?" Krak laughed again. "Come over here and tell me about it." He pointed to a small office in one corner of the room.

"Well, this is where I split." Targa clasped his hands together. "See ya around, Horn." He raised his voice and threw a kiss at Krak. "See ya, pal."

Horn started to say something, but Targa was heading out the door. He felt a huge hand on his arm and the next thing he knew, Krak was leading him into the office. "Let dat jerkwater bastard get outta here," the giant breathed, as he shoved Horn into a chair. "Now tell me da real goddamn reason you're here, asshole!" Krak shoved his face to within an inch of Horn's.

"I told you," Horn said, wiping the spit from his nose. "I'm with the New York—"

Krak shoved Horn back into the chair. "Tite dust make men mean..." he gritted out haltingly, a string of slobber running from one corner of his mouth. "You will die in dis place!"

Horn sprang up and grabbed Krak's collar with his right hand. "I see," he said, looking into Krak's eyes. "That was probably old Targa's intent all along, wasn't it?"

A grin spread across Krak's mouth. He glanced down at Horn's gloved hand. "You are one funny guy!" He suddenly reached up and grabbed the back of Horn's head with both his hands. "I am glad you love to suffer!" He pulled Horn toward him and opened his mouth.

Horn realized the terminal was getting ready to bite him on the face. The giant's foul breath wafted into Horn's face, and he exclaimed in disgust and shoved Krak's head back so hard that he felt skin get raked off the back of his neck where the large fingers had been gripping him. The sudden motion had a whiplash effect on Krak's head that caused his mouth to slam shut violently, and Horn saw a couple of the big yellow teeth fly out of the cavernous mouth.

Krak's face twisted in shock. Blood poured from his mouth and ran down his chin in a crimson stream. A sound bellowed from his throat as he cocked a high fist. Horn shoved the crazed terminal again, his E-modified arm driving like a superconducted piston, but this time, Horn released his grip. Krak flew backward across the desk, his legs flipped up over his head, and his body slammed face-first into the wall. He slid to the floor in a crumpled heap.

Horn dusted off his gloved hands. "Nothing personal there, Krak." He turned to walk out of the office, but instantly froze in his tracks. The other terminals had gathered outside the door and now blocked Horn's escape route. He had never seen such a collection of burned-out humanoid hulks. Their dead staring faces were a bright cherry red under veil-like layers of the powdery tite dust.

"Come with us," one of the terminals ordered.

"Why should I?" Horn asked, but he figured he'd better get out of the dead-end office before he made a move.

"Come on, you asshole." Another terminal waving a huge brass wrench moved a couple of steps forward and issued the order.

"Oh, all right," Horn said. "I don't want to make waves. Where are we going?" He could hear Krak trying to struggle to his feet and felt a little stab of anxiety. He sure as hell didn't want the big zombie breathing down his neck after what he'd just done to him. "Come on, I'll go, no sweat."

Horn moved toward the twenty or so terminals, and they immediately surrounded him like a herd of sick animals. They led him down the center of the room, bumping him along with their bodies. He could feel intense heat bleeding off the fuel rods, which were lined up in front of each chute like so many stretched-out torpedoes. The moving herd came to a shuffling stop in front of the Reactor Transfer Only chute. A terminal pushed a button on the wall and the door spiraled open. Horn felt heat belch out of the opening and could see a dull red glow emanating from somewhere deep within the chute.

One particularly loathsome terminal gazed at Horn and drawled, "Looks kind of like a big asshole, don't it?" The rest of the terminals broke up in howling laughter.

Horn slowly slipped the glove off his right hand and stuck it in his jacket pocket. He elbowed his way by a couple of terminals until he was next to one of the racks holding the fuel rods. None of the terminals seemed to be too concerned with his maneuver; after all, he was vastly outnumbered. Horn placed his titanium hand on an irradiated rod and tried to look casual.

Unexpectedly Horn felt good. He knew the terminals intended to force him into the burning hole, but he started to feel energized and self-possessed despite the desperate situation.

The danger tuned Horn's mind and nerves to what was now the leading edge of his body: his E-mods. He could feel the servos and actuators tightening up the control linkages in anticipation of something. He didn't know what, but he knew it would be violent.

Krak staggered through the crowd now, his eyes fixed in a death stare on Horn. "I have come to kill you—" Krak's final curse was turned into a hideous scream of pain as Horn took two quick steps toward the approaching terminal and latched his right hand onto the giant's face. The palm of the modified hand had absorbed enough of the heat from the fuel rod that it was frying Krak's face. The scream continued ripping from the giant's throat despite the dull green mechanical hand that muzzled his gaping mouth. The terminals stared in awe at the combat-colored hand and covered their ears in an attempt to shield them from the high-pierced shrieking. The screaming struck an unknown chord in Horn's spine, which caused his E-mods to react. Before he could stop it, his hand moved of its own volition, and Krak's head was crushed.

Horn dropped Krak's 250 pounds of dead meat to the floor. Snapping out of their amazed stupors, the crazed crowd stared at Horn like a collective death wish. Without hesitating, he reached into his jacket and pulled out the 9 mm. Horn went into target acquisition, squeezed the trigger and, nanoseconds later took out a terminal, making the others leap on Horn lethargically.

Five more times Horn pulled the trigger, firing point-blank into the churning flailing bodies. He cleared a way in the mess of flesh, but one zombie had summoned enough energy to leap onto his shoulders. Horn spun 180 degrees, grabbing the terminal by the belt. He took three steps toward the Reactor Transfer Only chute and threw the terminal straight into the opening. The scream faded into nothing, as if dropped into a deep well.

Horn headed for the door. Out of the corner of his eye he saw a terminal moving on an intercept course. The 9 mm swung around automatically, its beam tracking on the terminal's skull, then Horn squeezed off a round, perfectly on target.

Finally Horn dived through the door and put a bullet through the cipher lock to slow down the pursuing survivors. He launched his body down the tubelike hallway, kicking up a rooster tail of red dust. The sound of the rod room door crashing open reached Horn's ears just as he reached up to open the trapdoor. It was locked.

"Targa, you son of a bitch," Horn said between gritted teeth. He swung an E-modified fist up and punched through the quarter-inch steel. The microactuators in his hand squealed briefly as he clamped down onto the edge of the metal and ripped the door off its hinges. He stuck the 9 mm into the shoulder holster, grabbed the ladder and pulled himself up into the shaft.

Once he emerged on the surface, Horn took stock of himself. He felt sunburned and knew he'd gotten a pretty stiff dose of rads. His neck felt torn and bruised from Krak's attempted death grip, and when he touched the sore spot his fingers came away covered with blood. But that didn't merit priority. He had to get the radioactive dust hosed off his body. And then figure out why happy-go-lucky flirtatious Robin Silver had set him up.

CHAPTER THIRTEEN

THE ALL-COMPOSITE Lear Needle had been on autopilot for the entire trip. Its sleek, black form resembled the edge of a knife blade that had been married with a bullet. The four-man crew didn't have to worry much about Steller during the sortie. As soon as the ship exited its orbital pattern around earth, Steller had strapped his body onto a padded bulkhead and plugged his mind into one of the on-board electrical sedation systems. In accordance with his instructions, the crew disengaged him from the system as the bird went into its auto retro sequence on final approach. The captain took control for the first time in more than five weeks and docked the ship at the dedicated security port.

"Welcome to New Pittsburgh, sir," one of the crew said as Steller exited the bird, stepping into the air lock. "It's been our pleasure, sir."

Steller didn't respond to the crew member and barely appeared to notice Frank Wand's effusive greeting, either. "Good trip, sir?" Wand asked hopefully.

"The place looks worse every time I come back," Steller said, ignoring Wand and taking in the view from the security dock overlooking the domed city. He turned and finally acknowledged Wand's presence. "There's only one consolation for my being here, Wand," he said without smiling.

"What's that?" Wand brushed an imaginary speck of dust from the sleeve of his uniform, carefully avoiding Steller's eyes.

"We get to kill the cop, then flush this turd." Steller grinned humorlessly.

"I may have already taken care of the cop for you," the security chief said enthusiastically.

"You were not supposed to take him out!"

From Steller's icy tones, Wand had picked up his cue that he was in trouble. "Wait a minute." Wand held up a hand and tried to inject a degree of authority into his speech. "Your message said to surveil, the intent being to eliminate the subject."

"Wand—" Steller's voice suggested disgusted anger "—you just told me the message said to kill the guy by keeping an eye on him. It's no goddamn wonder you wound up on this stinking rock!"

Wand felt compelled to say something. "But didn't you want him wasted?" Sweat broke out on his upper lip, which had begun to quiver.

"The message said to keep tabs on the bastard and that he would be terminated at my command. You moronic son of a bitch!" The veins stood out on Steller's forehead beneath the dead-white skin. "A goddamn terminal has more sense than you do!"

Wand was worried; he'd heard the stories about Steller's rage when he was crossed. "What should I do?" he asked meekly.

"You said that you *may* have already taken care of the creep. What do you mean?" Steller placed a gloved hand on Wand's shoulder.

"I mean I don't know yet." Wand rolled his eyes and stared at Steller's hand. He nearly fainted when the corporate emissary reached over with the deadly hand and stroked Wand's thinning silver hair. "I—I can find out," he stuttered.

"When did you order this attempt on the cop's life?" Steller backed away a couple of steps and crossed his arms.

"Ah, yesterday, last night." The look on Wand's face said he was glad Steller had taken his hands off him, but he still had trouble speaking calmly. "I, ah, we had two of our informants lure the cop into the Hot Zone. Krak was supposed to do the rest."

"Did they take Horn out?" Steller asked.

"Who?" Wand looked puzzled, then held up a hand before Steller could answer. "Horn...oh, the cop, right. I don't have a report yet, but I'm sure they nailed him. The terminals are always willing to—"

"Let me tell you something, Wand," Steller said in a low and menacing voice. "If you managed an unauthorized hit on a New York cop—and I don't give a good goddamn if it did happen up here—I'm going to personally see that you never set foot on Earth again." Steller glared at Wand, who shifted his eyes awkwardly. "Since you ignored my first order, I assume you didn't arrange to have Lieutenant Roach available either."

Wand perked up. "Oh, no, sir, we have Roach standing by in the control station just as you requested."

"Ordered," Steller corrected before adding, "but if you've already masterminded the death of Detective Horn, why would I need to see Lieutenant Roach?"

"Huh?" Wand was obviously missing the point.

"Wand, you stupid bastard." Steller wanted to take the security chief's head off then and there, but held back. "I'm going up to the control station. I want you to find out what Horn's status is, and I don't give a damn if you have to go into the Zone yourself. Now get your head out of your ass and meet me upstairs in thirty minutes." Steller looked at his watch, then at Wand, who carefully avoided making eye contact. "And, Wand, you better have a status report on Detective Horn when you get there."

"Yes, sir." Wand bolted from the dock like a frightened rabbit.

Steller took the long, curving tube to the apex of the dome, which housed the drone control station, the laser aiming system and the Titus Steel Security executive offices. Since the station was at the apex, it was dome-shaped itself and about seventy-five yards in diameter. About a fourth of the area was dedicated to Titus Steel Security offices and the other portion to the drone control functions and the laser beam aiming device, which stuck out from the top of the dome into the atmosphere of the asteroid. The inhabitants of the colony called it "the tit," since it stuck out like a nipple from the dome. When mining operations were in effect, the beam was directed to the tracked drones working the rutile beds and then vectored by mirrors into the ore, breaking it apart. The beam drilling could only take place when the smelting operation was shut down, since an atmosphere filled with slarr wasn't conducive to transmission of a high-energy beam of light. When mining operations were under way, the old pros would say in the charming local style that the tit was flashing or that it was milking light.

Steller harried the control room for a while, putting the staff through their paces by demanding impromptu reports and solutions to worst-case scenarios. He left them sweating, then stalked into Wand's office and installed himself behind the desk.

When Wand reluctantly reported that Horn was still alive, Steller felt almost happy. He mulled over the news and tried to decide what to do with Wand. It was merely a question of timing. He looked at the quivering security chief and decided he would get Wand later, after Horn.

"Bring the Roach in here; we need him for an errand," Steller ordered with a small tight grin.

Wand walked to a side door in the office and pulled it open. He motioned to two guards, who escorted Lieutenant Roach into the room and deposited him in a chair in front of the desk. Wand waved the two guards out of the room and stood next to the trembling Roach.

"You don't look too damn good, Lieutenant Roach," Steller said, almost casually. "Remember me?"

Roach nodded and said weakly, "Mr. Fine's, ah, business associate."

"That's pretty funny," Steller said without laughing. "Business associate? Let's just say that I take care of Mr. Fine's problems. I'm a handyman of sorts." He raised his eyebrows. "That's it. I'm a handyman." Roach didn't react. "Hey, wait," Steller said, swinging his legs down from the desk. "Where are my manners? Would you like a drink, Lieutenant Roach?"

Roach jerked his head around, looking at Wand, an expression of surprised confusion plastered on his face. He turned back to Steller and spoke nervously. "Yeah. Yeah, sure." His lips curled into an apprehensive smile.

"What would you like? Wine, whiskey, Dorfin ale?" Steller returned Roach's smile.

"You got any vodka?" he asked hesitantly, running a finger around the inside of his dirty sweat-stained collar and licking his lips.

"Get Lieutenant Roach a drink," Steller said to Wand. "Red Square vodka." He turned back to Roach. "On the rocks?"

"Ah, no. No thanks." Roach flashed another cheesy smile. "Straight up is fine. Ice kills the taste."

"No doubt," Steller said, as Wand walked to a corner of the room and opened a liquor cabinet. He returned with a tall beakerlike glass filled with a good six ounces of clear liquid and set it on the desk in front of Roach.

Roach licked his lips and swallowed several times before extending his shaking hands toward the glass. "Wait a minute," Steller said, gesturing with his black-gloved hand, and Roach froze in midreach. "Did you forget the custom here on New Pittsburgh?" Steller said in mock embarrassment. "I'm surprised, Lieutenant Roach, you of all people, and a representative of New York's finest."

"What?" Roach pulled back his shaking hands and stammered in confusion. "I, ah, don't know what custom you're talking about."

Steller shook his head. "Wow! You are in bad shape. How long has it been since you had a drink, anyway?" Steller looked at Wand. "Doesn't he look bad to you, Mr. Wand?"

Wand, who was still standing next to the quivering boozer, glanced at him. "Yeah, he does look like hell." He patted Roach on the head and addressed Steller. "Let me answer your question for Mr. Roach. We've had him back here in our, ah, guest room for the past two days and, well—" Wand shrugged as though he were embarrassed "—I guess we just flat forgot our goddamn manners. Never thought once to offer Lieutenant Roach here a drink. I'm sorry as hell, I really am."

"Well, I'm sorry, too," Steller said, directing his speech to Roach, who looked like a starving mongrel in a dog pound. "The custom, though, dictates that you be in our favor in order to share our liquor. Are you in our favor?"

"I—I hope so," Roach answered, wondering what the hell was going on. He was shaking badly and couldn't keep his eyes off the tall glass of 120 proof Russian vodka. It was making him salivate like a starving dog in a butcher shop. "Can I have a drink now?" he asked tentatively.

"Not so fast," Steller said, standing. He walked around the desk and sat on its edge, facing Roach. "To be honest with you, Lieutenant," Steller said solemnly, "you're not in our favor." Roach looked as if he were on the verge of tears. "But you're not exactly in our disfavor, either." Steller raised his voice optimistically. "To set things right, you need to do us a favor. Understand?" Steller grinned and picked up the glass.

"I get it." Roach bobbed his head up and down like a cork, his eyes glued to the glass like radar. "I'll do whatever you want. Just give me a shot, man, I need a drink, please...."

"It involves your new on-site detective," Steller said, holding the glass of vodka in front of Roach's face. "Horn, that's his name. Right?"

Not waiting for Roach's answer, Steller went on. "I want you to send him on a mission outside the dome." Steller moved the glass to within an inch of Roach's nose. "Interested?"

Roach nodded furiously, and his shaking hands moved up toward the glass. "Sure, go ahead and take a shot." Steller let Roach grab the glass. He got up and walked around behind the boozer as the 120 proof liquid touched the quivering lips. The instant Roach's Adam's apple started to yo-yo down its first swallow, Steller grabbed the top of his head, snapped it to one side, leaned over and bit off his right ear.

Roach's scream was muffled as he choked on the vodka, spraying it across Wand's desk. Steller grabbed the glass from his hands, moved a half step to the side, then threw the remainder of the vodka onto the bleeding wound. The choking scream broke into a full-fledged howl. Steller turned his head and spit the ear out of his mouth.

"Get the bottle of vodka," Steller ordered. Wand quickly fetched it and started to hand it over. "Open it, for Christ's sake," Steller said. Wand fumbled nervously with the cap, still shook up over what he'd just witnessed. He finally got the cap unscrewed just as Steller ripped the bottle out of his hands. The big blonde tilted the bottle and filled his mouth. He swished the liquid around a couple of seconds before spitting it on the floor. He then filled the glass and placed the bottle on the desk.

"Sorry about that, Roach," Steller said, turning back toward the lieutenant. His howling screams had subsided, and he sat whimpering like a whipped puppy. Steller put a hand on his shoulder and said, in a soothing manner, "There, there, pal. No hard feelings. I just had to make a point, that's all. Here, look at me." He put his gloved fingers under Roach's chin and lifted his head. "That's better. You see, I had to show you what's in store for your head if you fail to do this small favor... correctly. Understand?" Roach nodded. He held a hand over his wound. Blood trickled through his fingers. "Now here, have a real drink." Steller shoved the glass forward.

"Th-thanks," Roach said, grabbing the glass. He drank heartily, little streams of Red Square running from the corners of his mouth.

"Listen, Roach," Steller said. "Mr. Wand is going to fill you in on the details. If you screw it up, well, just remember what happened to your ear."

"No sir, Mr. Steller. I won't screw it up," Roach answered, as he raised the glass to his lips. The booze in his gut had already filtered a calming warmth to his half-dead brain. He didn't want Horn there, anyway. He took another hard-core belt of the vodka and repeated to himself what really counted—he was starting to feel a whole lot better.

HORN HAD MADE a stealthy back-alley approach to his bungalow. He quietly entered through a side window and with considerable relief found no one waiting. The place appeared to be undisturbed. He was mildly surprised, however, to find a message from Lydia on the telemonitor's LCD scratch pad: the one word *Call*, followed by her code. He punched the sequence of numbers into the keyboard and rubbed the back of his neck with one hand.

Lydia's face appeared on the screen. Horn commented that she looked distraught. "You don't look well yourself," was her answer.

"Probably not," Horn replied. "I was ready to hop into the shower when I saw your message."

"Whatever happened to you?" Lydia asked.

"It's a long story—you'd find it boring." He smiled as Lydia flashed an incredulous look. "Let's just say I'm not cut out to be an occupational safety inspector."

Lydia looked briefly puzzled, then her expression grew serious. "I must talk to you, and soon," she said.

"This evening?"

"Right now, if you can manage." Lydia appeared to be debating whether to add anything further. Finally she said, "It's about Alice."

"Can it wait until I shower?" Horn asked. The heavy dose of radiation was making his skin crawl.

"It won't take long, I promise." Lydia almost pleaded. "I've been waiting several hours...."

"Okay," Horn acquiesced. "At least let me stop by the dispensary. I got roughed up." He gingerly touched the wound with his fingertips.

"Did you forget I'm a nurse?" Lydia responded with a sort of irritated urgency. "I'll look at it right away."

"See you shortly," Horn said, and the screen immediately went blank. He figured he could stand the rads another hour or so. Besides, he didn't want to give Lydia time to change her mind about confiding in him. He felt pretty good about his earlier perception that she had more on her mind than she was initially willing to tell. Horn chalked it up to his being a good cop.

He took a circuitous route to Lydia's apartment and made certain he wasn't being followed. Even with the added precautions, it took less than twenty minutes to get there. He pressed the buzzer.

"Come in," Lydia said, swinging the door open. She bolted the electrolock after Horn entered, then turned to him with a shocked look. "You look like—"

"Yeah, but I'll tell you about it later." He stepped back to caution her. "Don't you get too close; I got a good dose of rads." He smiled. "Now you know I didn't just want to smell good before I came over."

"I didn't realize that's why you wanted to shower." Lydia's voice carried a noticeable degree of concern. "Use my shower. You should get that dust off your body as quickly as possible."

When Horn protested, Lydia became adamant. "I insist," she said stubbornly. "Please."

Horn had to admit a shower would go a long way at that moment to put out the fire that was soaking into his skin. The heat seemed to be increasing exponentially. "Are you sure you don't mind?"

"Of course not," Lydia answered.

"What was it you wanted to tell me about Alice?" Horn asked.

"I'll tell you after your shower," she said. "I'll deal with your neck, too—now go on. And I'll run your clothes through the cleaner down in the laundry room."

"I'll be quiet," Horn said, as he moved toward the bathroom.

"Don't worry," Lydia said. "Zack's spending the night at another nurse's place. As you can see, I just got off my shift." She gestured at her uniform.

Horn heard Lydia enter the bathroom and retrieve his clothes once he had the water going. He examined his body as he showered; except for the marks on his neck, he was in pretty good shape. The radiation had turned his face a sunburned red, but his clothing had done a fair job of protecting the rest of his body. He turned and raised his modified right arm to let the water reach his side.

He cursed aloud when he realized that Lydia was unaware of his mods and that she would want to treat his injured neck without a shirt on his back. And anyway, he figured, the cleaning cycle wouldn't have his clothes done before she would expect to check him out. "She's going to think I'm some kind of goddamn freak," Horn said to himself in frustration.

Horn heard Lydia come back into the apartment as he toweled himself off. "Do you have my clothes?" he yelled out.

"Not yet," Lydia's voice answered. "I'm running them an extra cycle for another thirty minutes. Just wrap that big blue towel around you and get out here so I can examined your neck."

Horn wrapped the towel around his waist and looked at his reflection in the mirror over the sink. His right shoulder, arm and hand were in perfect proportion to the rest of his well-built body, but they were wildly in contrast with the flesh and blood to which they were attached. The combat-green titanium was covered with little drops of water from the shower and glistened in powerful silence like a staged weapon. Horn glanced down at his modified knee and below that his real lower leg and foot. They all appeared strange and familiar at the same time. Horn looked himself in the eyes. "Here goes nothing," he said, then turned and walked out of the bathroom.

Lydia was sitting on the edge of her bed going through her well-equipped first-aid kit. She had placed a chair at the foot of the bed, which was obviously meant for Horn while she provided medical attention. "Sit in the chair," she said, without looking up. Horn was about halfway across the room when Lydia said, "Oh, there they are." She held up a pair of surgical scissors and looked at Horn, who stopped dead in his tracks. "I thought I lost these— My God!" Her voice had been casual, but suddenly expressed astonished fright. She quickly covered her mouth and stared at Horn's modifications.

Horn managed a crooked grin and tried to safety-valve Lydia's shock by saying, "Don't worry. The radiation didn't do this."

Lydia continued to stare, her eyes two pinwheels of bewilderment. "I've never seen—"

"They're mods, that's all." Horn was embarrassed, not because of the mods themselves, but because they had come as such a surprise to Lydia. "I'm sure you've seen mods before, being a nurse."

Lydia dropped the hand from her mouth and looked up at Horn's eyes. She was almost back to normal. "Yes, I've seen body modifications before, but they never looked like this."

"Like they were taken from a battle tank?" Horn smiled his best and it worked. Lydia even laughed a little.

"You scared the hell out of me," she said, in obvious relief at having an unknown explained. "When I saw you—well, your mods—I didn't know what to make of it all."

Horn casually straddled the chair, sitting so he faced Lydia. "Now, what was it about Alice you wanted to tell me?"

Lydia's expression turned grim. "I didn't tell you the other day because I wasn't really sure," she started quickly, as if her words were unloading a mental burden. "And anyway, I didn't know you."

"You don't know me now," Horn replied calmly.

"Let's just say I'm scared and I'm taking a chance." She looked Horn straight in the eyes. "For all I know, you may work for Titus Steel."

For a split second Horn wanted to tell her about himself. He almost began the story of how he'd got the mods to his body—about his family, his partner, the entire edge of the razor. But he didn't. He just stuck with his current status and said, "I'm a cop. My job hasn't changed since the last time I saw you."

Lydia seemed to relax a bit. "Okay, I believe you. Alice told me she was being directed to falsely inflate New Pittsburgh's revenue projections."

"I don't understand," Horn said. "What does that mean?"

"She said it made the company's worth more than it really is. She was concerned that what she was doing was illegal, and approached the manager of the finance department."

"So?" Horn responded, raising his eyebrows slightly.

"I think they killed her," Lydia said flatly.

"Why do you think that?"

"Because she knew too much," Lydia answered. "Alice told me she could get killed for what she knew."

"Over some numbers?" Horn asked skeptically.

"Alice said the projections would change the value of the operation by more than fifty percent—on paper, that is. She was talking about millions." Lydia took a deep breath and let the air out slowly.

"Still," Horn replied, "they could deny ever having told her to falsify the data."

"She had a memo," Lydia said. "I found it hidden in her dresser when I was packing her things."

"Can I see it?"

Lydia got up from the bed to go into the living room. She returned moments later and handed Horn the yellow envelope. He took out the memo and read it. "Do you think this was enough to get Alice killed?" Horn asked, looking up at Lydia, who stood at his side, hugging herself with her arms.

"She's dead, isn't she?"

Horn didn't answer immediately. What Lydia was saying made more sense than anything else. The circumstances surrounding the Stenhaus woman's death were too out of place to make rape the motive behind her murder. "I'll keep this," he finally suggested.

"Good, I don't like having it around." Lydia sat down at the foot of the bed. "Do you think I'm right?" she asked.

"You may well be right," Horn answered slowly. "At least, you may be pretty close. I've been conducting an investigation that involves a Titus Steel executive. What you told me, and this—" he held up the envelope "—may have a connection. If the company's responsible for Alice's murder, I'll be in a position to find out."

"What should I do?" Lydia asked.

"Right now, just stick with your normal routine. The Titus Steel Security people know I've been talking to you, but they probably think I'm not getting anywhere. They've left you alone, so don't do anything unusual that might attract their attention." It was Horn's turn to look Lydia straight in the eyes. "However, I think it would be a good idea if you and Zack got off this rock, permanently."

"I'd already decided to do that." Lydia seemed to brighten up a little. "As soon as I can figure out how."

"I'd be glad to help," Horn offered. "Arrangements, credits, anything."

Lydia didn't respond to his offer, but stood and pulled the envelope out of Horn's hand. She tossed it on the bed and leaned over his shoulder. "Thanks." Her voice was sincere. "But right now, I'm supposed to be helping you. Bend your head down, please."

He did as he was told and felt her fingers gently probe his neck. "This is pretty nasty." Lydia's breath brushed across Horn's ear, and a pleasant, warm electric current ran up his spine. "I'll put something on it in a second, but first, I want to look at your knee." She squatted in front of Horn, and he could look down on her gleaming blond head.

Horn watched as Lydia ran her fingers over the exotic metal's hardness. He could see the smooth valley between her milky-white breasts, and where her skirt had ridden up, he had a view of her shapely thighs encased in white stockings. He was instantly filled with a need to reach down and gather her into his arms.

Lydia looked up and smiled. "I better put something on your neck," she said, and as she caught his eyes, a blush spread across her face. She rose and smoothed down her dress.

Horn returned the smile as she walked behind him, propping one of her knees on the edge of the bed. He felt her cool fingers again touch the burning flesh on his neck and winced slightly. "Did I hurt you?" she asked.

"Don't worry about it," Horn answered. He could feel Lydia rubbing a salve on his wounds. "What is that?" he asked.

"It's a steroid ointment," she said, moving her fingers down to his shoulder. "You've got a nasty bruise back here." He felt her fingers feather down the middle of his back. "This will help it heal in a couple of days."

Horn slowly turned to his right until he could look into her eyes. He put his hand on her waist, then slipped it around to her back, following the curve of her spine. Sliding off the chair, he gently pushed her backward onto the bed. She ran her fingers through his hair to the back of his head and pulled him down, drawing him into a deep, warm kiss before he could answer. Her tongue sought his, and his mind was awash in a soft, white light.

Horn moved his right hand up the front of her uniform and undid the top three buttons. She was wearing a low-cut bra, and as he ran his hand across the silk, her nipples tautened in response. Lydia moaned in pleasure and turned Horn's head to one side. She kissed his ear wetly before probing with her tongue. He quickly slid the top of her uniform away from her shoulders and unhooked the bra. They separated momentarily, as Lydia pulled her uniform off and dropped it next to the bed. She then reached up and pulled the towel from Horn's waist, her eyes never leaving his.

Horn unhooked her stockings, then started to work off the garter belt and panties. She took over and slipped them downward, then pulled him back down, to let him hungrily devour her mouth. She moved her leg up and hooked it around Horn's thighs. He felt a strange, lightly scraping sensation and realized she still had on her stockings.

A cold chill crawled up Horn's neck and over his scalp as he suddenly remembered Ashley's long stockinged legs sliding across his waist. He licked his lips and swore there was a salty taste on his tongue.

There was a deep twinge in Horn's spine as Lydia moved her hand down and squeezed him. He felt his mods jerk slightly. "Are you all right?" she whispered into his ear, flicking her tongue across the lobe and down the side of his neck.

In answer Horn stretched his body out to make full contact with hers. He gathered her tightly against his hips, and she writhed in anticipation. "Right now—" his voice was strangely distant, but Lydia was too far gone to notice "—I couldn't be better." Then Horn closed his eyes and let the soft spell of the woman overwhelm his senses.

CHAPTER FOURTEEN

"WHAT THE HELL happened to your ear?" Horn asked, as he stood in front of Roach's desk. The lieutenant had a big white bandage scabbed to the side of his head like an old tire patch. Blood had soaked through the gauze in a spider-shaped red stain that matched his bloodshot eyes. "You look like a train wreck." Horn couldn't resist jerking Roach's chain.

"None of your goddamn business," Roach snapped, raising a cup of half vodka and half coffee to his lips. He took a huge gulp before addressing Horn. "Where have you been the past week and a half?"

"Working the Stenhaus case," Horn replied. "You told me to stay out—"

"I know what I told you," Roach interrupted, scratching the six days' worth of stubble on his chin. "You've bled that dead-end job for about all it's worth. I've got another case that should make your time a little more productive. I got a goddamn dead drone tender out on the Flats. Don't know all the details." Roach propped an elbow on top of the desk and rubbed his forehead. "But the report says he didn't exactly die of natural causes."

"What's that supposed to mean?" Horn said irritably. "Is that what the report says—'not exactly of natural causes'?"

"No, the freaking report says the bastard had his head ripped off—" Roach suddenly broke into a fit of coughing. Horn wondered if he were going to gag till he threw up, like last time. He picked up the wastebasket and held it toward his boss, who shook his head. Horn tossed the wastebasket back on the floor while Roach managed to get himself under control. The lieutenant picked up the cup and downed the rest of the contents. "It's all in the damn report." He tossed a folder across the desk. "And don't blame me if you can't read it. I'm not responsible for teaching those corporation security assholes how to write reports." Roach wiped his mouth with the back of his hand. "They ain't cops, you know."

Horn flipped through the folder, which held, as usual, a single copy of a Titus Steel Security interoffice memo. The brief report stated that the maintenance technician had been found, decapitated, next to a mining drone in a sector of the rutile beds known as the Flats. "This doesn't cover the disposition of the body," Horn said, looking up at Roach, who was gingerly poking at his bandage.

"That's because it's still out there," Roach answered. "And that's where you come in."

"What do you mean?" Horn asked, placing the folder back on the desk.

"I mean you gotta go out there and check it on site before it's moved." Roach grinned as if he'd just cheated someone out of their change. "Steel Security won't move a body without an official release form signed by you or me. After all, we *are* the only two *real* cops on this rock." He picked up the cup and tilted it back, letting the few remaining drops roll onto his tongue.

Horn asked, more out of curiosity than anxiety, "Is there some kind of special vehicle, like the moonwalkers?"

Roach snorted. "Hell, no. You wear just what those jerk-off tenders wear." He pointed to a hooded silver suit hanging from a peg on the wall behind Horn. "There's yours, rocket man.'' Roach snickered as though he were holding back a ten-megaton laugh.

Horn walked over to the suit and removed it from the peg. It was a lightweight, one-piece, self-contained human protection device. At least that was what the tag said. There were two flat packets the size and shape of decks of cards, which were marked Liquid Oxygen. ''Have these been charged?'' he asked.

''Yeah, yeah. They've been charged. Now, go see the security guards at the drone port, they'll give you directions and a goddamn maintenance bug to drive.'' He glanced at his watch. ''The smelting operations director said he would hold off firing up the furnace until 1800. That gives you more than five hours to do a one-hour job. Think you can handle it?''

Horn didn't answer. He draped the suit over his shoulder and headed for the door. ''One more thing,'' Roach said, as he turned the knob, ''you'll have to bring back the body. The head, too, if you can find it.''

Roach's wheezing laughter followed Horn out the door. He wondered if Roach was telling the truth. From what he'd seen of New Pittsburgh, he was certain fatal accidents were commonplace. The requirement for NYPD to stamp off on a body being moved seemed peculiar. By the time he got to the drone port, he was ninety percent convinced that his trip outside the dome was prearranged. The fact that he might be walking into a trap didn't concern him: he figured the best way to catch the trap setters would be to wait nearby until they showed up to claim the kill. Horn would bait the bait and see who had primed the wire.

After identifying himself to the guards, Horn was given a two-minute lesson on how to drive a one-man tracked vehicle that was controlled by two handles operating the brakes. After receiving simplified directions on how to get to the suspected crime scene, Horn donned the protective suit and drove the maintenance bug into a garagelike air lock.

As Horn emerged and drove the bug toward the Flats, he noticed how much more barren and desolate the asteroid looked from outside the dome. No wonder they use drones, he thought as he steered the bug through the maze of tracked roads. There were drone-made hills of slag and ore everywhere. And the red dust fallout, the aftermath of the slarr, was a blanket of rustlike powder several inches thick. The sky was a hazy, blood color, as though the light were filtered through red cellophane.

Horn finally broke out of the hills and hit the Flats, which stretched to the asteroid's horizon. Across the wide expanse of strip-mined rutile beds, he could see dozens of tracked drones moving along, scooping up the ore and dumping it into the self-contained holding bins. Every minute or so, a beam of blue-white light would flash out from the direction of the dome and strike a mirror fixed on the mast of each drone. As soon as that occurred, Horn could see a cloud of red dust billow up from the front of the drone, after which it would remain stationary for several minutes, chugging away, scooping the blasted ore up into its bin. The drone would then move forward ten yards or so and wait for the beam to make its rounds. Horn saw several of the drones heading for the dome, their bins nearly overflowing with chunks of ore. He also saw empty ones heading back to the leading edge of the current stripping layer.

Horn examined the Plexiglas map given to him by one of the guards. He was in the area where he was supposed to find the disabled drone and the headless body of its tender. He drove to the edge of one of the strips and saw the distress beacon flashing on the mast of a drone that had

apparently high-centered its undercarriage on the ridge between the strips. Horn could see an object next to the vehicle that looked like another maintenance bug, but he was
too far away to tell for certain. He couldn't see anything
that looked like a body. Releasing the brakes, he headed up
a gradual incline and followed the ridge toward the beacon.

THE TECHNICIANS were holding their breath in the control
room.

"What's the power level?" Steller demanded as he
walked forward to the console to peer over the operator's
shoulder.

"It's at eighty percent, sir."

"Bump it up to one hundred. I want to make sure the
asshole winds up looking like a piece of burned toast."
Steller grinned.

"But, sir," the technician said, turning around in his
chair, "we don't run the laser at one hundred percent.
Never have."

The grin fell from Steller's face like a dropped curtain.
He grabbed the tech by the neck, jerked him backward out
of the chair and flung him across the tiled floor of the control room.

Steller took the vacated chair and motioned for Wand to
approach. He reached down and reset the digital power
setting to one hundred percent. Wand stood tentatively by
his side. "Listen, Wand, how do you activate the beam?"

Wand pointed to a covered safety switch marked LASE.
"That's it," he said, then pointed to a digital control sim-
ilar to the one used for power control. "That's the lasing
duration control. At that power setting you can activate the
beam for up to five seconds. After that, there's approximately a two-minute wait while the gas recharges."

"How do I aim?" Steller asked, smiling like a kid with a new toy.

"That joystick." Wand pointed to a rotating control stick on the right side of the console. "Just move the cross hairs on the screen." He reached down and spun the knob, making a set of thin lines on the monitor dance around.

"Great." Steller brushed Wand's hand out of the way. He centered the cross hairs on the image of the drone and watched as Horn's maintenance bug tracked up the incline, leaving a small cloud of red dust in its wake. "Zoom the camera in on the drone," he ordered. "I want to see his reaction when he finds the body."

Another tech at the camera console followed orders, and the image doubled on the screen. A body was visible on the blind side of the drone, away from Horn's approach. It was propped up against one of the treads. Cradled in the corpse's lap was a small metal plate. Steller centered the cross hairs on it, then sat back, his eyes never leaving the screen.

THE CLOSER HORN GOT to the disabled drone, the more suspicious he became. The vehicle appeared to have become stuck on the ridge, but there were no indications that the treads had dug in, or disturbed the dirt. It looked as though it had been parked on the ridge purposely. Horn stopped the bug about twenty yards out and took in the situation. Except for the drones plodding along in the distance and the flashing distress light on top of the disabled drone, nothing was moving. Something was wrong, but Horn couldn't put his finger on it.

He looked around the barren asteroidal wasteland once again and realized the laser had stopped flashing. He felt a little spooked, then remembered that the laser was shut down when the smelter was in operation. He figured they must be getting ready to fire it up, which meant he had to hurry. Slarr didn't look like the type of stuff he'd want to get caught in; suit or no suit. He released the brakes.

Horn pulled up beside the dust-covered drone. It was beat to hell and, except for the mast, looked like one of the old-style nuclear-hardened combat tanks that had been sliced in half horizontally. Horn got out of the maintenance bug and walked up to the machine. He didn't notice anything peculiar, other than an inordinate number of footprints made by feet inside environmental suits. Footprints, not people. He also noticed another set of bug tracks out and back, vectored from the dome.

Horn started to walk around to the blind side of the drone, but stopped dead in his tracks before he cleared the nose. He could see two silver-suited feet sticking out from the side of the vehicle and thought that the tender had been run over. Then he stepped into a clear view, and Horn jumped backward in shock at the drone tender's headless body. In its lap was a sign that read: New York City Cops Suck. Horn crouched instinctively and looked around, half expecting an attack.

Horn swiveled back toward the body and was suddenly blinded by a flash of light followed by an explosion. For an instant he thought he'd been struck by lightning. He was blown backward in a violent slow-motion shower of sparks, plowing up the red dust with his body. A crazy time warp occurred, and Horn watched as a brilliant beam of light burned through the side of the drone effortlessly. The beam seemed to stay on forever, then a secondary explosion erupted from within the vehicle, sending more than two tons of burning rubble into the sky like a deadly volcano.

Horn rolled over on his side, covering his face and head with his right arm, as the slow motion was sucked into real time. The chunks of ore rained down like meteors. Horn

fended off the projectiles the best he could, but got hit
enough to make him feel like a piece of meat getting ten-
derized.

The deadly fallout finally stopped, and he scrambled to
his feet. The red dust was so thick he could hardly see beyond the end of his nose. Figuring it would make good
cover for an escape, Horn headed in the direction of the
maintenance bug, but tripped on a large piece of the ore
and fell flat on his face. Cursing under his breath, he
crawled on his hands and knees, feeling his way to the bug.

The dust began to settle, and Horn knew it wouldn't be
long before the death beam struck again. He moved quickly
to clear the fallen chunks of rubble off the bug. One particular piece of the ore felt odd, and Horn looked down—
into the staring dead eyes of the drone tender's helmetless
head. It looked as if it had been beaten with a chipping
hammer and then shot out of a cannon. It had evidently
been tossed into the ore bin after being severed from the
body. Horn hesitated a second before tossing it to one side,
and a chill ran up his spine and through his fingertips as he
released the chunk of flesh and bone.

As Horn leaned into the bug to pull out the last of the
debris, his inner alarm went off like an exploding super-
nova. A voice in his head screamed, Move! He took two
steps toward the smoldering wreckage of the drone and
dived, flexing his right knee, which shot his body out like
an arrow from a gas-powered crossbow. As he slid to a stop
behind the tread carriage, another beam tracked straight to
the maintenance bug and destroyed it in a blaze of light.
Horn covered his head once again as flaming pieces of the
junked-out machine flew out like shrapnel.

"Son of a bitch!" Horn said aloud, as he grabbed hold
of one of the treads and pulled himself to his feet. He knew
where the beam was coming from, but didn't know what to

do about it. Turning in the direction of the dome, Horn could see the beam controller sticking up from the apex of the dome. He turned back again and his eyes focused on the mast at the front of the drone's remaining hulk. It looked like a masthead from a foundered ship. The shiny, round mirror was still intact, pointing toward the ground in front of the flattened nose. A thin thread of survival logic connected inside Horn's brain, and he immediately moved toward the mast.

"GODDAMMIT!" Steller screamed at the top of his lungs. "Get on the com to whoever the hell is running the goddamn laser plant and tell them to charge this son of a bitch faster!" He banged his fist into the console next to a flashing red light labeled Hold-Laser Charge Mode.

"But, sir," Wand said meekly, fear audible in his voice, "you can't override the laws of physics—"

"I'll override your worthless life if you don't do what I tell you to!" Steller barked as he swung his head back toward the monitor. He moved the cross hairs joystick around rapidly and squinted into the screen.

Before Wand could make the call to the laser plant, a green light flashed on the console, indicating the beam was once again fully charged. The light caught Steller's eye. He gazed down, and a satisfied expression spread across his face. "Horn, you're mine," he said in a whisper, looking up at the screen. "Wand, get on a monitor and help me spot this target. Go to a larger scale," Steller added out of the side of his mouth. "He may be making a run for it."

Wand moved to an empty console and keyed in on the sector where Horn was under attack, increasing the scale and scanning the surrounding area before reporting, "No sign of him making a break, sir. He has to be right around the drone, or else you nailed him."

"I didn't get the son of a bitch yet," Steller answered. "I can still *feel* him. He's hiding out there in the junk like a goddamn rat." He punched the LASE button and drove another five-second burst into the rear quarter of the drone, blowing off the back armor panels and carriage wheels.

THE TRASHED-OUT HULK slid sideways several feet, nearly crushing Horn, who had crouched next to the machine when he saw the laser flash from the dome.

Red dust swirled up to fill the stagnant air like smoke. This time Horn moved as soon as the debris quit falling. He climbed onto a surviving piece of tread and used it to pull himself up to the scorched deck of the vehicle. The dust began to settle as he climbed the mast, which had tilted at an odd angle. In spite of the damage, it still rose a good twenty feet into the hazy atmosphere. Horn reached the mirror and tried to swing it up, but found it slaved to a servo that was frozen solid. He grabbed the two-inch-thick steel linkage with his right hand and tore it off easily. He then turned the mirror in the direction of the dome and lined it up the best he could with the nipple.

Horn swung the thing up and down, then finally let it rest in a down position. "Come on, you son of a bitch, give it a shot," he gritted out, determined to get back at the bastard. His words echoed strangely in the helmet as the dust settled to reveal his silver-suited body hanging on the mast like a battle flag.

"THERE HE IS!" Wand screamed, finally feeling as though he had contributed something.

"I already have him," Steller spit out. The cross hairs were marked right on the waving silver flag, but his eyes were glued on the flashing red Hold light. "Wand! Did you tell the laser plant to charge the goddamn gas faster?"

"Yes, sir," Wand lied.

Steller wasn't buying it. He shot out of his chair and kicked it back. The techs cringed as the chair hurtled across the room before hitting the wall and splintering like kindling. Steller turned his head toward Wand, and his eyes drilled into him. "Get your worthless ass down to the laser plant and take off some heads!"

Wand ran out of the control room, and Steller resumed his position at the console. The status light flashed green, and he centered the cross hairs on the silver-suited body, then moved his gloved hand toward the lasing button. "Give me a zoom on my mark," Steller ordered the camera operator, then lowered his voice. "I want to see the bastard a little more closely before he smokes."

The image of Horn hanging on to the drone's tilting mast grew larger on the screen in front of Steller's face. He watched in avid fascination, his hand poised above the firing button, wanting to get as clear a view as possible of the beam turning the cop into vapor. "Wonder what he's doing up there?" Steller murmured to himself, more out of curiosity than anything else. "What the—" Steller's mouth fell open in dumbfounded amazement. Horn was holding out his right hand, the middle finger extended in a universal gesture. "You son of a bitch!" Steller raged. "Fry, asshole!" He slammed his hand on the button so hard the plastic shattered.

THERE WAS A CLICK in Horn's mind, an anticipatory sort of chemical reaction that heralded danger. He grabbed the mirror and flipped it up just as the laser flashed from the nipple. The beam hung its deadly rope of light across the barren landscape and struck the mirror dead-on. It was immediately redirected straight back to the control tower's

aiming device, overloading the circuit breakers and blowing out the massive gas charging generator.

INSIDE THE CONTROL TOWER, all the monitors flashed
white, then violently imploded in a shower of sparks. Steller
backed away from the panel, covering his face with his arm
as the control circuitry cooked off in a smoking electronic
fireworks display. Several of the technicians screamed as
entire electrical systems went berserk, shocking and burning hands in contact with the controls.

Wand noticed the lights dimming and ran out of the
men's room where he had gone to be sick after leaving to
carry out Steller's order. He went to a firebox and activated the emergency lights just as the primaries went out.
He then ventured into the control room. "What happened?"

"Horn," Steller said, brushing Wand out of his way and
walking out the door. He headed straight down the hall and
burst into the smelting operations control center. "Who's
in charge?" he demanded, as the five or so uniformed
workers turned toward him, surprised looks plastered on
their faces.

"I guess I am," answered a bespeckled operator, who
turned toward Steller.

"Guess again, asshole," Steller spit. "I'm in charge now.
Got a problem with it?"

"Ah, no. No, sir," the guy answered, removing his
glasses and glancing around at his fellow workers.

"Good." Steller walked over to the smelter's controls,
which covered an entire wall in the huge room. "Fire up the
son of a bitch and make it fast."

"But, sir," the same guy said, "it takes—"

Steller turned toward the operator and grated, "Get on the goddamn stick or I'm going to ram it down your throat."

The operator hastily ordered, "You heard the man, fire all burners." Then he turned to one of the workers who was nearest a commo bank. "Lenny, get on the horn to Krak and tell him to make sure we're running at least eighty percent."

"You keep forgetting about Krak," Lenny answered.

"That's right." The man with the glasses snapped his fingers. "Call whoever the hell is running the rods and give him the word.

"And mind," Steller bit out as he jabbed a finger at the controls, "I want to see that red shit rolling out of those smokestacks in less than five minutes, or every one of you is going to spend the night out there." Steller pointed toward the control tower windows, through which the landscape of the asteroid could be seen. In the distance, thin plumes of red slarr were rising from the huge venting stacks.

Steller paced back and forth as the volume of the red gunk increased and formed clouds, which quickly covered the asteroidal sky. He walked to the windows and stared out as the slarr broke loose and began to rain down in heavy clumps on the dome. Weird blue lightning streaked down from the churning clouds and snaked across the dome in giant arcs and jagged fingers.

"Now he's a goner!" Steller said, shaking his black-gloved fist in the direction of the mining flats. "Nobody can survive that chemical hell."

CHAPTER FIFTEEN

It took him nearly an hour, but Horn finally reached the dome. He'd moved through the thickening slarr beneath the shell-like piece of armor skin he'd ripped from the remains of the drone, taking small steps like an old man. He'd seen the slarr start belching from the vent stacks shortly after he'd reversed the beam and short-circuited the control station. Had he panicked and made a run for the dome, more than two miles away, he wouldn't have made it more than a third of the way before the slarr would have eaten through the protective silver suit and stripped his flesh from his bones.

Now what? he thought, peering out from under his protective shroud as the slag rain pelted the thin armor, playing a maddening drum music. He looked up and down the skirt of the dome and racked his brain for an idea of how to break in.

Horn felt a tingling sensation in his feet and ankles. He looked down and was startled to see the silver fabric of the protective suit smoldering like a cigarette dropped in mud.

A wave of panic threatened to squeeze the air out of his lungs. He looked at the oxygen packs on his arm: less than fifteen minutes until a smothering blanket of hypoxia would cover his brain.

He waddled down the dome's perimeter, forcing himself to push the urge to panic out of his mind. A ray of hope reached his mind as he approached an air lock. He flipped down the cover for the door's manual override and pulled the yellow T-handle. Nothing. "Goddammit," Horn muttered, slamming the cover shut. The system had been locked down like a prison after a riot.

Horn drew back his right fist and drove it into the massive steel doors of the air lock. He grunted in pain as the shock of the blow recoiled into his neck and back. He brushed a hand over the spot where his mod had struck the steel. There was only the slightest dimple.

Horn suddenly jumped, almost losing the protective cover, as a loud hydraulic hissing sound seemed to engulf him. He swung toward the noise, which continued like air escaping from a giant tire, and watched the flat spiraling door of a garbage vent open next to the air lock. He moved toward it quickly, knowing an opportunity when he saw one, and almost got bowled over as all manner of waste blew out of the vent.

A feeling of shock slapped Horn in the chest as he realized one of the larger pieces of vented garbage was actually a human body. Horn started to move toward the naked form, but stopped as he saw the skin melting away from the bones. He heard a switch being activated. Without hesitating, he tossed aside the protective shell, turned and dived into the garbage vent just as it closed.

The interior of the vent was covered with slime, and Horn slipped the first time he attempted to stand. He managed to gain a dubious footing on the slick floor and turned to the inside of the air lock. This time the manual override worked, and he stepped into a large warehouse-like building that was obviously one of the garbage staging areas. Heaps of trash were scattered about, and a couple of small front-end loaders sat idle near the huge overhead doors at the front of the building. Horn could see no one as he took off his mask and immediately started gagging. The air was desperately foul, and he understood why no one was working.

As he shucked off the silver suit Horn stuck his head out of a walk-through door that was built into an overhead. There wasn't much traffic. His clothes had become sweat-soaked inside the protective gear, and he immediately became chilled as the air wafted around his body. He tossed the suit onto one of the garbage heaps and scrounged until he found a dry rag. He pulled the 9 mm from the shoulder holster and wiped it down. Pulling back the slide, he blew into the barrel before sighting in one of the front-end loader's hubs with the laser. Satisfied that the weapon hadn't suffered any ill effects from the steam bath, Horn holstered it and headed out the door, figuring he would stop by to check on Lydia.

As he hurried toward her apartment, Horn ran the events of the past several weeks through his head. While the dangerous situations that had befallen him lately seemed connected with the Stenhaus case, his cop's instinct was nagging at him insistently. He couldn't help feeling that the Stenhaus murder was but a small part of a grander scheme—something more than inflated revenue projections. As Horn pressed the buzzer on Lydia's door, he made up his mind to look up Robin Silver and Targa as soon as possible, that night if he got the chance. If they couldn't fill him in on the bigger picture, he was damned sure they could be persuaded to reveal who was behind the Hot Zone setup.

Horn was suddenly snapped from his thoughts as Lydia flung open the door. "Come in," she greeted him. "I was going to call you this evening."

Horn stepped into the apartment gingerly. "What's up?"

"Look at you!" Lydia suddenly exclaimed. "Have you been dragged through a jungle?"

"Just took a nice walk in the rain, that's all," Horn answered.

"Let me fix you a drink." Lydia went to the counter that divided the living room from the kitchen area, poured a healthy measure of straight whiskey into a glass and took it back to Horn.

"Thanks," he said, accepting the glass and sitting on the couch. "Now, why were you going to call?"

"I've got some information. Fine is on his way to New Pittsburgh."

Horn was straining his memory, but in the aftermath of his narrow escape, his mind was sluggish. "Who?"

"Oasis Fine," Lydia elaborated, "the CEO of Titus Steel. He's on his way here. Should arrive tomorrow night."

"Then something must be getting ready to come down." Horn stretched out his legs and took another drink. The alcohol burned his gut but spread a warm feeling throughout his body. At least a part of me can relax, Horn thought, as his mind continued to try to catch up. "Oasis Fine," he said aloud. "How did you find out?"

"A friend of mine who works in the communications center told me," Lydia answered.

"Does he come here often?"

"Rarely. The last time he came was more than a year ago when the union got busted. At least he's not bringing the Shadow this time."

"The Shadow?" Horn looked puzzled.

"Yes," Lydia answered, "his spectacular mother. I didn't see her, but I heard she's beautiful. They call her the Shadow because she's the one who really runs the company. She has a reputation for being ruthless." She fell silent and looked at Horn expectantly.

When he seemed still. lost in thought, she nudged him. "Why do you think he's coming here?"

"Could be connected with the numbers thing," Horn said, taking another sip of the whiskey. "He signed the memo, after all. But there's one sure way to find out why he's squandering his precious time on this place."

At Lydia's puzzled look, Horn went on, "I'll ask him— and get him to introduce me to his bodyguard." Horn smiled tightly.

"Listen," Lydia said, "I hate to change the subject, but you said you'd help if I wanted to get us off this place. Does your offer still stand?"

"Sure," Horn answered. "What do you need, money? Want me to arrange passage for you?"

"Both."

"I heard on the street that a freighter is coming through here in three or four days. The captain's a guy named Crossfield. He's a drinking buddy of mine. I'll get you both booked and make sure you make it out of here in one piece. It's probably a good thing you're leaving. I've got a feeling that things will heat up after Mr. Fine arrives."

A look of relief spread across Lydia's face. She put her hand on his shoulder and said warmly, "I appreciate this more than you'll ever know."

Horn looked into her eyes for ten full seconds before speaking. "I really enjoyed the other evening."

"So did I," she answered, flushing quickly.

"I'd like to get to know you better." Horn knew he was taking a chance, more with himself than the woman.

"Maybe someday," she answered, her voice almost becoming a whisper. "I really like you, but I came up here to cut ties, not make them." Lydia barely managed to get the words out. She had been attracted to Horn since they first met, but good sense told her that it wasn't the time nor the place. Those guidelines had never been truer, she thought regretfully as she saw Horn assume a mask of indifference. "I'm sorry."

"Don't worry about it," Horn replied, and a feeling of loss squeezed his chest. He placed the drink on the coffee table and stood. "Where's Zack?" he asked, going to the door.

"He's spending the night with one of his friends." Lydia got up to follow Horn to the door, then reached out and lightly touched his arm. "You want to stay?"

"I don't think so," Horn said. "I'll call you tomorrow and make sure you're okay. You and Zack should have your things packed and ready to go. I don't think Crossfield is too accurate when it comes to schedules." He smiled his good-night and left her lingering by the door to gaze after him.

Horn headed back toward his apartment by way of Ringo's Nightowl. It was getting late, but Ringo's was just becoming really lively. The place was jumping, packed with miners and street people. The band was wound for sound, and it appeared to Horn that one would need a big shoehorn to get another couple onto the dance floor. He elbowed his way to the bar and ordered a beer, then looked around the joint as an edge of recklessness worked its way into his mind. Knowing it was a spin-off from what he'd just gone through with Lydia, he tried to check it, but it was easier not to.

"Hey, Ringo!" Horn yelled out, and waved at the mustachioed owner of the bar.

Ringo shuffled through the crowd and worked his way in front of Horn. "What's shakin', Horn man?" he asked, twirling one end of the massive mustache and glancing about the crowd.

"Buy you a drink?" Horn raised his voice above the din.

"No. No, thanks," Ringo answered. Horn thought the man's dark little eyes looked like a weasel's, the way they darted about constantly.

"Listen," Horn said, moving his face closer to Ringo, "have you seen Robin Silver or Targa?"

"Targa?" Ringo jerked his head around and glared into Horn's eyes. "Why would I give a good goddamn where that sawed-off asshole is? For all I know he's in a good place as long as it ain't in my sight." Ringo turned his head and spit on the floor.

"Well, I don't exactly want to make a social call on the guy, if you know what I mean." Horn tilted back the mug and downed a hefty swallow.

"I don't know where the bastard Targa is." Ringo grabbed the front of Horn's jacket and pulled him closer, whispering loudly into his ear, "If you're looking for the hooker, she's in a booth near the dance floor."

"Thanks, Ringo." Horn set his half-full mug on the bar and started to move toward the back of the room.

"Wait a sec," Ringo said, still holding on to the jacket. "She's got a couple of big dudes with her. Look like a couple of double-tough mothers." He released his grip on Horn's jacket and glanced in the direction of the band before turning back around. "Watch your ass, cop. That badge ain't going to cut shit with those two."

Horn was smiling strangely. "I guess I won't bother showing them my badge."

He made it back to the dance floor and immediately spotted Robin in a booth with two hulking miners. One guy sat on the outside of the booth right next to her. His greasy black hair hung over his filth-covered shoulders, and a large patch covered one eye. He had his arm around Robin, who appeared rather put upon.

The other miner resembled a sewer rat. He had red hair covering his face and head, more like fur than hair. He kept reaching across the table and squeezing one of Robin's breasts with a grime-covered hand.

Horn didn't feel like beating around the bush. He walked up to the booth and leaned forward on the table, resting on the knuckles of his gloved hands. "Hello, Robin," he said after giving her a long and silent look, ignoring the two miners, who stared at him in astonished anger. "I've got to talk to you about a mutual acquaintance of ours." Horn leaned closer to her face. "You remember Targa, don't you?"

Robin looked shocked. She'd looked as if she were seeing a ghost from the moment Horn had leaned on the table. Her lips started to move, but Ratface spoke first. "You barkin' up an occupied tree." He grabbed Horn's right sleeve with his left hand and picked up an empty beer mug with his right. He brought the mug down on the edge of the table, breaking off a portion of the glass, then held the jagged remains of it to Horn's face. "Want another scar on the left side of your face, asshole?" He pressed the broken glass to Horn's cheek, and a trickle of blood immediately ran down and dripped to the table.

Horn's right arm was a blur as it moved in a circular motion, knocking the miner's arm away. In the same instant, Horn grabbed the fist that still gripped the mug's handle and squeezed. The miner yelped in pain like a kicked dog. Horn looked at the miner next to Robin and asked, "This guy a friend of yours?"

The guy didn't answer, but just stared at Horn with a look of extreme hate emanating from his single eye. "I thought so," Horn said. Robin shrank down in the corner of the booth like a scared rabbit. Suddenly the miner moved his hand inside his sleeveless vest. Horn's movement was a deadly reaction that even surprised him. His right arm immediately straightened out and whipped up. The jagged edge of the broken mug was jammed into Ratface's upper lip and then jerked up, shearing off the long nose. Blood erupted from the wound and sprayed across the table.

Robin screamed loudly as Horn released his grip. He swung his arm down just as the miner with the eye patch pulled a shotgun pistol from inside his vest. Horn's gloved hand raked down the man's face like a tiger's claw, ripping away the patch, revealing a dead-white orb. The miner still tried to raise the 12-gauge pistol but Horn's modified hand clamped onto it like a vise.

"I'm going to kill your scurvy ass," the miner hissed and then reared back his head. He spit right in Horn's face with such emphasis that his ugly head and grease-soaked hair swung forward as if he'd been rear ended.

Horn looked into the man's good eye calmly as the spit ran down his face. He slowly turned the shotgun pistol around until the barrel was pointing straight into the guy's gut. Panic filled the miner's face as he used both hands in a vain attempt to turn the barrel away. "Hey, I'm sorry, p-pal," he stuttered, realizing he couldn't budge Horn's hand. "Don't d-do it, please—"

"Wipe your spit off my face," Horn ordered. He turned his head and glanced at Ratface, who had slouched down on the red vinyl seat, his bleeding face in his hands. "Come on," he ordered again, raising his voice slightly. "Wipe your goddamn spit off my face." Horn found the twin hammers with his thumb and simultaneously cocked them both. The ominous click caused the brow above the miner's good eye to arc up dramatically.

"Sure," he said, letting go of the gun and patting his vest pockets nervously. "I—I ain't got nothing to wipe it off with." He seemed to be on the verge of tears.

"Here." Horn was a little taken back as Robin spoke up and handed the miner a bright red handkerchief. He raised the cloth tentatively and rubbed the spit from Horn's face.

To most the movement would have gone without notice, but Horn caught it out of peripheral vision he never knew he had. He immediately pulled one of the triggers on the shotgun pistol. The big man screamed as Horn swung the pistol toward Ratface, who held a six-inch switchblade over his head. The ten-inch steel barrel of the pistol struck him in the temple as the point of the knife stabbed Horn's right shoulder, breaking the blade in half. Horn's finger automatically squeezed the second trigger and a load of lead BB's drove into the barrel chest. The crowd on the dance floor had crouched at the sound of the first blast, and now they scattered in panic.

Horn grabbed the gut-shot man by the shoulder of the vest and pulled him out of the booth. The big miner held on to his midsection and collapsed into a heap on the floor. Tossing the pistol onto the table, Horn reached for Robin's arm and jerked her out of the booth roughly. "This place isn't too conducive to conversation tonight, is it?" he said, not expecting her to answer. "Let's go outside where your customers won't bother us."

Horn led Robin out of the bar. He stopped long enough to toss Ringo a one-hundred-credit wafer. "Sorry about the mess," he said. Ringo just smiled and waved him on.

Once outside, Horn dragged Robin down the street a couple of blocks before pushing her into the doorway of an abandoned liquor store. "Targa," Horn spoke calmly. "Why did you help him set me up?"

"He tricked me," Robin said, her voice shaking. "He told me you were going to bust me." Robin pulled a package of cigarettes from her purse and managed to light one.

"Bust you?" Horn raised his eyebrows. "Come on! How much did he pay you and where is he?"

Robin took a deep drag on the cigarette and crossed her arms. Her eyes glistened in the dim light from the street. "If I tell you, will you let me go?"

"Sure," Horn answered. "I guess I can't blame you." He looked up and down the street. "As the shrinks would say, the environment probably has a lot to do with your behavior. It's kind of like you are what you eat." Horn's voice was slightly sarcastic. "I guess you could only stomach so much of this red dust before it got into your head." He looked into her eyes, but she turned her head away. "All right, where the hell is he?"

"He's back at the Chain. He sleeps in a room in the back." Robin tossed her cigarette butt into the street. She reached into her purse again. Horn figured it was for another smoke and was surprised when she pulled out a shiny stainless steel snubnose. "Sorry, Horn," she said, her voice no longer shaking. "I kind of liked you." She licked her lips seductively and smiled.

"I guess I still don't get it!" Horn looked with genuine curiosity at the barrel pointed at his chest.

"Bullshit!" Robin laughed wickedly. "You cops are just too—I don't know." She shook her head. "Too human!"

"Then it was credits," Horn said more to himself than her.

"Of course it was credits," she said. "Look around you. You weren't all that wrong with your observation about the red dust. I was supposed to get ten thousand credits if you wound up dead. Now maybe I'll get a bonus for pulling the trigger myself." She glanced up at Horn's face, but avoided his eyes. "I really am sorry, but you're the highest-priced ticket off this rock. Believe me, one night with a couple of sweating hogs like those two back at Ringo's, and you'd do anything—"

"No doubt," Horn said, suddenly pivoting off his right knee and shifting his body to the left. Robin's snubnose barked, and sparks and flame shot from the barrel. Horn felt the chunk of lead drive into his upper right arm. It ricocheted off the titanium and slammed into the brick doorway, exploding in a cloud of red dust. He reached out and grabbed the revolver as Robin struggled to pull the trigger again. She lunged forward just as the hammer fell. There was a muffled shot, and she slumped against Horn's chest.

Horn relaxed his grip and let her body slide to the ground, and a pool of darker red spread around it atop the rust-colored grime. Horn's mind spun like a high-speed reel. He felt as though he were trapped in a bad movie that could only get worse.

CHAPTER SIXTEEN

TARGA WAS SLEEPING on a sweat-stained cot in the sweltering back room of the Chain Reaction Lounge. He was cradling a half-empty bottle of Rojo Gato mescal in his arms, and there were a number of empties scattered about the room.

Targa was sweating in his sleep despite the fact that he was dreaming about ice. In his dream he was lying naked, spread-eagled on his back, in the center of an enormous block of ice. It was so cold that Targa shivered, making the bottle of rotgut roll out of his sweaty arms and onto the floor. It hit a big ashtray made from a lead rod cap and broke.

"Bejesus," Targa slurred as he raised himself up on one elbow and peered around the dimly lit room. He had awakened just in time to see the flimsy door of the room come off its hinges and fly to the wall above his head with a loud crash. "Goddamn!" He recovered his voice with a scream of shock as his eyes fell on Horn's foreboding figure silhouetted in the doorway.

"Targa." Horn held out his hands and spoke as though his feelings had been hurt. He moved toward the cot and scanned Targa's body for weapons. There was a big gas-operated .44 automatic on top of a wooden crate next to the cot. Horn kicked it to the far side of the room, splintering the wooden box into a thousand pieces.

"Where did you go, Targa, old boy?" Horn continued with the mock friendliness. "Your buddies down in the Zone wondered where you ran off to, and come to think of it, I'm kinda curious why you bugged out so fast, too." Horn knelt and patted Targa on the side of his face, then looked at his black leather glove, which was dripping with sweat. "Look at you!" Horn said, wiping his glove on Targa's chest. "I think that claw is gripping your head with too much force. It's squeezing all this saltwater out through your face." Horn put his right hand on top of Targa's bullet-shaped head and gave it a little squeeze.

Targa screamed and grabbed Horn's wrist with both his hands. "Let go of me, you son of a bitch!" He wrestled with Horn's arm and flopped around on the cot like an ugly fish. Horn squeezed his fingers together and sort of popped Targa's head out of his grip as if it were a big Ping-Pong ball. The maneuver left angry red welts covering the tattooed eagle claws.

"Now, listen to me." Horn grabbed the jaw and turned the sweating face toward his. He could see his reflection in Targa's mirrored contacts and was mildly shocked at his own facial expression; he looked as if he were almost enjoying himself. "Who hired you to set me up?" His face was less than six inches from Targa's, whose mescal-laden breath rolled out as he panted heavily.

"I don't know what you mean." Targa's answer wasn't given with much conviction.

Horn shifted his weight to the other leg and picked up the lead ashtray. Targa raised his hands and covered his face. But all Horn did was to dump the ashes and cigar butts onto Targa's heaving chest. "See this?" Horn held the ashtray in his right hand as Targa slowly lowered his hands.

"What about it?" Targa responded reluctantly.

"If you don't tell me who hired you and what's going on
in the Hot Zone, then I'm going to do this—'' Horn
squeezed the lead ashtray, and the gray metal extruded from
between his fingers and fell to the floor in misshapen lumps.
"—to your head." Horn opened his hand and allowed the
remaining pieces of lead to drop to the floor. He smiled at
Targa. "Come on, talk is cheap. Especially for someone
like you."

"You got it, chief." Targa licked his lips and wiped his
forehead with the back of his hand. "It was Wand."

Horn wasn't surprised. "The chief of security?"

"Yeah. He was gonna pay the woman and me ten grand
if you never came out of the Zone. As it stood, we ended up
getting jack shit."

"Robin told me she would have collected the ten thousand credits herself if I was offed in the Zone."

"Hell, I'm not surprised." Targa spoke as though Horn
should have known from what type of cloth Robin had
been cut. "I'm sure she planned to kill me, once Wand had
paid us off."

"Well, I'll be gone to hell!" Horn shook his head.

"You are in hell." Targa laughed weakly. "That chick
wasn't really a hooker, man." He spoke quickly, wanting
to distract Horn. "She was more like a freaking barra-
cuda, a bona fide man-eater."

"That's enough," Horn said, waving a hand and remembering Robin's crumpled form in the desolate doorway. "Listen, Targa," he said flatly. "I don't want to, but
I'm going to have to waste you. You haven't really told me
anything I couldn't have guessed."

Targa's mouth dropped open like a trapdoor for a couple of seconds. "I thought we was getting to know each
other here." He waved a hand around the trashed-out

room, a look of fear on his face. "You can't just kill me. You're a cop!"

Horn almost laughed as he pulled the 9 mm from the holster. He shone the red beam of the laser into one of Targa's eyes and watched it scatter around the room. "Kind of pretty, don't you think?"

"Okay, okay." Targa moved a hand in front of his face as if to brush the beam away. "They're going to cook off the goddamn reactor. Titus Steel is going to do the job and make it look like an accident. Got something to do with insurance, I think."

It suddenly made sense to Horn. The inflated revenue projections weren't intended to make the mining and smelting operation look better for purposes of selling the business. The numbers scheme was meant to increase the payback from an insurance claim—a very large insurance claim, according to what Targa was saying.

"How are they going to do it?" Horn asked, dancing the beam between Targa's eyes.

"One of the terminals in the rod room is going to slip the reactor a mickey," Targa answered.

"Do what?"

"Sabotage the big piece of junk," Targa explained. Then he added, "You're just a kid, ain't ya?" In spite of the barrel between his eyes, he flashed his oversize teeth in a stupid grin.

"You keep making comments like that, and I'm going to lose my patience." Horn moved the beam down to Targa's chest.

The smile dropped from Targa's face. "Let's see, is there anything else I can tell you?"

"When are they planning on dumping the reactor?"

"I don't know exactly." Targa seemed to be concentrating. He rubbed the top of his head in a circular motion. "It's going to be soon, though."

"How do you know?" Horn stood up from his crouch, holding the 9 mm loosely at his side.

"I heard Wand telling Krak—now deader than a wedge, thanks to you—to have the fixed rod prepped and on standby in the auxiliary system." Targa snorted a couple of times. "Mind if I smoke?" he asked.

"Go ahead," Horn answered, as he walked over and leaned against the wall.

Targa scrounged around among the trash on the floor next to the cot until he found a butt long enough to smoke. He lit it with the lighter in his glove and eyed Horn. "Thanks," he said, shifting his eyes over to the corner where Horn had kicked his big automatic. He spotted it and got its location fixed in his head. Swinging his legs around, Targa moved into a sitting position before continuing his explanation. "Like I said, you took care of Krak, so they got a terminal named the Crank, or some dipshit name like that, to fix the rod." Targa took a deep drag on his cigar and blew a smoke ring into the air. "Anyway, it's all set up for the hotshot from New York to fly in and pull the trigger."

"Oasis Fine, of course," Horn said, more to himself than to Targa.

"Huh?" Targa grunted.

"Nothing." Horn turned toward Targa. "How the hell are you going to get off this rock?"

"What do you mean?" Targa looked dumbfounded.

"I mean," Horn said as though he were explaining something to a four-year-old, "don't you know what's going to happen when the reactor goes?"

"Well, it just burns up." Targa shrugged. "Don't it?"

"Yeah, it burns up." Horn laughed. "It also burns up everything underneath it. Does that tell you anything?" Targa just shrugged again.

"Well, let me explain it to you." Horn shifted his weight and watched Targa out of the corner of his eye. "When the reactor goes, the whole rock goes."

Targa chanced another glance at the pistol and calculated it would take him one and a half diving steps to reach it. It was already cocked, so he figured he might be able to get off a shot before Horn could aim his piece.

"Well," Horn asked, "what the hell are you going to do?"

"It's simple," Targa said matter-of-factly. "I'll just take one of the little business ships the executive jerks use."

"They're not going to haul your ass out of here," Horn said. "Especially after your pals in the Zone botched the attempt to kill me."

"Screw 'em," Targa answered with a grin. "I'll commandeer one of the sons of bitches, pilot or no pilot. The goddamn things ain't nothing more than drones, anyway. Any monkey could get one of those thing outta here and back to earth."

Horn was suddenly very interested in what Targa was saying, but he maintained his casual demeanor. "I guess you say any monkey could fly one because you've had the experience."

"Yeah, cop." Targa blew smoke in Horn's direction. "I got a ride on one. It ain't no big deal. Once you get in an earth orbit a shuttle will pick you up. The computers do everything. Even a cop could do it."

"Where do they dock these machines?" Horn had lowered the automatic drop to his side. "I didn't see any at the main port when I got here."

Targa kept his eye on Horn's weapon. "Of course not. They park 'em at the security dock next to the control tower tube. There's one there now."

"How come you know so much?" Horn asked.

"I'm not as stupid as you think I am," Targa answered, as he slid down the cot, positioning himself closer to the corner and his gun. "I know the fat cats are planning to smoke this place. I'm going to make sure I got a way out. That is, if you don't kill me."

He threw back his head and laughed.

Horn thought he heard something in the hallway and jerked his head around, looking out the door. Targa took the opportunity and dived for his weapon, his barrel-shaped body belly flopping on the floor and sliding head-first into the corner. Horn automatically raised the 9 mm and swung around just as Targa got his finger through the trigger guard of the big automatic.

Horn squeezed off a round as Targa took aim with the .44. The big 9 mm bucked violently in his hand, and a lethal projectile tracked the beam straight into Targa's neck making the bald head flop to one side.

Horn stuffed the automatic in the shoulder holster and walked out. The few patrons in the bar didn't look up from their drinks as he walked to the exit. It was as though the sound of a weapon exploding were an everyday occurrence.

Horn stopped outside the bar and took a deep breath. He was a little surprised that he didn't feel any remorse over the way he'd baited Targa into going for the gun. He tried to feel something, anything. The only thing that struck him as unusual was how calm he felt.

It was five in the morning when Horn got back to his apartment. He waited for more than an hour before calling Lydia. "I'm probably going to have to get you and Zack off this place sooner than I'd expected," he said. "How long will it take you to get ready?"

She looked distraught, and she touched her hair with a trembly hand before speaking. "Just a few hours."

"Something wrong?" Horn asked, his eyes locked onto the screen searchingly.

"I got word a while ago that Fine has arrived." Lydia's voice was a little shaky.

"Even more of a reason to move now," Horn said. "I want you and Zack to meet me at the staging area for the tite shipments near the main shuttle port. Know where it is?"

"Yes," she answered. "But why are you moving us so quickly? I thought a freighter was coming through in a couple—"

"I've got some new information," Horn interrupted. "If what I've been told is correct, the sooner we get off this rock the better."

"I guess I don't understand." Lydia looked puzzled. "And you said 'we'. Are you coming with us?"

"Yeah, I guess I've had enough, too." Horn avoided telling her about the pending sabotage, figuring she didn't need to have the thought complicating her preparations to leave. Anyway, he didn't know when the reactor was scheduled to cook off. Also, he hadn't forgotten who gave him the information. Maybe he'd been misled.

He was, however, relying on another piece of information Targa had given him. He planned to get Lydia and Zack off the asteroid via one of the Titus Steel business shuttles. Horn planned to commandeer a crew using his NYPD official police business authority. If that didn't work, he'd use the 9 mm.

His own decision to leave was based on the rationalization that he had the beginnings of the evidence to implicate Fine, at least circumstantially, in the Stenhaus woman's death. If the reactor did blow, the murders of everyone who went down with the asteroid would be added to the charges.

Horn had to be in New York to deal with such matters. He also thought it would certainly be safer on his own turf. Life on the roid, so far, had exhibited a level of risk that hovered near the top of the lethality scale. But the real reason driving Horn to leave floated unacknowledged in the back of his mind. He wouldn't admit it to himself, but the reason was the woman.

Lydia's clear blue eyes were staring at him fearfully. "The staging area is a big place. Can you be more specific? And what time do you want us to meet you?"

"There's an old abandoned scoop drone near the big ridge that runs through the center of the field. It looks like an antique scoop shovel. Hey, you couldn't miss it." He looked at his watch. "It's almost seven. Let's meet there at three this afternoon. I'm going to take care of a couple of things and finalize our transportation."

"Three o'clock," Lydia repeated and smiled weakly. "And Max," she said, "I know what a risk you're taking for us."

Horn started to say something, but stopped himself. He wanted to tell her that she was the only reason he was really concerned about what happened to anybody on the asteroid. He longed to tell her that she had complicated his originally simple mission to unravel the mystery associated with the deaths of his family and partner.

"Nothin' to it," he said. The dark green titanium finger moved on its own and punched off. He watched Lydia's image fade to black, and he felt the ending of what hadn't even really begun.

CHAPTER SEVENTEEN

FINE WAS TIRED, bored and wired as he stepped out of the Lear into the small lobby of the security dock. After his five dull weeks on autopilot, an electron microscope would have been needed to measure the thickness of his skin. "Where in the hell is Steller?" he snapped at Wand, who was standing sloppily at attention just inside the air lock's doors.

"He's up in the control station," Wand answered, avoiding the CEO's copper-colored glare.

"I hope he has some good news," Fine muttered, as he walked toward the transport tube. He'd felt himself becoming nearly insane during the trip, having ordered restricted radio communication for the duration. During the first ten days or so, he had tried to knock himself out with barbiturates, but they had had little effect other than his droopy eyelids. His mind had continued to race madly on a track that centered on Horn. Fine had spent the past several weeks of the trip doing a slow burn in a hellish sort of hyperspace. Now Steller's name was ready to be launched from his lips as soon as the cylindrical doors of the tube began opening into the control station.

"Steller!" Fine's voice echoed in the circular hallway that connected the rooms of the station.

"Let me go find him, sir," Wand said meekly, as he followed the CEO into the hall.

"Hurry the hell up!" Fine barked.

"No need for the agitation, Oasis." Steller's voice was followed by the man himself, stepping into the hallway from the reactor control center. "Think I was hiding from you?" Steller smiled. He wore his usual black uniform, along with the leather shoulder holster containing a massive .44 Automag, and as always the black gloves stretched across his huge hands. The contrast between his clothing and the snow-white skin of his face was intensified by the short blond hair raked across his head like a stiff golden flame.

The sight of Steller seemed to have a calming effect on Fine, whose voice dropped several decibels when he spoke. "We need to talk."

"Come in here." Steller nodded toward the reactor room. "I was just getting the fuel sequence set up to make the auxiliary insertions. I wanted to have it ready for you."

Fine followed him into the control center. Wand tagged along behind like a faithful dog waiting for its next beating. "I want to know one thing before we start this show," Fine said as Steller studied a clipboard handed to him by one of the many technicians.

"What's that?" Steller asked, looking up at Fine.

"Where's the cop's head?"

"Huh?" Steller said, crossing his arms as a puzzled expression flashed into his eyes.

"Horn." Fine lowered his voice. "The cop, where's the goddamn head?"

"Ah, I think it's out there." Steller turned his head and nodded toward the windows. "Attached to the rest of his body—or what's left of it."

"What do you mean?" Fine asked, his forehead wrinkling severely.

"I mean we cranked up the sauce while he was stuck out there." Steller shrugged as though his explanation should have been more than sufficient.

"No, goddammit!" Fine's voice increased in volume as well as pitch. "You said *think* it's out there. So you don't know for sure. I wanted to see this cop's head rolling around on the goddamn floor when I got here. Now where the hell is it?"

"There's no question he is dead," Steller said confidently, but he was a little embarrassed. He *had* agreed to provide physical evidence of Horn's death; at least he had intended to provide it to himself. "You're right, Oasis," he heard himself say. "I can't be certain that the cop is dead."

"Have you sent anyone to check out, or stake out his apartment? Did you send anyone out of the dome to see if his body could be found? Have any of those things been done?" Fine appeared to be struggling to control his anger. "I'll answer for you. Hell, no!"

"I can't argue with that," Steller agreed again. He turned to Wand, who shrank back a couple of steps. "Get some of your men over to Horn's apartment. I don't expect him to be there, but check it out anyway. If he is stupid enough to fall into your hands, try not to kill him. And put the word out to the drone tenders to keep an eye out for the body." Steller paused a second. "But I doubt if any body they find out there after a rain will be recognizable. Get moving."

"Yes, sir," Wand answered, then turned and hurriedly left the room.

"I have a suggestion," remarked Fine, who had calmed down when he saw that something was going to be done. He sat in an operator's chair and crossed his legs.

"I'm anxious to hear it. May I order you some coffee?"

"No, thanks." Fine rolled his head around as if he were trying to work the stiffness out of his neck. "I've got a feeling—'' He stopped to clear his throat, and swallowed again.

"Excuse me, sir," Wand interrupted, as he walked back into the room.

"Any news?" Steller asked curtly.

"I just got a message from one of the stations near the old section." Wand was nervous to the point that his voice was cracking.

"Come on, spit it out," Steller said impatiently.

"Targa'a body was found in the back of some bar down by the Hot Zone."

"So what?" Steller had an edge of disgust in his voice. "Targa was an idiot. And we know idiots die on this roid every eight minutes or so."

"He had a 9 mm hole through his neck," Wand reported. "Some of the patrons in the place saw the guy who did it. The description matched Horn to a tee."

Steller's expression changed from irritation to concern. "A lot of people on this rock fit the bill."

"Not all of them would take on Targa," Wand said.

"Or have a reason to," Steller added, speaking aloud to himself. He nodded his head slowly. "The cop is alive."

"I strongly suggest you get your ass over to the woman's place. What's her name?" Fine said as he rubbed his forehead.

"Lydia Kline," Steller answered, and a look of regret passed over his face. His reports lately had said Horn was keeping in touch with her on a regular basis. He wished he'd checked her out.

"Yeah, whatever," Fine said. "Pick her up and take her to the Zone."

"What about the kid?" Wand interjected. "She's got a kid."

"Take the kid, too, for Christ's sake." Fine shook his head. "Anyway, Horn may head to her place, or they may be meeting somewhere. Set up an ambush at her apartment, or wherever they plan to meet."

"What if she won't talk?" Wand asked, and he looked slightly uncomfortable.

"Really, Mr. Wand." Fine was annoyed. "She's got a kid. Can't you figure it out? Steller will take care of the hard part. Don't worry about it." Fine glanced at Steller before turning back to Wand. "Now, you better get the hell over there and hope she hasn't left already. I'll tell Steller the details, and he'll follow."

"Yes, sir, Mr. Fine." Wand nearly tripped over his own feet getting out of the room.

"What makes you think he'll hook up with the woman?" Steller asked as soon as the security chief had left.

"I've got a feeling, Mr. Steller." Fine almost smiled. "Something's keeping Horn here. I'm sure he hasn't been hanging around just for the exercise involved in dodging your futile attempts on his life."

"What if the woman and the kid are gone?" Steller asked, ignoring his boss's comment.

"I know how badly you want to personally eliminate the cop. Believe me, I would love to have you waste him." Fine cast his eyes toward the windows as he spoke. "Anyway," he said, turning to face Steller, "If we can't find them before the reactor goes, we'll watch them burn from space."

"Don't worry," Steller said. "Once you bring the auxiliary fuel system on-line, we've got forty-eight hours. It shouldn't take me more than six to find the woman and kid. Hopefully, Horn will be close by. Where do you want me to take them?"

"If you find them, call me. Then take them to the reactor." Fine stared at Steller. "Level nine. I'll meet you there."

"Level nine?" Steller looked back uncomprehendingly. "I thought the reactor only had eight levels."

"Level nine," Fine explained, "is the secondary containment area below the reactor's main chamber. Hardly anyone here knows it exists, since there should never be a need to go there."

"How do you access that level?" Steller asked.

"When you get to level eight, punch Ring 9 on the cipher, and a hidden door next to level eight's door will open. Just follow the stairs."

"Stairs?"

"Yes," Fine answered. "It's plain to see you've never been down there. Remember, the old elevator system only goes to level five. You'll have to walk down the rest of the way. Ring 9. You like the code?"

"The code?" Steller was a little confused. "Ring 9. I'll remember it."

"No." Fine shook his head. "Do you *like* it? It was my idea. Ring 9 as in the ninth ring in hell."

"Yeah," Steller said uncertainly. "Wasn't that from one of Janson Zinke's classics?"

"Not really." Fine looked disappointed. "But never mind. Just take them down there. Also, make sure to tell whoever is manning the ambush, where you'll be taking the woman and kid."

"I understand." Steller nodded. "Horn will wrench it out of whoever tries to take him out. There's an unexplained quality about that cop..." His voice trailed off as if he were lost in thought.

"What is it? You worried about something?"

"It's just that the cop should have been sunk a long time ago," Steller answered. "He's scraped through . . . and in a way I don't understand. Could be he's got some extra edge. . . ."

"Bullshit!" Fine laughed. "You're getting old, Mr. Steller. I doubt if Horn could handle it. He's just lucky, that's all."

"You're probably right," Steller said, moving toward the door. "I'll contact you from the woman's place and give you a status report."

"Good!" Fine seemed to cheer up. "You better get moving. You know how Wand and his crew always manage to screw things up."

"One more thing that's bothering me," Steller called back from the doorway. "Horn always wears gloves." But Fine's attention was no longer there, and Steller didn't try anymore.

He found Wand and his squad of styros at Lydia's apartment in a state of elation. They were all jammed into the small living room, crowded around the woman and young boy, who were cowering on the couch. Lydia had her arm around Zack, and a look of fear masked their faces. Several of the styros held automatic weapons on the two hostages.

"Jesus Christ, Wand!" Steller said disgustedly, as he stepped over the splintered door and stood in the center of the room. "Get your goddamn kill squad out of here. Tell them to wait in front of the building. What the hell is the matter with you? Afraid the kid was going to mount a counterassault?"

Wand motioned to the styros and they promptly left the room. "Want me to leave?" he asked.

"No, you stay," Steller said, as he turned toward the sofa and knelt. He rested one knee on the floor and smiled at

Lydia and Zack, who cringed like lambs before the slaughter. "So, you are the cop's woman—at least so Oasis thinks. And a boy as well." Steller looked from Lydia to Zack, then back to Lydia. "A sort of ready-made family, kind of like the one he used to have." Steller reached out and ran the gloved fingers of his left hand down the side of Lydia's face. She quivered in fear and stared mesmerized into Steller's emotionless eyes.

"Now, I really don't want to cause you any more pain then necessary." Steller's voice was soft and low. "But I would like you to tell me where you were going to meet Mr. Horn. Was it here? Someplace else? You would be wise to tell me without delay. I don't have much patience."

"Why would we be going anywhere?" Lydia's voice wavered as she spoke.

"They have bags packed in the bedroom," Wand interjected.

Steller raised his eyebrows in mock surprise. "You are treading on very thin ice, Ms Kline." He suddenly stood and grabbed Zack away from Lydia.

"No!" Lydia screamed and tried to rise from the couch, but Steller shoved her back into the cushions. Zack kicked and screamed, but Steller held him like a squirming puppy. "Let him go, please, let him go!" Lydia cried in an anguished voice.

"You were going to meet Mr. Horn. Now tell me where?"

"No, you're mistaken," Lydia answered.

"Too bad," Steller said, holding Zack upside down by the ankles. "I was afraid your mind would become clouded." He turned toward Wand. "This is drug award day down at the Zone, isn't it?"

"Ah, yes, sir," Wand answered nervously.

"What do you think the terminals would do with the boy here if he happened to show up?" Steller slowly swung Zack back and forth.

Wand shrugged. He had a pained look on his face, which reflected exactly what he was thinking. He was wishing he was someplace else. "I guess they would, ah..." Wand ran a finger around the inside of his shirt collar.

"It would probably be like sharks during a feeding frenzy," Steller said, grinning and turning back toward Lydia, whose pale face matched her white uniform. "Ever see sharks go after a bloody piece of meat? The terminals are worse." Steller looked at Zack meaningfully. Looking back at Lydia, he added, "The terminals don't really care if the meat's human or not, just as long as it's moving."

"All right!" Lydia buried her face in her hands. "I'll tell you!"

"I knew you would." Steller tossed the boy onto the couch. "I don't like these theatrics any more than you. Give me the particulars."

"Three o'clock this afternoon," Lydia cried. "Near the titanium shipping area. There's an abandoned mining drone. We were to meet him there." She broke down into uncontrolled weeping.

"Know what she's talking about?" Steller asked Wand, who nodded affirmatively. "Go set up an ambush for the bastard."

"Do you want him eliminated?" Wand asked tentatively.

Steller put his hand behind Wand's head and spoke straight into his face. "Listen to me, Mr. Wand. I am going to hold you personally responsible for getting Horn. You bring me his head." He looked into Wand's fear-stricken eyes. "Brief your men that they are to meet Mr. Fine and me in the main reactor building, level nine. You got that?"

"Level nine?" Wand shook his head. "I didn't know there was a level nine. Anyway, the reactor's in the Hot Zone."

"I know where the hell it is." Steller lowered his voice. "Write it down."

Wand nervously pulled a pen and small notebook from one of his pockets. "I think I'd remember—"

"Shut up and write," Steller interrupted. "Punch R-I-N-G-9 into level eight's cipher. That will access you to level nine. Tell your men in case Horn gets lucky during the ambush and drills your ass." Steller watched Wand cringe. "Meet us there right after you do Horn in, got it?"

"Yeah, I got it," Wand answered. He was also afraid to know the answer. "Level eight, Ring 9," he said, writing down the data. "Meet you there after the ambush." He closed the notebook and stuck it in his pocket. "Anything else?"

"Yeah," Steller said, releasing his grip on Wand's head. "Don't fail me. I want Horn dead. If you and ten of your crew can't do him, then I'm going to do you. Slowly."

"Yes, sir," Wand said mournfully as he turned and left the room.

"This is a true comedy," Steller said, as he faced Lydia and her son. "I have no doubt that your boyfriend cop will win any confrontation with Mr. Wand and his dupes. By the time he gets done with them, he'll know exactly where we're holding you and the kid. Don't you see the humor in it?" He laughed as a look of horror spread across Lydia's face.

FINE PUNCHED OFF the telemonitor after receiving Steller's status report. He turned to the head reactor technician, a tall skinny man named Butler, and ordered the auxiliary fuel rods loaded into the insertion chambers. Butler passed the order on down to Hank the Crank and his pals, who immediately began the dangerous process of loading the auxiliary rods. Even though the task exposed the terminals to more radiation in ten minutes than most people receive in a lifetime, they went about their jobs with smiles blistered across their cherry-red faces. A fresh fix of the drug of their choice flowed through their veins.

Once the loading process had been completed, Fine ordered Butler to initiate the insertion. The tech spoke up for the first time since Fine had assumed command. "Before I do that, could you please explain why we're deactivating the current fuel load less than fifty percent through the cycle?"

"Sure thing, ah, Butler," Fine answered, looking at the man's badge. He walked toward the tech, pulling a .357 Composite Magnum from his inside pocket. He aimed it between Butler's startled eyes. "We're doing it because the current fuel load is clean. The aux load isn't."

"I—I don't understand," Butler stammered as he stared at the barrel of the .357, which stared back at him from a range of less than six inches.

"I'm sure you don't, but let me explain it this way." Fine glanced at the other technicians, who stared at the scene in disbelief. "This piece of rock called a mining colony does me no good by existing. Therefore, it must come to an end. One of the auxiliary fuel rods has a little surprise that is going to flush the reactor straight through the bottom of the roid, a sort of radioactive suppository."

Butler looked as though he were going to say something, but Fine held up his free hand. "Let me finish answering your question," he said. "When the rod hits the reactor pool, it's going to work just like this caseless hollowpoint works when it scrambles your brain."

Just as Butler opened his mouth, Fine pulled the trigger. The lead rocket punched into the tech's skull, spraying brains and blood across the control consoles. The other technicians crouched and covered their heads. Butler teetered back and forth a couple of times before finally falling backward. His dead body hit the hard floor with a thud as the rest of the techs made a break for the door.

"Hold it!" Fine yelled, pointing the pistol toward the lead escapee. He walked over and grabbed one of the men by the sleeve and pointed the .357 to his head. "Okay, the rest of you can leave," Fine said, steering his captive toward the main fuel control console. "Insert the aux rods," he ordered.

The tech obeyed, his hands shaking badly as he moved the levers into position. "Now lock them in place and run the steam flow up to 110 percent."

"But sir!" the tech protested in a birdlike whisper. "The reactor always runs at 80 percent; 110 is for emergency power requirements only!"

"Just do what I tell you to do and you can get out of here," Fine answered calmly. He watched the tech go through the sequence, finally punching the mechanism that locked the controls in place. "Who else knows the code to unlock this?" Fine nodded toward the panel.

"Ah, just Mr. Wand, myself and Butler." The tech looked over at Butler's body, which seemed afloat in its own pool of blood.

"Good," Fine said. "Get the hell out of here." He let the man go three steps toward the door before shooting him in the lower back. The technician fell across Butler's body and twisted grotesquely for several seconds before Fine put a terminating round in the back of his head.

Fine then went quickly to the drone control center and waved everyone out. Using three carefully placed rounds from the big handgun, he disabled all the shuttle port controls, rendering impossible any conventional means of escape from the asteroid. The exception was the dedicated security port where Fine's own Needle was docked. He punched the port up on a telemonitor and ordered his crew to stand by. As he headed out of the dome's control center, every warning buzzer, siren, flashing light and klaxon that had been wired into the system tripped on. Fine smiled to himself, knowing that once and for all he was going to rid himself of the asteroidal profit sink.

While Fine was climbing into a tracked security drone for the ride to the Zone, Horn was getting out of the tube and stepping into the circular hallway of the dome's control center. The buzzers, sirens and flashing lights made the place look and sound like the test section of a fire alarm factory. He pulled the 9 mm and moved cautiously down the hall.

Through the limited descriptions he'd received, Horn had a vague idea of what Fine looked like. And, if his suspicions were correct, he would recognize the CEO's blond bodyguard, too. He was sure he'd met the man before. The picture of that meeting was burned forever in his mind. Something like fire was running through Horn's veins as he moved down the hall. He could almost smell the solution to his agony as his mind ran clear, humming along the razor edge of revenge.

Horn was furious when he found the control center deserted. He went into the reactor room and checked out the bodies. Then he moved on to the control consoles to find out what was causing all the racket. "Holy shit!" he gasped, his eyes scanning the electronic wreckage. "That hellhound has done it!" His eyes focused on the inlet water temperature gauge and watched the digital readout as it moved into the critical zone.

Horn knew it wouldn't help, but he went ahead and tried to unjam the controls. The reactor was clearly headed into a meltdown with no hope of shutting it off. He could tell that much. It would take a miracle to turn the sequence of events around, and Horn knew that wouldn't happen, because, he suspected, there was nobody around anymore who was knowledgeable in nuclear physics.

He had to grab Lydia and Zack and get off the short-fused roid, Horn thought as he started for the tube. His quest for revenge had to be momentarily suspended. Suddenly he stopped dead in his tracks. He turned and walked into the drone control room. His heart skipped a couple of beats as he viewed the control systems for the shuttle ports. He ran his hands over the buttons and levers, trying to get a response out of the air lock indicators. Horn banged the console in frustration. His heart fell to the pit of his stomach as he realized the extent of the lockdown.

In a flash he remembered the security port and hoped it hadn't been sabotaged. He moved to one of the drone control terminals and called up the menu. He scanned through most of the control modes, which mainly covered the tracked vehicles associated with the mining operation. One particular routine, Docking Valet, caught his eye. He called it up and quickly surmised it to be the control mode for moving docked vehicles outside the dome. Horn punched in the overlay of the dome and saw two vehicles docked at the dedicated security port. Each had the distinctive outline of the Lear Business Needle.

"Bingo!" Horn said aloud, picking up a mouse and centering the valet mode's cross hairs on one of the machines. Following the instructions on the screen, he punched in an engage command and slowly moved the spacecraft away from the port. He took it down the perimeter of the dome and parked it next to a garbage vent near the mining drone port. Horn smiled, wondering if it was the same vent he had used to escape the slarr. Engaging one of the tracked surface drones, Horn maneuvered it directly in front of the security port air lock and punched in Forward Cruise.

Down in the security port air lock, two maintenance workers were sweeping several weeks' accumulation of red dust into a pile. Suddenly the outer doors caved in, sounding like a train crash. The scoop of the drone tore through the heavy steel doors, and the pile of red dust was immediately sucked out, followed by the two workers, whose bodies slammed into the jagged edge of the eight-foot scoop before being dragged over the excavating teeth and into the deadly asteroidal environment.

As soon as the pressure in the air lock blew out, the inside doors were automatically activated. Six huge hydraulic rams moved the two big doors toward each other at an emergency closing speed of nearly 150 miles per hour. It wasn't fast enough for Stick Perry, one of the Lear pilots, who was walking from the rest room back to the crew lounge. His lean flight-suited body was sucked exactly halfway through the inner opening when the grooved edges of the stainless steel doors slammed closed on him with a hideous finality.

Horn heard a couple of extra alarms go off as the drone breached the doors. He brought his right hand up, then swung it down, his fingers extended in clawlike fashion. The five titanium projectiles drove three inches into the control terminal. More alarms went off, adding to the din, as the electronics shorted out, smoke curling up around Horn's gloved hand. He pulled it out and headed for the door with one thought in his mind: get Lydia and Zack off the asteroid. His plan was so thin it was crazy, but he hoped with an all-out determination that his momentum would carry him through. And, he acknowledged, that his luck would hold.

CHAPTER EIGHTEEN

ON THE WAY to the ambush site, Wand and his squad of styro hit men stopped off at a security substation to pick up extra firepower. The security chief was so intent on loading up his men with every kind of weapon the station's small arsenal contained that he didn't quite catch the manager's report about a disturbance at the main security port.

Wand figured that his ticket off New Pittsburgh was dependent upon his ability to pull off the ambush, and he wasn't about to fail because his men were short on arms or ammo. Each one of the killers trudged away from the substation weighing at least fifty pounds more than when he'd strolled into the place. Eleven pros, counting Wand, against one cop? Piece of cake, Wand thought. He wondered why he didn't feel so confident. He wondered why he was sweating profusely as he marched his men, route step, up to the half-buried, burned-out hulk of the old scoop mining drone.

The gigantic relic of a drone had been resting in the red dirt of the staging field since New Pittsburgh was founded. Titus Steel had purchased but one of the behemoth scoopers, which was more than fifty yards long and twenty-five yards wide. Its massive steel treads were broader than a street and towered above a man's head when tracked around the huge drive wheels. The maintenance costs associated with the ore-grinding beast had been astronomical, and the company had abandoned the machine after using it for less than a year. In fact, Titus Steel had ended up suing the manufacturer for misrepresentation and managed to recover the transport costs, which were ten times the price of the hardware.

But the rusting scoop had stayed squatted in the staging area, more than one-quarter covered with the red tite dust. A twenty-foot ridge of hard-packed waste ore ran down one side of the machine and curved around its front end in a hook shape. The scarred-up nose of the scoop stuck out from the drone a good fifteen yards on a hydraulically operated conveyor system. It was still raised, the wedge-shaped bucket hanging ten feet above the ridge like a monument to the death of technology.

Wand grew even more fidgety as he stood on the ridge next to the riveted steel carcass. He called Franz, his lead styro, over to give his first order since they left the substation an hour earlier. "Send two of your men into the machine and check it out. I want to make sure the cop hasn't gotten here early."

Franz smiled into Wand's eyes. His big square jaw stretched out sideways, exposing a narrow view of teeth the size of a beaver's. "Yes, sir. Anything else, sir?"

The styro's voice didn't match the weapons-clad, uniformed appearance of a professional killer. It was soft and low, almost effeminate. It gave Wand the chills. He'd always suspected that Franz had the hots for him, and just about then, Wand figured it was all he needed to complicate his already wired-for-sound anxiety. He was certainly going to be happy when he got away from the weird rock.

"No, just check out the drone," Wand ordered and looked at his watch. "It's almost two-thirty. Position the rest of the men on the machine to make the ridge here the field of fire." He waved his hand, indicating the area on which they stood. "I'm going to be up in the control cab.

Tell your boys to hold their fire until they hear my .308.''
He patted the stock of the assault rifle slung under his arm.

"No problem, Chief Wand." Franz joined the rest of the
styros and instructed all but two of them to deploy along
the inside rim of the drone's ore bin. He waited until the
first man had crawled over the steel lip before asking, "Is
it clear in there?" The styro looked around a couple of
seconds before giving Franz the thumbs-up.

Wand crawled up into the control cab, which was elevated high above the ore bin. Most of the glass had been
broken out of the closet-size cockpit, which had been used
for manned control of the vehicle inside the dome. Many
of the controls and levers were rusted, and everything was
layered with red dust. The floor of the cab was littered with
broken bottles and other trash, left behind by workers who
were probably no longer alive. Probably as good a place as
any for a cop to die, Wand thought, as he scanned the
staging field for a sign of his intended victim.

Down below, Franz had finished checking out the inside
of the drone. He crawled up to the bin and made sure his
men were well concealed and in the optimum position to
catch anyone on the ridge in a murderous wave of lead.
Each styro carried an automatic weapon and extra ammo.
A couple of the elite security squad brandished autoload-
ing shotguns capable of firing a round magazine of thirty
caseless 12-gauge shells in less than four seconds. While the
weapon was capable of throwing out buckshot in such a
blistering manner, the operator often had trouble controlling the jackhammering effect, which made aiming the
death stick somewhat difficult. It was most effective in a
crowd.

Satisfied that the ambush was properly staged, Franz
gave Wand a wave before taking a position behind a piece
of disconnected tread that lay across a portion of the ridge

near the nose of the drone. Assuming a prone position behind the tread, he unhooked two concussion grenades from
his web gear and placed them in the red dirt, within easy
reach. He took a deep breath, stared up the trail along the
ridge and waited.

HORN MOVED along the ridge quickly, relying on his instincts as well as his senses to warn him in case the unex-
pected happened. In the distance he could see the tilted
form of the drone, partially submerged in the red dirt like
the rotting body of a dead dinosaur. The sight of it made
him quicken his pace.

Horn knew he would breathe easier once he had Lydia
and Zack aboard an earthbound ship. He had come to feel
responsible for Lydia, though he knew a big portion of her
allure was the vacuum of his life. At first he had thought
she was making a play for him, but after their last couple
of conversations it became clear she had been using him. It
was in a way, however, that was not unkind. She was simply taking care of her child, protecting him as any parent
would. Horn would keep his word and get the two off New
Pittsburgh. Perhaps, he hoped more than rationalized, she
would look upon his intentions in a different light once they
got off the desolate asteroid. As for the mystery behind his
personal misery, Horn figured he would be satisfied knowing the puzzle pieces would float in space forever once the
sabotaged reactor turned the asteroid into another cloud of
debris.

As Horn moved in on the drone, a subtle alarm went off
in his head. He stopped on the ridge and pulled the 9 mm
from its holster as the hair on the back of his neck bristled.
Nothing seemed extraordinary as he scanned the trash-
strewn area. There were footprints in the red dust, but that
didn't signify much. He moved forward cautiously, skirt-
ing the drone, keeping to the ridge. As his lips parted to call

Lydia's name, a shot rang out like a cracked bell, shattering the silence.

The .308 X-nosed bullet struck Horn square in the right
shoulder like a pile-driven spike. The impact spun his body
around in a semicircle, knocking him off the far side of the
ridge in a billowing cloud of red dust. The last thing most
of the styros saw after Wand fired were Horn's boots flying
over his head. They all opened up anyway. The sound of
automatic weapons filled the air in a hot swarm.

Franz was livid. He stood and waved his hand, yelling for
the squad to quit firing. Up in the control cab, Wand
breathed heavily and leaned against one of the grime-
covered operator panels. Sweat ran down his face, making
little streaks in the powdery red dust. "I got that S.O.B.,"
he said hoarsely.

Horn immediately regained his feet and crouched. He
blew the dust off the 9 mm and scanned the area, pointing
the automatic in the direction his eyes moved. His heart was
like a stone in his chest. The realization that he'd been set
up screamed through his brain, and his blood turned to ice
water. But his shock was instantly replaced by anger. He
knew Lydia and the boy were prisoners.

Horn started to move out of the immediate area to take
a position farther down the ridge line when he heard a soft
swishing sound. His weapon automatically followed his
eyes, and the red pencil beam of the laser sight came to rest
on the forehead of a styro with an HK Airborne Assault
Special to his shoulder. Horn squeezed the trigger and the
top of the styro's head was detached from his skull. The
body rocked back and forth for a couple of seconds, and
Horn was twenty yards down the back side of the ridge
when the dead man hit the dirt.

The sound of the gunshot had alerted Wand, and he
jerked up, striking the roof of the cab. He peered out

through the broken glass and watched the Styro's body flop into the dust. "Franz!" he yelled at the top of his lungs. "The bastard is still alive!"

No shit, Franz thought, shifting nervously. He picked up one of the lemon-size grenades and pulled the pin. Releasing the lever, he counted to three, then threw it over the ridge where Horn had disappeared.

Horn chuckled a little when the grenade cooked off behind him. Crawling on his belly, he moved up the side of the ridge and peered back toward the drone. He saw Franz looking along the trail, craning his big neck over the steel tread. Several of the styros were gazing tentatively over the edge of the ore bin, aiming their weapons in the general direction of their fallen comrade.

Taking a deep breath, Horn moved in a running crouch across the top of the ridge and down the other side. He took cover beneath the steel lip that ran across the nose of the dead machine and listened. In a high-pitched voice Franz was ordering a styro named Joel to scout ahead on the other side. Horn looked around, thinking it was time to set up his own ambush. He scooped out a shallow grave in the dirt beneath the lip of the drone and lay down in it. Covering all but his face, he burrowed his right arm beneath the dirt so that it lay in the path that anyone circling the drone would follow. He looked out from the shadow beneath the machine and waited for someone to come within range.

"There ain't nobody down here!" Horn heard one of the styros yell. He assumed it was Joel. "There's just a hole in the dirt where your frag went off, Franz," the guy added in a squeaky voice.

"Goddammit!" Franz got up from behind the tread and waved at the men in the ore bin. "I need two crackers posthaste," he chirped. A couple of styros called Larry and Bob stumbled down the side of the machine and stood in front of Franz. "I want you boys to take a look-see around the drone here." Franz nodded toward the machine. "If you see the cop, kill him."

Wand watched the whole scene from the cab and felt sick. A growing dread crept into his mind like an ominous shadow. The words of the substation manager suddenly came to him as sweat dripped into his eyes. Some disturbance at the security port. "Shit," Wand gasped, remembering that the security port was the last doorway out of New Pittsburgh. He cowered in a dirty corner of the cab and clutched his assault rifle with sweaty hands. The cop bastard has more lives than a freaking cat, Wand thought, as he shivered in a burning fever of fear.

Beneath the dull red blanket of dirt Horn made an effort to control his breathing. He could see the mound across his chest rise and sink with each breath, and little tracks formed in the packed dust like miniature earthquakes. Trickles of sweat ran down his face, and his eyeballs ached from staring at such an extreme angle. In spite of the discomfort, three things felt good to Horn: his two E-mods and the butt of the 9 mm in his right hand.

The two styros, Larry and his buddy, rounded the corner at the nose of the drone and crouched, waving their weapons like a couple of hotshot gunslingers. Larry was carrying one of the automatic shotguns, aiming it from the hip. When they saw a clear path to the other corner of the drone, they stood and laughed. Larry patted Bob on the head. "That goddamn cop is probably sucking down a beer on the other side of the Hot Zone by now."

His partner continued down the path, with an air of relief. "Let's just get the place checked out and get back to the base. It's no good hanging around here."

Horn heard the two styros moving toward him, their composite-soled boots crunching in the ore-based dirt. His eyes finally latched on to their legs ten yards out, and he could feel his mod twitching mildly in anticipation. Horn relaxed, remembering that the mod's function was to be the leading edge of his body. His mind became extra alert as Bob stepped directly into the titanium palm of Horn's hand.

The styro thought something felt odd as he put his weight down. He was looking at his boot when Horn clutched hard. The titanium fingers squeezed, crushing the bones in the styro's foot. Horn emerged upward out of the dirt, then flipped his wrist, and Bob was slammed facefirst, his assault rifle trapped beneath him. Horn swung the 9 mm around then and aimed it at Larry, who stared at Horn's dirt-covered form as though he were looking at a ghost.

"What's the matter?" Horn asked, his finger squeezing the trigger, causing the red dot of the laser beam to appear on Larry's chest. "Haven't you ever seen a slag monster?" His words seemed to snap the styro out of his shocked daze. The barrel of the shotgun started moving up just as Horn pulled the trigger into the death zone. The weapon bucked and Larry was knocked backward, the weapon flying from his hands. Automatically Horn brought his gun to bear on the back of the other styro's head. Bob was struggling, trying to wrestle his weapon into a firing position. Horn fired from a range of less than four feet and blew his head apart.

Right away Horn jumped up, grabbed the shotgun and ran to the center of the machine. The other styros were yelling for the two men Horn had just killed. He crouched beneath the base of the big conveyor boom and holstered the 9 mm. After checking the shotgun over, Horn crawled up the machine and peered into the ore bin. He could see six styros crouching among the chunks of red ore. Periodi-

cally one of them would peek over the edge of the machine
nervously, then turn and shake his head at his buddies.

Horn flipped the selector switch on the side of the
shotgun to full auto and placed his hand on the lip of the
bin. Using the mod of his right knee, he sprang up and
swung himself into the bin. Just as he landed, Wand's voice
echoed out from above. "Look out, you fools!" Horn
glanced upward momentarily, but his finger was already
squeezing the trigger of the shotgun. The weapon barked,
with Horn easily controlling the severe bucking as all six
styros were shredded by the lead pellets. He had fired a
burst of less than two seconds, but it was enough to make
the inside of the ore bin look like a slaughterhouse.

A rifle shot rang out from over Horn's head, and the
bullet ricocheted off the steel sides of the ore bin just behind him. He flipped the selector switch to semiauto and
fired a quick round into the bottom of the cab before leap-
ing onto the conveyor boom. He crawled up the structure,
holding the shotgun in his left hand.

As soon as he cleared the upper edge of the machine, a
burst of automatic fire barked out from the ridge. One of
the high-caliber rounds struck the shotgun, knocking it
from Horn's hand, and he nearly fell from the boom. He
yelled out and moved around to the side of the structure in
an attempt to escape the flying lead. Suddenly the firing
stopped, and Horn moved into a position to jump down
into the ore bin. He figured himself to be too easy a target,
hanging on the conveyor like a flag.

He was just getting ready to jump when a loud thunk
caused him to look down. An egg-shaped fragmentation
grenade rolled directly beneath him. Without hesitating, he
pushed off with his left leg and dived completely over the
side of the drone, landing on a section of the tread. He
rolled off and hit the ground running just as the grenade

cooked off in a deafening explosion. Horn sprinted to the front of the drone and pulled out the 9 mm. He glanced up at the cab, which was framed in a cloud of red ore dust and smoke, but couldn't see any movement. He scanned the ridge before peering around to the side of the machine.

Franz's body was a blur as he plunged over the top of the ridge and rolled down its side in a cloud of dust. Horn fired a round at the form and watched it disappear into one of the side doors. He ran in a crouch, stopping next to the door for a couple of seconds before spinning around and aiming into the opening. No result. He could feel his heart pounding as he gazed into the shadowy guts of the huge machine.

Horn took a deep breath and slipped into the cramped steel aisle that ran tunnellike throughout the big drone. He had to hunch over to keep from hitting his head. Moving down the tunnel slowly, he allowed his eyes to adjust to the darkness.

Up ahead a loud bang rang out, echoing in the darkness. It sounded like the slam of a heavy steel door. Horn felt his way around the corner and could make out a door at the end of the coffin-shaped hallway. Faded yellow letters on the rusting steel door pegged it as the engine compartment. Horn pulled on the handle, but the door wouldn't budge. He put his right foot on the wall next to the door and grabbed the handle with his right hand. The steel creaked loudly as he pulled. A sharp snapping sound suddenly filled the cramped space, and the door flew open, causing Horn to stumble backward a couple of steps. He immediately aimed the 9 mm into the darkness, letting the red beam track and hunt through the gloom. No movement, no sign of life.

Horn stepped forward, then cautiously crossed the threshold. Instantly a sharp pain sliced down the left side of his chest near his neck. He cried out as Franz's two hundred-plus pounds of muscle and bone dropped on his head and shoulders. The styro grabbed him around the neck with one hand while he tried to drive the fingers of his other hand into Horn's eye sockets. Horn twisted his head away from the prying fingers. Inches from his face he could see the pearly handle of the stiletto, driven to the hilt just below his left shoulder.

Gritting his teeth, Horn knew he'd better take care of the problem on his shoulder before worrying about the knife sticking out of his chest. He swung his right arm up in a reverse roundhouse. His titanium fist struck Franz in the ribs, shattering six of them, one of which was driven into the styro's left lung. Franz tried to scream, but instead he coughed. Blood shot from his mouth and nose and ran down the front of Horn's shirt, mixing with the blood flowing from the knife wound.

Franz grunted loudly as Horn slammed his fist three more times into the stomach and chest area. The third time he swung, the impact of the blow knocked Franz's grip loose and he felt the big styro start to slide down his back. Horn grabbed his neck with his right hand and bent over. He flung the choking body onto the floor, and without thinking, brought his right boot down on Franz's face. He felt the strain on his ankle and foot as the servos kicked in, crushing the styro's head.

Horn backed out of the engine compartment and leaned against one of the steel walls. Blood was running from his wound, over his left arm and hand. He grabbed the 9 mm, carefully uncocked it and shoved it into the holster. Taking a deep breath, he gripped the handle of the knife. The five-inch piece of steel came out in a flash, and Horn was surprised by the lack of additional pain. He leaned back into the engine room and ripped a piece of cloth from the front of Franz's uniform. After wadding it up, he stuffed it beneath his own turtleneck, covering the wound. He applied some pressure for a couple of seconds before flexing his arm. The wound hadn't affected his movement, but he realized he'd better limit the arm's activity. He turned and headed for the exit, in a hurry to leave the steel tomb.

Horn made it back to where the styros had been holed up. Silently he prowled until he located his prey through a window of the machine, then stared at him intently.

It was Wand. The security chief turned to look out one of the side windows and suddenly screamed. Horn's face was less than three feet away. Even closer was the business end of the 9 mm. From Wand's angle, the barrel of the huge weapon looked like an atomic cannon. "Where the hell did you come from?" he squawked.

Horn was standing on the narrow steel mesh walkway that ran around most of the cab. He moved closer to the window before speaking. "Throw the rifle out before I air-vent your head." Wand did as he was told, quickly tossing the weapon outside.

"Are you g-going to kill m-me?" Wand stammered, his knees shaking so badly that his whole body seemed to sway.

Horn stuck his head through the window and made sure Wand wasn't wearing a side arm. "You must be Wand, right?" He waited for the man's nod.

"You asked a question, and now it's my turn. Do you deserve to die?"

"I—I don't think so." Wand was sweating like mad.

"Where are the woman and the boy?" Horn asked.

"Who?" Wand barked, apparently caught off guard by the question.

"The people who were supposed to meet me here. Where are they?" Horn lowered his voice. "The answer to the question of whether or not you deserve to die depends one hell of a lot on how you answer.''

Wand didn't think about spilling his guts. "Fine has them," he answered. "He had Steller take them to the reactor."

"Reactor?" Horn didn't try to hold back his surprise. "Why the hell are they being taken to that goddamn place?"

"Bait, I imagine," Wand said calmly, the fear suddenly absent from his voice. "I imagine they want to bait *you*. Otherwise, I don't think Steller would have made a major point out of telling me and my men exactly where they were taking her and the kid."

"Tell me about it," Horn commanded.

"Level nine of the reactor. At level eight you key in Ring 9 on the cipher and a side access will open. They're probably there by now." Wand's face looked tired and hopelessly worn-out, matching his voice.

Horn rubbed the scar on his cheek with the barrel of the 9 mm. "I would guess that Steller is a big, blond guy, always wears black—"

"Always enjoys the kill." Wand picked up Horn's sentence. "He was the one who tried to smoke you out in the ore fields."

The vision of Steller bringing violent death to his New York apartment filled Horn's mind. He forced the image out as his right arm twitched mildly. "And were you planning on getting off this rock?" he asked, stepping onto the rungs of the steel ladder running down one of the braces.

"The business Lear is at the security port," Wand said, "but I can write that off. Looks like I'm a dead man." He was surprised he admitted his fate so calmly.

"Nobody's leaving out of the security port," Horn said, moving down. "It had an accident."

Horn reached the bottom of the ladder and stepped onto one of the treads. Wand's voice made him look back up to the cab. "Watch out for Steller," the security chief yelled. "Fine, too. They're both ruthless—will stop at nothing. You hear? At nothing!"

Horn turned and jumped off the tread. He climbed up the ridge and stuck the automatic back in the holster. Making a beeline for the Hot Zone, Horn moved out in a fast trot. When he'd gone about a quarter of a mile, the sound of a single shot came from the direction of the abandoned drone. Horn figured it was Wand answering the question of whether he deserved to die.

CHAPTER NINETEEN

HORN ENTERED the Hot Zone via the same route he had used with Targa.

While the shaft drew him in deeper and deeper, he allowed the craving for vengeance to burn through his mind. It gave him energy. He had found a fine line between reality and the nightmare visions of those deaths in New York. The longer he walked the line, the stronger the desire for revenge became. As he dropped out of the shaft into the stifling hallway, Horn could feel his mods flex. They felt ominous, like a loaded gun. He focused in on the energy, drew the 9 mm from its holster and headed down the long hall.

The first level of the reactor complex was sheer chaos. Terminals were everywhere, stumbling around and speaking incoherently. Horn figured the reactor was showing the effects of the contaminated fuel and had locked down. The first stages of the meltdown were taking place, and the terminals were helpless. They were like a bunch of animals trapped in a forest fire. At first, Horn was concerned he'd have to waste his time warding them off, but they ignored him or just stared through him.

The place was even hotter than Horn had remembered. Sweat ran down his back, soaking his turtleneck and light jacket. He stopped next to the rod room and shed the jacket, wiping it across his face before tossing it to the dirt-covered floor. Horn continued down the hall, finally reaching the service elevator for the complex. A handful of terminals milled around in front of the pitted steel door as though they were waiting for it to take them somewhere.

Horn elbowed his way past the crowd and pressed the button with his left index finger, then yelped in pain. The button was like a soldering iron. He looked at the smoldering leather covering his finger as the big door slid open. Horn was swept into the elevator as four or five terminals ganged into the box, apparently excited by the sudden opening of the door. Horn wondered if one of them had thought to push the button.

Horn pulled the 9 mm from the holster and waved it in front of the terminals, who showed no sign of reacting. "This elevator is going down. You'll have to get off."

"Up," one of them grunted. "We go up, away from fire."

"Sorry, pal," Horn answered, shoving him toward the door. "I said down."

The terminal suddenly let out a growl and lunged at Horn, who easily sidestepped the slow-motion charge. The zombie ran facefirst into the steel-plated wall. He screamed at the top of his lungs and clutched his burned face, which gave Horn the opportunity to grab him by the back of the neck and fling him into the hallway. The others backed off, and Horn herded them toward the door with the barrel of the automatic. They moved out slowly, staring at the red beam of the laser sight as Horn flashed it back and forth across their chests. When he was alone, he pushed the button for level five, the last one on the panel.

The loud humming that had saturated the hot air space in level one increased as the ancient elevator dropped into the bowels of the reactor complex. The hum turned into a rumble as the elevator came to a stop on level three. Horn punched the red emergency override button in an attempt to abort the unplanned stop, but it didn't work. The door slid open, and Horn gazed into a huge room filled with a maze of twisted and broken pipes spewing steam with a hiss that sounded like a million snakes. The sound temporarily drowned out the underlying rumble as Horn raised his left arm in an attempt to shield his face from the intense heat. Suddenly a body stumbled out of the shroud of vapor and fell facefirst into the elevator. Horn continued pressing the close button as the form twitched on the floor. After what seemed to be endless seconds, the door slowly closed. Horn grabbed the back of the guy's shirt and pulled him in a couple of feet to keep his legs from jamming the door. He flipped the body over and gasped when he saw the parboiled face of the terminal.

Horn looked up at the panel and watched the old digital readout indicate the elevator was creeping down through level four. It showed no sign of stopping there, which was a relief to Horn. He didn't want any more surprises.

The door to the elevator finally opened on level five. Horn locked it open by propping the terminal's body against the steel jamb. He looked around the large warehouselike room and took it for a storage area. Hundreds of drums were stacked to the ceiling on pallets. Horn noticed the air was considerably hotter now.

The place appeared to be deserted as Horn moved toward a door marked Stairs. He grabbed the door handle with his right hand and pulled. It was apparently locked. He ripped it open, the flat piece of steel tearing off its hinges. Horn stepped back as a wave of hot gas belched out of the stairwell. He could hear the reactor rumbling down in the pit like a giant beast. Taking a deep breath, he headed down the stairs.

Horn forced himself to concentrate on the mission at hand as he went deeper and deeper into the claustrophobic

belly of the complex. As he passed level seven, he thought
he heard screaming. He nearly went back to check it out,
thinking it might be Lydia or Zack. But after listening a
couple of seconds he knew that the piercing scream of pain
was a man's. It wailed up to a pitch so high that it no longer
sounded human. The hair on the back of Horn's neck stood
on end, and he felt himself getting spooked. He moved on,
finally reaching the door to level eight.

Without checking to see if it was locked, Horn did a half-
spinning kick and planted his right boot in the center of the
steel door. It blew into the main chamber area like a leaf,
striking a steel beam twenty feet away. Level eight resembled a postbattle kill zone in hell. The bodies of at least fifty
terminals lay on the floor. At first Horn thought they must
have died from the heat, but at second glance, he noticed a
number of the bodies had their hands clutched around the
necks of other cadavers in death grips. It was a grim scene
of madness and despair.

In the center of the huge room, the stainless steel cylin-
der of the main reactor chamber squatted like the gleaming belly of a gigantic silver Buddha. Steam shot out from
several ruptured pipes, and red warning lights flashed
madly through the haze. Horn located the cipher box for
the access door and punched Ring 9 on the alphanumeric
keyboard. He heard a loud creaking sound above the din of
the cooking reactor and watched as a panel slid open next
to the original doorway, revealing a hidden staircase. A
bright light emanated from the stairwell, and he headed
down without hesitation. His heart raced, and adrenaline
flowed through his body in an unabating stream.

The door to level nine was unlike the other accesses. It
was a solid piece of black steel with a big red 9 painted in
its center. Below the number, also in red, were the profes-
sionally lettered words: Your Soul Dies Here Forever. Horn

stood to one side of the door and balled his titanium hand into a fist. He leaned away momentarily before swinging his right arm around in a blur, striking the center of the 9 with the forearm. The sound was like a bomb exploding as the door burst away, and pieces of the reinforced steel hinges flew through the air.

Horn stepped into the ninth level, holding the automatic chest-high, his eyes taking in the scene like microprocessed radar images. Suddenly his eyes found what they were searching for, and as the meaning of what he saw registered in his brain, his heart stopped. Four people stood staring at Horn from across the vast room. Lydia and Zack were huddled together in front of a huge blond man, who was holding a massive .44 pistol to the boy's head. An electrical alarm system went off in Horn's head that nearly caused him to pass out. He recognized the huge weapon as well as the malevolent grinning face. He started to raise the 9 mm, but quickly checked the motion.

Standing off to one side was a short man in a business suit, whose face was also plastered in a grotesque smile. Horn didn't need anyone to tell him it was Oasis Fine. "Come closer, Mr. Horn, we've been looking forward to your arrival. As you can see—" Fine gestured toward the stainless steel ceiling "—we don't have much time to conduct our business with you."

Horn glanced up at the ceiling. It appeared to be vibrating and caused the light in the auditorium-size room to shimmer strangely. He moved toward the group of people cautiously, not wanting to invite premature action. He moved to within twenty feet before Fine raised his hand. "That's close enough, Mr. Horn," he said. "Now throw that weapon down."

Horn flung the 9 mm off to one side. It hit the concrete floor and skidded into a stack of eight-foot sections of steel pipe. "You've got me, now let the woman and the kid go," he said.

"Well, but of course, Mr. Horn. You don't think Mr. Steller or I would hurt them, do you?" Fine said with a sickly smile.

"You son of a bitch." Horn took a step forward, but stopped as Steller cocked the hammer on the .44.

"Now, Mr. Horn," Fine admonished, "don't do anything stupid to screw this up. We've worked too long to get you in this position. Mr. Steller would be sorely disappointed if he had to kill you with his pistol."

From the confident manner in which Fine was speaking, Horn was getting the impression that he was unaware of the sabotaged security port. "Why am I getting all the special attention?" he asked.

Fine brushed back his hair with the tips of his fingers. "Let me put it this way," he answered. "You have stumbled into a wave of darkness that will swallow you forever." Fine pointed his finger at Horn. "You are going to die by my command, as did your wife and child." He let his revelation soak in, watching Horn for a reaction.

Horn forced the vision of Steller's death march through the New York apartment from his mind. He had to control himself to be effective, especially with Lydia and the boy around. "And don't forget that scum-sucking detective partner of yours." Steller's voice sent a charge of electricity up Horn's spine that nearly forced a shout from his lips when it hit his brain.

"I'd almost forgotten about that," Fine said. "You see, Mr. Horn, you are the last set of eyeballs that I was really worried about. Now, Mr. Steller says you have to be pretty damn good to have survived the several attempts on your life, even if they were bungled. So I think I will let him see

just how skilled you really are." Fine smiled as he pulled the
.357 from inside his jacket.

Fine tracked the weapon on Lydia and Zack. "Ms Kline,
you and the boy come with me." Steller shoved Lydia toward his boss, and Zack stumbled after her, clutching the
hem of her dress with one hand.

"What are you going to do with them?" Horn asked,
figuring Fine might tell him just to torture him because
there was nothing he could do.

"Look at it this way," Fine said. "It's a long way back
to New York. I'm certain Ms Kline and her son will offer
Mr. Steller and me some degree of entertainment."

Horn wanted to scream at Fine that he was going to burn
with all his victims, that his escape via the security port was
gone, but held his tongue. Not telling Fine would at least
give Lydia and the boy a little extra time. To what purpose, though, he didn't know.

"Come on." Fine grabbed Zack roughly by the neck and
stuck the gun to his frail back. "You know the way, Nurse
Kline."

Horn watched the trio disappear out the door. He turned
toward Steller, who had the .44 aimed at his chest. "Just
you and me?" Horn asked, raising his eyebrows.

"You got it, cop." Steller smiled. "I'm almost glad you
didn't buy it that night. Now it's going to be kind of like
getting to kill you twice."

The strobelike flashback invaded Horn's mind again, and
once more he forced it out. Soon, he thought, feeling his
mods jerking like horses at the starting gate.

"Are you ready to die, cop?" Steller asked, cocking his
head to one side.

Horn looked into Steller's eyes without showing a trace
of emotion. "You talk pretty tough with an advantage like

that in your hand." He nodded at the .44. "Too bad you don't have the guts to try me for real."

A flash of anger briefly illuminated Steller's face. "I have more guts than you have brains," the blond giant said slowly, tossing the big pistol to one side. Horn was surprised that his goading had worked. "I'm going to kill you with my body," Steller said, stripping off the empty shoulder holster. "Fine thought there wasn't enough time for me to kill you just with my own hands and still make the Lear before the reactor goes, but I'll manage."

Horn recognized the mad grin on Steller's face. It had been imprinted on his mind on the most gruesome night of his life. Horn started to move toward the killer, but stopped cold in his tracks as Steller stuck his gloved fingers into the collar of his turtleneck and ripped the shirt from his body. Everything that was visible below the man's neck was solid titanium. Unlike Horn's combat-green mods, Steller's enhanced body was polished to a high gloss. The hard metal looked almost liquid.

Steller plucked off his gloves as Horn watched in a grim sort of awe. He then kicked off his boots and removed the black parachute pants. The only parts of Steller's body, besides his head, that weren't modified were his left leg below the knee and, Horn assumed, the assassin's crotch. A line of flesh could be seen around the black briefs.

"You like my body?" Steller asked, flexing his mods into a blur of flashing titanium. He was intimidating, a deadly, invincible superman who had been primed to kill. "You should be honored that I'm going to use it to finish you off instead of just putting an ignoble chunk of lead into your brain." Steller grinned and took a step toward Horn, who suddenly made a running dive toward the 9 mm.

Steller's derisive laughter floated after Horn as he slid headfirst across the smooth concrete and slammed into the steel pipes. He grabbed the automatic and swung it toward the big blonde's head, seeking out flesh with the laser sight. His trigger finger pulled three quick times, but Steller's huge titanium hands beat the bullets to his face, and they ricocheted off in a shower of sparks.

Horn got to his feet and tracked the laser across Steller's body, trying to get a shot at real skin. He fired a round at the assassin's crotch, but Steller bent over slightly, catching the bullet on a titanium section of the abdominal area. In the same movement, he picked up one of his heavy-high-topped boots and flung it at Horn's chest, knocking him backward over the stack of pipes. The 9 mm flew out of his hands and clattered across the floor somewhere behind him.

Steller moved toward Horn, flexing his gleaming armor of titanium. The big blonde laughed again as Horn struggled to his feet. "What's the matter, cop?" Steller asked. "Feeling a little wimped out?"

Horn reached down and grabbed one of the sections of steel pipe with his hands. He grunted as though he were struggling to lift the heavy tube. Steller took another couple of steps toward Horn, the insane grin still etched into his face. Horn slipped his right hand under the pipe and in one swift motion swung it around like a bat, striking Steller across the chest with a loud bang. The blow caused the blond killer to stagger back a couple of steps, and a look of concerned surprise replaced his grin.

"You son of a bitch!" Steller said, sounding almost satisfied. "You do have something other than flesh and bone under those clothes." His hand shot out like a bolt of lighting and ripped the pipe away from Horn. He flung it across the room. "This is good," he said, closing in on Horn, who matched the move in a backward direction. "I've always wanted to kill one of my own kind."

Horn felt a trickle of blood running down the front of his chest from the reopened knife wound and looked around for something to use as a weapon, even while knowing that it wouldn't be much use against a mechanical superman. He fought the panic out of his mind and backed up another couple of steps as Steller advanced.

"How are you going to like going up with this chunk of ore?" Horn said to get Steller's attention off track. He'd noticed that the stainless steel dome over their heads had begun to develop a crack. It started in the center and ran out like a spiderweb.

"You've got it all wrong. I do the killing, you do the dying. It's your job as a fool."

"That's not what I mean." Horn threw his head back and forced himself to roll out a peal of mad laughter. "I'm afraid your boss is finding out about now that the outer air lock of the security port has been destroyed. Looks like we're all stuck here."

A look of grave concern washed over Steller's face. "You're lying," he said, then lunged at Horn, his huge titanium hands extended to cut off all escape. Horn tried to sidestep the attack, but wasn't quick enough. Steller grabbed him around the waist and flung him across the room. Horn landed a good thirty feet away, rolling on his shoulders, and finally skidding to a stop next to a support beam.

Horn stood up as Steller approached, cocking one of his gleaming fists like the trigger of a bizarre weapon. The big blonde was grinning and triggered Horn's flashback, gripping his mind with a demented intensity. This time Horn didn't force the bloody scene from his mind. He let it play itself in his head and immediately felt his mods go uncontrolled.

Feeling strangely detached, Horn got the impression he was watching the scene from somewhere else. Steller's big metallic fist came down in an arc, burning in toward Horn's head like a laser-guided warhead, but Horn's own modified arm rose up on an intercept course and deflected the blow in a shower of sparks. The crash of the titanium appendages sounded like a train wreck. Horn immediately brought up his right knee and drove it into Steller's groin. The big blonde gasped loudly and doubled over, then erupted in a drawn-out howl.

Horn fell back against the steep support beam and attempted to get into position so he could deliver the death-blow to Steller's head. The blond assassin wrapped both his arms around Horn's chest, and they collapsed onto the floor. Steller tightened his grip, and Horn could feel his breath being squeezed out of his chest. He managed to wedge his right arm between the titanium death clamps and pry them apart enough to keep breathing. Steller's face was inches from Horn's, and a trickle of blood ran from the corner of his mouth.

Horn figured the blow he had inflicted with his modified knee had done some good. He quickly used it again, and felt it strike hard metal. Adjusting the angle Horn swung the knee up three times in rapid succession, moving his aim after each thrust in a saturation pounding strategy. It worked. On the third strike he felt his knee penetrate soft flesh. Horn watched as the color drained from the man's face. He went ahead and delivered two more blows for effect before knocking Steller's polished arms away. He felt a sharp pain, and knew he'd started to bleed heavily again from the knifewound.

Gasping for air, Horn struggled to his feet. He grabbed the edge of the beam with his hand and raised his right boot over Steller's head. Just as he slammed it down, Steller's hand shot up like a rocket and grabbed the leather sole. Horn tried to jerk his leg away as the pain shot up to his brain. "Damn!" Horn yelled out and suddenly felt himself hoisted into the air.

Steller slowly started to get up, while he maintained his grip. Horn was jammed upward against the side of the beam as the man-machine below raised him like an elevator. He kicked out with his left foot and caught the blond head with a glancing blow. It didn't seem to faze Steller, who simply stretched up his arm, taking Horn out of kicking range.

Cold chills ran up Horn's back as Steller laughed in a high-pitched, metallic shriek. Horn looked up for something to hold on to and was startled to see a bright orange molten substance slowly begin to drip from the crack in the ceiling. "Hell," he gasped. It seemed everyone's time was just about up.

Steller suddenly gave Horn's leg a twist that twirled his entire body around, slamming the side of his face into the smooth steel of the beam. He quickly jerked his head back from the heated metal.

Steller violently twisted the foot again. This time Horn resisted, and pain engulfed his right leg and hip like a flame. The modified parts were twisted like pretzels as the servos strained, the whine of their linkages splitting the air, adding to the cacophonic din. Horn slipped his modified hand down along the beam in an attempt to get more leverage. Something stopped his movement and he ran his titanium fingers along a three-inch-thick, steel-jacketed cable that was riveted to the side of the beam.

Horn ripped the cable away from the steel structure, and the round clamps popped off like torn stitches. He then jerked down with all the strength he could will into his modified arm. The cable came apart less than three feet above his hand in a blaze of sparks that showered down on Horn's and Steller's bodies. Despite the burning electrical storm over his head, Horn forced himself to concentrate. He pulled more of the heavy cable away from the lower part of the beam, then swung the torched end down, aiming for the face.

Steller screamed as the hot end of the electrical line struck his right shoulder. Ten thousand volts of pulsed power were shocked through his electromechanical systems like a bolt of lightning. Steller's mods glitched madly in an uncontrolled burst of conflicting motion. His entire body shot away from the beam as though they were opposing magnets, and Horn's body was thrown twenty feet through the air in a slow somersault. He managed to touch ground with his feet for a moment before tumbling onto his back and sliding across the concrete with great speed.

Horn struggled to his feet and ran back to the cable, which was dancing around on the floor, creating a crazy fan-shaped pattern of orange sparks. Steller was lying on his stomach, his arms and legs jerking around in a staccato rhythm. Horn waited a couple of seconds, timing the flopping cable, then reached down and grabbed it just below the fire-breathing head. He turned toward Steller, holding the cable in his hand like a garden hose. The titanium assassin twisted his head around and stared at Horn, his eyes wide, reflecting the sparks from the burning electrical line.

Vengeance welled up in Horn's chest. For the first time he saw fear spread across Steller's face like the epitaph on a hangman's tombstone. He moved forward and stood over the twitching titanium body, letting the sparks fall across the gleaming hard metal back. Steller twisted his head farther around and stared up at Horn, begging with his maniac eyes.

"So long, asshole," Horn said simply as he shoved the end of the cable into the middle of Steller's back. The huge titanium body bucked violently as the electricity screamed through its maze of circuitry. Horn kept the connection pressed hard until he felt the end of the cable burn into a weld with the titanium skin. He backed off as Steller's body continued to bounce around on the floor.

Horn watched a couple of seconds longer, letting the adrenaline born of revenge pump through his body. It felt good, and he didn't deny the pleasure.

Suddenly a sound like the twisting of heavy steel caused Horn to look up. A thick stream of burning liquid shot from the crack in the ceiling. It struck the concrete floor and drove straight through with an explosive sound. Smoke spread upward from the fire-drilled hole to shroud the room.

Horn raced for the stairwell, wondering if it was too late to carry out the rest of his fragile plan. As he reached the doorway, he couldn't help glancing back at Steller, whose titanium body continued to buck and jerk, fueled by the burning current.

Turning away, Horn wondered if anybody would make it off the asteroid, or if they would all be consumed in a fireball more spectacular than the shower of sparks that had enveloped Steller.

CHAPTER TWENTY

HORN POUNDED up the stairs with the gurgling screaming sounds of the reactor following him. He paused briefly to punch the elevator button at level five but didn't wait, calculating that Fine probably smoked the controls once he reached the upper level with Lydia and the kid.

After what seemed like an eternity, Horn reached level one. The place was a madhouse, but he ignored it, running the hallway like a gauntlet, shoving terminals out of the way.

He was nearing the section of the hall that contained the overhead trapdoor of the shaft when he unexpectedly found himself flying headfirst through the air. The red dust billowed up as he struck the floor in a diving position, skidding ten feet before coming to a stop. Horn rolled over and looked back down the hallway. He saw the thin trip wire stretched ankle high. As he rose to his feet, a terminal stepped out of a doorway and raised a fire ax over his head. Horn noticed the steel blade was covered with glistening red liquid that dripped off the edge and into the terminal's mangy hair. He could guess that it wasn't paint.

"Listen, pal," Horn said, holding up his right hand as the terminal moved toward him. "I don't have time for this shit." The big zombie growled and swung the ax down, aiming it straight for the center of Horn's head. Instead of dodging the blow, Horn checked his titanium hand over a couple of inches and caught the handle just below the wedge-shaped head. The terminal grunted loudly as the ax slammed to a stop, and the vibration carried back up the aluminum handle, making the terminal howl as the shock ran through his arms.

Ripping the ax away from the attacker and swiveling around, Horn swung his right foot at the barrel-shaped chest. The big terminal was knocked backward down the hall to land on his butt, and rolled into another two terminals, who were going at it with pipe wrenches. They both looked down at the intruder, who was gasping for breath, and started beating him on the head with their wrenches. Relieved that he didn't have to waste more time, Horn hurried for the trapdoor.

He was exhausted as he stumbled out of the abandoned warehouse and into the dilapidated streets of the old section. The area seemed deserted. No doubt everyone had trooped down to the docking ports as soon as the warning sirens had gone off. He could hear the mournful wail echoing in the dome eerily. Taking a deep breath, he set his hasty course in the direction of the security port.

FINE, despite his having to prod Lydia and Zack along, had made the main security port smoothly. He didn't have a problem to get the woman following his orders, especially when he had a gun jammed to the kid's head.

Fine's trouble began once they accessed the security facility. A cold doubt assailed him unexpectedly. Something was seriously wrong. There was no control.

Bile rose up in Fine's throat as a wave of panic flushed through his mind. He tried to order one of the styros running helter-skelter in the halls to fill him in on what had happened, but they all ignored his threatening weapon. He managed at last to clothesline a skinny little guard and shoved him into a doorway. Fine slammed the frail body up against the door and shoved the barrel of the .357 into the soft skin beneath his chin. Sweat streamed down his face as he slapped the styro on the side of the head.

"Listen to me, you son of a bitch!" Fine screamed into the scared face. "What the hell is going on around here?"

Before the guard could answer, Fine suddenly remembered Lydia and the kid. He jerked his head around. They were gone, having taken the opportunity to disappear into the teeming mass of styros. "Screw 'em," he said turning back to the guard, whose eyes darted back and forth fearfully.

"I asked you a question, goddammit!" Fine glared at the man demandingly as he shucked the dirty jacket off his shoulders. "Did something happen?" Fine's voice rose to a fever pitch as a fine spray of spit flew into the styro's face.

"Yeah!" the guard answered frantically.

"Well, what is it?" Fine shoved the gun harder, then realized the man probably wouldn't be able to talk with a steel tube jammed two inches into his neck. He eased the weapon out and added, "You better hook your tongue up to your brain this time, or I'm going to blow them both to hell."

"A mining drone rammed through the outside air lock," the styro blurted, his eyes nervously avoiding Fine's snake-like stare. "All the other ports in the dome have had their controls wrecked. We... we're trapped, and now the god-damn smelting reactor is getting ready to shit its load clean through the bottom of this rock!" The guard's wild eyes suddenly locked onto Fine's as the futility of the situation dawned on him. "You may as well go ahead and pull the trigger, mister! We're all going to die anyway!"

"Shut up!" Fine barked, backing away. "Or I will shoot you!"

"Go right ahead!" The styro grabbed Fine's gun hand and jammed the barrel back under his chin. "Shoot me!"

"You crazy bastard!" Fine said, as he rammed a knee into the styro's groin. The little man grunted, releasing his grip on Fine's hand. He slid to the floor and Fine backed away, pointing the Magnum at his head. "Since you want it that bad..." The CEO lowered the barrel of the weapon and fired a single round into the abdomen. He turned and headed toward the control station's tube, knowing the gut-shot styro would agonize for several hours before death would put an end to him.

Fine was somewhat more merciful to the lone styro who guarded the entry to the overhead transport tube. He shot him point-blank between the eyes. Kicking the body away from the sliding door, he stepped into the cylindrical chamber. He pressed the Engage button, and felt himself propelled upward in the long arc that led to the control station at the top of the dome.

On the way up, Fine tried to get a plan together in his head. He was crazy with anger, knowing that Horn had somehow wrecked the security port, but found logical thought elusive while panic ruled his mind. Then a black veil of hopelessness suddenly fell upon Fine's scrambled thoughts. It sucked them into a whirlpool, making the CEO finally experience what he'd put his victims through. He knew that he'd become just one of the fifteen thousand other doomed souls on the asteroid who were facing the empty despair that was making his heart feel like a block of lead. He waited for tears to well up in his eyes, but instead a shrill laugh welled up in his throat. Fine realized he couldn't bring himself to weep...even when it was over his own death.

"Goddamn!" he said aloud and leaned against the side of the tube. The finality of the situation washed through his mind like an electrical storm. It was such a new experience for him that he found he was almost enjoying it. Finally, something confronted him over which he had zero control. It was exciting. The feeling was suddenly turned off like a tripped light switch as a survival plan jumped into his head. A weak plan, but a plan just the same. Fine figured he would grab an environmental suit and use a drone to smash through both air locks of a sabotaged port. "At least I'll make it to one of the Lears if I'm lucky," he said to himself.

HORN STORMED the security port bloodhound fashion, tearing through the place as explosions rolled like thunder from the Hot Zone. He kicked open doors, checking every room, not wanting to think about what Fine might do to Lydia and the boy once he figured out what had happened to the air lock. Anguish gripped him as the sound of a woman screaming hit his ears. He followed the sound down a hallway and kicked in a door marked Day Room.

The sight that greeted Horn's eyes made him wince. Several styros were holding a woman down on a table while one of them rocked between her legs. Her head hung over the edge of the table, but he couldn't see her face.

When the door ripped open, the styros had turned their heads toward the sound. The rapist kept at it, but yelled, "Get the hell out of here!" When he saw Horn moving quickly into the room, he slurred, "You'll have to wait your goddamn turn—"

Horn didn't let the styro finish the sentence. He leaned over the table and backhanded the grinning guard across the mouth with his right arm. The guy's head snapped back, his neck breaking with a loud crack like a piece of dry wood. While he was swinging his arm, Horn reached down with his left hand and pulled a Composite .45 Automag from a styro's side holster. The dead guard was just rolling off the back edge of the table when Horn swung the automatic up and aimed it between the surprised eyes of a styro. The big weapon jumped in his hand as he squeezed the trigger, and a third eye socket appeared in the man's fore-head.

Moving around the table counterclockwise, Horn pulled the trigger four more times, having to aim down at the last guard who was crouching for cover. The he looked at the woman, who had pulled her head up onto the table and was curled in a fetal position, wrenched by sobs. Horn still couldn't see her face, but he'd known it wasn't Lydia. The woman spoke up unexpectedly, her voice muffled by her tears. "Throw me a gun."

Horn stopped and looked at her for a couple of sec-onds. He realized what she wanted to do, and he also knew she was doomed. He couldn't stay around or take her along to help her, or they would all be lost. He tossed the auto-matic onto the tabletop, turned and walked out the door without saying a word. He hadn't taken ten steps down the hall when the .45 barked once.

Horn made a hurried check of the security port before heading up to the control station. He figured Fine would be there, trying madly to reverse his earlier sabotage. And he hoped that if he found Fine, he would also find Lydia and the child.

A feeling of anticipation ran through Horn, and his mods twitched slightly. He felt calm, almost good. He felt sure Fine was waiting in the control station; he could sense it. His mission to destroy the link to his nightmares was al-most complete. Horn forced himself to concentrate, to fo-cus in on the final ghost.

The door of the tube slid open, and he stepped into the trashed-out hallway of the control station. Bodies and de-bris were scattered everywhere. Smoke filled the corridor like thin fog, creating an eerie environment as the red warning lights in the ceiling spun their beams to the music of impending disaster. Horn acquired another pistol from the holster of a dead styro. He charged the chamber and moved toward the drone control center.

Horn gave in to the strange pulling sensation his modifications were exhibiting. In the past he had flirted with the power, yet always denied its full control over himself. Now he didn't resist any longer, thinking it ironic that his mods were going to eliminate the entity responsible for their creation.

He found Fine bent over the keyboard of a remote controller, cursing aloud, trying to program a loop to unjam the controls. He wasn't having much luck. Instinctively he raised his head and looked out the window. It was then that he saw Horn's reflection in the doorway and froze. What little color there was drained from his face. He stared as though he were seeing his own face in a coffin.

Horn let Fine gaze at his reflection in the glass for a full minute, wanting it burned into the man's brain like a brand. "You look a little surprised," he finally said, his words making the CEO flinch. "Aren't you going to say something stupid like 'What are you doing here?'"

While Horn was speaking, Fine moved his right hand infinitely slowly to the .357, stuck into his waistband. Horn raised the .45 Automag and fired a round into the console next to Fine, who cringed and gasped. He jerked his hand away from the handgun and went stiff. The metallic taste of fear filled Fine's mouth. "What are you doing here?" he asked shakily and immediately cringed again, realizing he'd asked what Horn had anticipated.

Horn laughed strangely, his voice echoing in the trashed-out control center. But he was deadly serious when he spoke. "Turn around slowly and keep your hands where I can see them." Horn could feel his mods twitching mildly.

Fine turned toward Horn, keeping his trembling hands extended before him. "You're the one who ruined the security port's air lock, aren't you?" Fine asked, his voice shaded by an unreasonable and angry anxiety.

"I really couldn't have you missing out of the big light show. After all—" Horn walked a couple of steps toward Fine as he spoke "—you're the one who set it up." He stopped about ten feet away from the CEO.

"How did you overcome Steller?" Fine suddenly asked, his nervous fear seeming to disappear.

"Let's just say his circuit breakers broke," Horn answered.

"The man's body cost me more than 950,000 credits," Fine said and he sounded strangely objective. "You didn't stand a goddamn chance, unless—" He stared at Horn, remembering that Steller himself had alluded to the possibility that the cop had something extra. "Have you been modified?"

"Thank yourself for it," Horn answered. "Where's the woman and kid?"

"You *have* been modified." Fine almost looked surprised. "I'll be damned."

"No doubt." Horn's voice signaled his growing impatience. "But answer my question," he snapped, coming a step closer.

Fine had to try to throw Horn's mind off track. He estimated he only needed a split second and hoped his answer would shock the cop. "They're dead, like your family!" He barked out the false confession like a mad dog and went for the .357.

Like a straight razor, the words sliced into Horn's mind, tripping every trigger that wired the E-mods into his spine. His right arm was already in motion as Fine grabbed the pistol, pulling back the hammer as he aimed. Sparks flew from the barrel and Horn's hand moved, slapping the bullet away like an annoying gnat. Fine's eyes grew wide, and his mouth dropped open as Horn closed in on him. The CEO pulled the trigger three more times, and the lead projectiles bounced off Horn's titanium arm as he moved it in a blur, blocking the shots. Frantically Fine aimed the gun at Horn's head and dropped the hammer on a spent chamber. He jerked the trigger several more times, but nothing happened.

Fine cocked his arm and hurled the pistol at Horn, who caught the weapon with his right hand. "I guess you're used to more helpless victims, aren't you?" Horn said, crushing the Magnum and letting it clatter to the floor.

"Wait a minute!" Fine held up his hands in surrender. "It was Steller! That bastard's idea of a good time was doing that sort of—"

Horn watched Fine grovel, going full circle in his madness. "What difference does it make?" he asked, pointing the .45 at Fine's head, feeling his trigger finger tighten automatically. "You're dead any way you look at it."

"Oh, I knew it," Fine said, moving his hands as though he were trying to settle things down. He took a couple of half steps toward Horn, and a look of insane desperation crept into his eyes like a wild fire. Horn could see it coming a mile away. Fine was winding up like a cobra getting ready to strike.

In a slow motion that bordered on freezing, Fine made his move. He lunged, his hands outstretched, going for Horn's eyes. Horn's mods seemed to overrule the want to fire the automatic as his right hand flew up and grabbed Fine's skinny neck. The CEO's body swung in midair, his hands immediately grabbing Horn's titanium wrist. "You bastard!" he gurgled. "Go ahead and kill me!"

Horn turned and walked out of the control room, dragging Fine by the neck. He effortlessly maneuvered the kicking body down the hall and into the control station's lounge. The debris-strewn room had a circular glass floor through which the entire area of New Pittsburgh could be seen below.

Horn flung Fine's body onto the center of the floor. The CEO lifted himself up on one elbow, rubbing his neck with his free hand. He glared at Horn a couple of seconds before speaking hoarsely, "What's the matter, cop, don't you have the guts to execute someone?"

"I want you to see New Pittsburgh one last time, a sort of visual eulogy for the accomplishments in your life." Horn swept toward the view with the barrel of the .45. The mining colony was visible in patches through an increasing cloud of reddish smoke that was billowing up from the Hot Zone. Thousands of people milled through the streets like ants in a burning field.

Getting down on one knee, Horn raised his right hand in a fist and plunged it into the floor. Pieces of the four-inch reinforced glass flew up like shrapnel as Horn's titanium wrecking ball drove completely through the clear slab. A little plume of red smoke snaked into the room from the hole, permeating the air with the smell of sulfur.

Fine's eyes were wide, glazed in paranoid wonder, as Horn went ahead and smashed out a larger circular hole in the floor. When he had it punched out to the approximate size of a manhole, he stood and looked at his right hand. He held it up, flexing the titanium fingers, the shredded leather glove hanging in strips like a rag. "Don't quite make them like they used to, do they, Fine?" Horn looked at Fine and smiled strangely. The CEO just shook his head in a jerking manner, and a little stream of spit dribbled from one corner of his mouth. "Maybe you're right," Horn said, motioning Fine to get to his feet. "Maybe I don't have it in me to execute you."

"What do you mean?" Fine croaked as he got shakily to his feet. His eyes were glued to the hole Horn had smashed into the floor.

"Do I really have to say it?" Horn sounded calm and reasonable. "I think you already have the idea."

"You, you wouldn't want me to—" Fine pointed to the hole, then swung his eyes toward Horn.

"You know—" Horn shook his head "—now I know how you got to be president of Titus Steel. It was your brain."

"No!" Fine backed away from the hole a couple of steps. "I'm not going to die that way."

"Then you'll go like this." Horn held up his right hand, palm toward Fine, and closed the dull green fingers into a fist.

Fine looked at the massive titanium hand and licked his lips. He glanced over at the smoking hole, then back to Horn as sweat ran down his face in streams. "My only choices?" he asked.

"Looking right at you," Horn answered.

Fine walked over to the edge of the hole and looked down. A strange fascinated expression turned his face into a waxy-looking mask. He turned his head slowly toward Horn and grimaced. "See you in hell, cop." Fine stepped out and started to drop like a stone. But he'd miscalculated, and as he fell through, his chin caught the edge of the jagged glass, snapping his head back with a loud cracking sound. Horn watched the body flip backward, end over end, as it plunged through the smoke.

Horn stared downward through the glass, trying to gain some satisfaction now that his vengeance was complete. Nothing came, and an emptiness gripped his spirit.

A vibration shook the dome. Horn realized he was feeling the reactor hitting critical. His final tussle with the asteroid was still ahead.

LYDIA HAD NEARLY JERKED Zack's arm out of the socket pulling him from the security port facility. She could only imagine what Fine had in mind for her and her son on the trip back to Earth. Her imagination was enough not to cause the slightest hesitation when the insane CEO momentarily forgot about his hostages. She pulled Zack down the hall and out the nearest exit, willing to resign herself and her son to die on the asteroid rather than be subject to Fine and Steller's manic fantasies.

Once Lydia and Zack were out in the streets, her mind went through a futile attempt to come up with some *safe* place to go. She thought about going back to her apartment or the hospital, but there wasn't any place on the roid that Fine didn't have his eyes or ears on. Suddenly Lydia laughed aloud, realizing the absurdity of her thoughts. People were running around like trapped rats. Fine would obviously be too concerned with other things to bother chasing them down. His concern had to center on how he was going to avoid becoming one of the rats.

Wanting to be clear of the area surrounding the security facility, Lydia led Zack to a small square several blocks away at the intersection of major streets. There was an old fountain in the square that had long fallen into disuse. It was covered with red tite dust and filled with debris. Lydia sat down on the ledge of the round structure and held Zack for a couple of minutes. He soon slipped down, put his head in her lap and, in spite of the chaos, went to sleep.

The sirens were still wailing in the distance. Lydia could see smoke rising to the top of the dome from the Hot Zone. As she sat there, an overwhelming feeling of loneliness drove through her heart like a sudden wind. She thought of Horn dying in the reactor's hell-like death chamber. It occurred to her that he'd been willing to die for her and Zack.

Lydia laughed to herself. She laughed as tears filled her eyes. She had never denied the attraction she experienced when she was near Horn. The physical passion was derived from that attraction, but she'd wanted it with no strings attached, no heartbreak, no added emotional baggage. She didn't need it, and guessed that Horn hadn't been ready, either. She had handled the situation objectively, maturely, the way it should have been handled; at least she thought so. Lydia put an arm around Zack and leaned over. She cried over him as a shudder rippled across the surface of the asteroid.

Lydia's heart stopped beating when she felt a hand on her shoulder. She jerked her head up, expecting to see Fine's distorted features and gasped in disbelief as her eyes fixed on Horn's face. "You're alive!" she said, clutching her hands to her chest.

"I could say the same thing," Horn said, brushing away her tears with his fingertips. "But right now—" he looked around as another tremor shook the asteroid, "—there's no time."

"But, there's no way—" Horn cut Lydia off in midsentence as he bent over and picked up Zack, holding the boy under his left arm.

"There's a way," he said, taking Lydia by the hand. "Hurry." He stared into the woman's eyes, wondering at the circumstances fate had thrown him in. He'd hardly been able to get his mind to consider what his eyes had registered when he saw the woman and boy on the ledge of the fountain. "Let's go." He forced the wonder out of his head and led the race toward the nearest drone port.

Horn kicked in a side door to one of the ports used by the tenders, while Lydia stood trying to catch her breath. She held on to Zack who stared around, obviously scared. "Wait here," Horn directed as he disappeared into the building. After a minute or so, Lydia suddenly jumped as a man's scream erupted from inside the building. Less than thirty seconds later, Horn emerged, carrying an armful of the silver, self-contained protection suits. "I'll show you when we get there." Horn grabbed her arm and pulled her and the boy after him. They ran along a dusty maintenance road that circled the perimeter of the dome. Horn suddenly found himself sprawled out in the red dirt, Lydia and Zack rolling head over heels next to him. A big wave ripped across the surface of the roid, and Horn felt himself tossed into the air.

Horn turned over and crawled to Lydia, who was brushing the red dirt from Zack's face. "Are you okay?" he asked. A loud hissing sound made him turn his head before Lydia could answer. The noise was coming from the base of the dome and Horn could see a crack running around the curved structure, less than a foot above the concrete base. "Come on!" He grabbed Lydia's hand and pulled her to her feet. "Grab Zack," he ordered, nodding to the boy.

It seemed to Horn that it took forever to reach the rundown building that housed the scum-covered garbage vent. He could hear a strange sound growing and rising above the wail of the sirens. The hair on the back of his neck rose up as his brain registered the high-pitched warbling as the sound of thousands of people screaming in unison. "Can't be," Horn said to himself as he slammed his foot against the steel door, nearly falling over when it caved in.

"Get into this," Horn ordered, tossing one of the silver suits to Lydia. "I'll help Zack." He helped the boy into the suit, which was huge on his small frame. Horn activated the oxygen system and explained that he should breathe normally. Lydia watched as she struggled into her own suit. After he'd clamped down the glass face plate for Zack, Horn walked over to Lydia and engaged the life-support module on the sleeve of her suit before slipping into his own.

Horn turned on his own system, then walked over to the vent controls. He activated the inner door to the vent and watched as the big steel slab slid open, revealing the slimy insides of the garbage chute. He waved Lydia into the chamber, grabbed Zack and followed, pausing long enough to trip the switch to close the inner door.

Once inside, Horn slammed his right hand down on the steel lid of the box housing the emergency controls, knocking it into the refuse-covered floor. Without hesitating, he pressed the override switch for the outer door, grabbed Lydia and Zack and braced himself. There was a violent blast of wind as the air inside the chamber was sucked out through the opening. The garbage on the floor of the chamber flew up and was suctioned out the door. The decompression ended as suddenly as it had started, and Horn led Lydia out onto the surface of the asteroid, carrying Zack, who was hampered in his movements by the suit.

The Lear was where Horn had staged it, resting on its triplex skids, looking as if it were in motion even when it was sitting still. Horn pulled down the inset handle to activate the external hatch and watched it open up on the bottom of the craft. The short aluminum ladder extended, and he motioned Lydia to get into the ship.

A booming explosion rolled over them, and Horn turned his head and watched as the far side of the dome blew out in a mushroom cloud of red smoke and flame. Horn figured the Hot Zone was gone. He glanced up at the towering vents, which were shooting blue flames into the churning red sky. The huge cooling towers were beginning to crumble and fall apart as a boiling mass of reddish foam rolled over the lips of the structures.

Something on the front of the aircraft caught Horn's eye and caused the tumblers in his head to spin crazily as they tried to unscramble the code. It was a name—the name of the sleek bird. Red letters, trimmed in gold were laid out in the black titanium near the nose: *Ashley White Fine II.*

"Well, I'll be damned," Horn muttered, staring at the name, his voice strange inside the helmet as it finally came to him: *Ashley White...Fine's mother.* The man had to like his mother, Horn thought in awe.

Horn felt his spine stiffen from the chill that moved up his back. A vision of Ashley's sinuous, muscular body and the unusual face floated before his eyes. He could feel a strange fascination; a repulsed sort of attraction as he recalled her blatant seduction. A trickle of sweat ran down his back between his shoulder blades.

Horn suddenly snapped out of the strange flashback and shoved Zack up and into Lydia's arms, who pulled him the rest of the way into the ship. He followed, closing the door behind him. Horn headed straight for the cockpit, hoping desperately that the machine was as simple to operate as Targa had said. He sat down in what was obviously the pilot's seat and activated the ship's computer. He breathed a sigh of relief as the menu flashed onto the LCD screen that covered most of the front panel. The logic was simple enough, and Horn punched in Engine Start, activated the on-board environment and went through the prelaunch checklist. Several items came up that Horn didn't understand, but each time he punched in Yes, hoping whatever it was wasn't broken or at least wasn't critical for getting the bird off the smoldering roid.

Then the spacecraft shifted, throwing Horn around in the seat violently. Screw it, he thought, calling up the launch sequence. Stand by: Engines at 83 Percent flashed across the screen. Horn watched for what seemed like a year and finally the 83 changed to 84. Can't wait, he thought and punched in the command to launch. He hoped Lydia and Zack were strapped down as the bird rocked up and out of the red dust, automatically turning 180 degrees. The rocket engine equivalent of afterburners kicked in, and Horn felt himself slammed back in the seat. The sleek machine blasted across the roid's surface at an altitude of less than one hundred feet and a ground speed of more than four hundred knots.

Horn grew nervous as the red chunks of rock, dust beds and craters became a blur outside the wraparound canopy. "I hope to hell this works," he said aloud as he punched in Standard 10 Mile Orbit and hit the engage key. The ship immediately went nose up, pulling over five G's, causing Horn to get tunnel vision. He felt the spacecraft break out of the gravitational pull of the asteroid and experienced a few seconds of weightlessness before the synthetic gravity system automatically engaged.

After Horn was certain the machine was stable, he checked the environmental status. All systems were in the green, so he pulled off his mask, then stood and stripped off the suit. He was just starting back to the rear of the ship to see how Lydia and Zack had handled the launch when a blinding flash drew his eyes to the windshield.

The asteroid was a ball of orange fire that appeared to implode for a few seconds before bursting out in a spectacular explosion of burning debris. Horn automatically brought up a hand to shield his face. He slowly lowered his hand and watched as the space-born rubble went spinning off into all directions. Small dinging sounds echoed through the ship as a number of pieces struck its black skin.

Horn turned and nearly ran into Lydia. She was half lifting, half dragging Zack along in the oversize suit.

Horn reached out and flipped up Lydia's mask before taking Zack off her hands and stripping the suit from the small body. He then helped Lydia out of hers. "Take a look," he said, pointing a thumb at the windshield. "Say goodbye to New Pittsburgh."

To his surprise, he saw her wipe her eyes. "There were some good people there, and anyway," she added tremulously, "what a way to die—for anybody." They looked at each other silently before she went to take care of Zack.

Fine was staring out the windshield into the vast emptiness when Lydia returned from bedding Zack down in one of the crew bunks. He turned and faced her, speaking in a voice that was strangely hollow, as though in his mind he'd already heard the answer to his question. "Lydia, I'd really like you to consider giving a shot at a relationship with me." Horn heard the halting awkwardness of his own words.

Lydia rubbed her eyes and suddenly looked very tired, but she managed a weak smile. "Max, I like you. But it won't work." Her voice dropped regretfully. "Let's avoid the pain."

"Why won't it?" Horn felt numb, as though he were slipping into a vacuum.

"Because you're a cop," Lydia said simply. "Cops don't live long."

Horn didn't respond. He stared as she slowly turned and walked out of the cockpit. After a couple of minutes he faced the controls, leaned over and punched up the navigation menu. He selected an autoroutine with Earth as the

destination, normal cruise speed. The estimated trip duration came up six weeks, two days, three hours and ten
minutes. He pressed the engage key and immediately the
Lear pivoted, heading into the blackness of space.

Horn looked down at the smooth titanium palm of his
hand. He knew he was looking into his future.

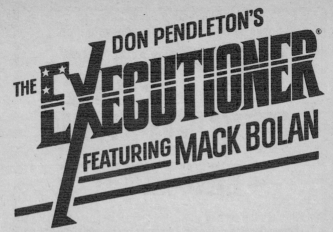

DON PENDLETON'S
THE EXECUTIONER®
FEATURING MACK BOLAN

Baptized in the fire and blood of Vietnam, Mack Bolan has become America's supreme hero. Fiercely patriotic and compassionate, he's a man with a high moral code whose sense of right and wrong sometimes violates society's rules. In adventures filled with heart-stopping action, Bolan has thrilled readers around the world. Experience the high-voltage charge as Bolan rallies to the call of his own conscience in daring exploits that place him in peril with virtually every heartbeat.

"Anyone who stands against the civilized forces of truth and justice will sooner or later have to face the piercing blue eyes and cold Beretta steel of Mack Bolan . . . civilization's avenging angel."
                                        —*San Francisco Examiner*

GOLD
EAGLE

Available wherever paperbacks are sold.

MB-2RR

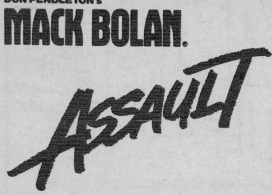